DEAD MAN SWITCH

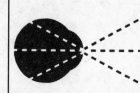

This Large Print Book carries the
Seal of Approval of N.A.V.H.

DEAD MAN SWITCH

MATTHEW QUIRK

THORNDIKE PRESS

A part of Gale, a Cengage Company

Farmington Hills, Mich • San Francisco • New York • Waterville, Maine
Meriden, Conn • Mason, Ohio • Chicago

LIBRARY OF CONGRESS CATALOGING-IN-PUBLICATION DATA

Names: Quirk, Matthew, author.
Title: Dead man switch / by Matthew Quirk.
Description: Large print edition. | Waterville, Maine : Thorndike Press, 2017. |
    Series: Thorndike Press large print thriller
Identifiers: LCCN 2017018970| ISBN 9781432842338 (hardcover) | ISBN 1432842331
    (hardcover)
Subjects: LCSH: Large type books. | GSAFD: Suspense fiction.
Classification: LCC PS3617.U5926 D43 2017 | DDC 813/.6—dc23
LC record available at https://lccn.loc.gov/2017018970

Published in 2017 by arrangement with Little, Brown and Company, a division of Hachette Book Group, Inc.

Printed in the United States of America
1 2 3 4 5 6 7 21 20 19 18 17

For Michael

CHAPTER 1

John Hayes stepped from the rear door of the two-and-half-ton truck. Four gunmen covered him, their Kalashnikov rifles braced against their shoulders.

He ignored them and looked to the sky. It was a good night for an execution, summer in the high alpine. The snow was soft, and the crevasses in the ice spread wide enough to make a man's body disappear.

He'd spent nine hours crammed in the back of the truck, and his legs were rubber. They had switchbacked up the valleys all night on a gravel path so narrow and pitted by old shell craters that the rear of the vehicle hung over empty space through each hairpin turn.

The highest pass had been well above fourteen thousand feet. They were slightly lower on the southern slopes now, and Hayes felt the blood that had frozen while trickling from his nose starting to melt again. He wiped it off, a long smear on the back of his hand.

"Let's go," the driver barked in Pashto, and the slanted muzzle brake of the rifle jabbed into Hayes's ribs just beside his spine. The cold burned his face as they marched him through a rolling door set in the hillside. They entered through a thick concrete portal into an underground garage. He climbed the steps, feeling the blood flush in his legs, the muscles regain their strength, the relatively rich air revive him.

A steel door opened at the far end of the garage, and they walked into an open courtyard. He had expected a mud-walled hut, or even a cave complex, but not this: an interior courtyard paved in marble with Moorish arches.

A man strode toward him, his hair gleaming. At first Hayes assumed the shine was due to the pomades popular among the officers in this country — he was wearing his regimental dress — but then Hayes realized that it was simply wet.

"I hope I didn't keep you," the man said as he stretched his right shoulder. "I was finishing a game."

Squash. It was a fetish among Pakistani military commanders. Imran Kashani was formerly ISI, the Pakistani intelligence service, an uneasy ally of the United States that still kept close ties with the Taliban and militant groups. But Kashani had gone to work for himself and become a power broker — a warlord, essentially — in the ungoverned lands along the Afghanistan-Pakistan border. He commanded a militia the size of a small army.

"Come in," he said.

This man had killed dozens of Americans. Hayes was here to make a deal with him.

They stepped through a long parlor into an office lined with books. Huge mirrors dominated one wall, windows with closed red drapes the other.

"English is okay?" Kashani said.

"That's fine."

"Excellent. I spent a year in college in the States. Arizona State University."

He sat back down at a desk at the front of the room, and Hayes stood between two guards on the carpet before him.

"Are you hungry? Tea?"

"No," Hayes said. He wasn't going to waste time on ceremony in this guano-reeking mansion. Kashani shrugged, and a moment later a third guard placed a glass cup of tea on the desk next to him. Kashani took a sip and examined Hayes.

"All business. Very American. I'll get to

9

the point. What do you know about Cold Harvest?"

Hayes knew it well. It was a small group, culled from the U.S. military's classified special operations units and the CIA's paramilitary forces. They were kill teams, in essence, run as independent contractors with no official relationship to their home government. They pursued the gravest threats to national security in countries, most of them American allies, where the U.S. would never be allowed to perform lethal missions. They were a last resort.

Hayes had once been a leader, a legend in those elite tiers of American special operations, but he had spent years in exile, hunted by his old teammates.

"What do you want to know?" he asked Kashani.

"I want to know their names. I want to know where they live."

"Their outposts? Safe houses? Covers?"

"No. I want their addresses inside the United States. Their homes. We have some, but not enough."

Hayes considered it, ran the back of his hand along his chin, felt the stubble scratch.

"I can get you that information."

"For how many?"

"All of them, give or take a few of the

most recent additions."

Kashani let out a short, startled laugh, like he'd just won something. The two men had no idea that from a hilltop a kilometer and a half away, they were being watched.

At the top of a glacial cirque overlooking Kashani's compound, Connor Burke slammed his gloved hand against his thigh, trying to warm up his fingers. After a minute he could feel pain buried somewhere in all the cold numb flesh. He huddled against his partner, Bryan Sanders. They were both former SEALs, senior chiefs in Team Six, but now they worked as contractors for the CIA. That allowed them to operate in the borderlands of a country like Pakistan, a nation with which the U.S. wasn't technically at war.

Sanders held the laser microphone steady and aimed it at the window of the formal office so he could pick up the conversations in the compound while Burke kept watch. They each had an earbud in and could hear everything Hayes and the other man said.

"I can get you that information."

"For how many?"

"All of them."

Sanders looked to Burke, eyes wide. Burke recognized the voice. He brushed the accumulating snow from his earpiece and raised the volume. Like most seasoned operators, they were half deaf from the tens of thousands of rounds they expended every year. But it was unmistakable. It was John Hayes. Burke had fought with him in Fallujah. It was Burke's second deployment, and Hayes had led the team through a baptism by fire in urban operations. Burke had since heard the rumors: Hayes had gone over to the enemy.

But Burke couldn't believe what he was hearing now. The flurries built into a steady fall, cutting through the laser's path and interfering with the microphone's operation. The audio broke up into static.

"Is Hayes going to sell them the names of our operators?" Sanders asked.

"More than that. The homes. The families. Jesus Christ. It's a kill list."

"It can't be. He was a good man."

"Was," Burke said.

Sanders looked over the compound, well defended and built into the side of the slope.

"I don't like it. Do we have the authority to kill an American if it comes to that?"

The batteries in the radios were dead. The cold drained them at twice the normal speed. They had been in the field for three days. There was no way to get authorization from above.

"You do the math. One life for how many? We've got to stop him."

Sanders nodded.

Burke slammed his hands together and flexed open his fingers. He lifted his rifle and started down the ridge.

In the office, Hayes waited for Kashani to absorb the full measure of what he was offering: a trove of intelligence that would allow him to destroy, root and branch, America's most effective defense against asymmetric threats.

Kashani's cool pose disappeared. He started blinking quickly and leaned forward.

"All of them? That information wouldn't be trusted to one man, or even put on one list."

"It's my business to know. They have been trying to kill me for a long time."

"Where is it?"

Hayes gestured to his temple.

"Memorized? All the names? Addresses?"

"Yes."

Kashani laughed again, regaining some confidence. "I guess you think that means I can't kill you?"

He said something in a dialect Hayes didn't understand, then waved a finger to the guard to Hayes's right, who approached Hayes from the side. Hayes's hand shot out, seized his wrist, and twisted it, wrenching the shoulder. A piece of black-and-tan-patterned fabric fell from the man's hand and landed on the floor. It was a *shemagh*, an Afghan scarf often worn by fighters over the head and neck.

The other two raised their rifles, but Kashani called them off.

"What is this?" Hayes demanded.

"Have you read Kipling?"

"It's been a while."

"It seems appropriate, given the circumstances. A test of your memory, to see if you can offer what you claim. Kim's Game," Kashani said. "Our instructors at the Farm used to use it."

Kashani had been trained in intelligence work by the CIA at its facility in Virginia, thirty years ago in this never-ending war. He had shaken hands with the vice president of the United States.

Hayes reached for the scarf. Kim's Game was a standard training exercise for spies and special operators. They would be flashed images of objects and told to recall them, or they'd simply be blindfolded for a quiz at random moments. They practiced until their senses were hyperaware and they could retain photographic memories of their surroundings at any time, recording every threat and exploitable piece of intelligence. It came from an old spy novel by Kipling called *Kim,* set not too far from these mountain passes.

If Hayes failed, they would most likely kill him. He folded the fabric into a long strip and tied it over his eyes.

"Arches in the courtyard?" Kashani asked.

"Thirty."

"Weapons on the guard to your right."

"AK-74M rifle. Beretta pistol on his hip. SOG dagger on his chest."

"Fruit on the table?"

"Four apples."

"Which direction are you facing?"

"Southwest."

"The red book on the shelf behind me. Is it to my left or my right?"

"There is no red book."

"Very good. And where are you?"

Nine hours driving in the dark, and Hayes had spent the entire time fixed on navigation: land speed, altitude, and the twisting azimuths of the stars that served as an endless unerring compass over his head.

When he stepped out of the truck he saw the Spin Ghar Mountains silhouetted against the sky: Sikaram, Barkirdar Sar,

Tarakai. They might as well have been street signs as he lined them up and fixed his location.

He knew where he was down to a few kilometers. Enough for an air strike. And he suspected Kashani knew he knew it too. The test was not only to evaluate his memory but to see how observant he was, to determine if he could identify this compound. If this deal fell through, there was no way he was going to make it out of here alive.

"You understand, I want the names of everyone in Cold Harvest."

"I'm not going to give them to you."

Kashani's jaw tightened.

"I'm only going to deal with whoever you're working for."

"There is no one above me."

"You're a go-between. This is too big for you to handle on your own."

Kashani rolled his cup between his hands. "John Hayes," he said, shaking his head. "I have to say, you live up to the stories. Follow me."

The guards led Hayes back through the hallway, underground, and down a long concrete corridor. Then they left him in a room with a simple table and chair lit by a dim desk lamp.

CHAPTER 2

He sat there for forty-five minutes, wondering what the odds were that this gamble would work, that he might be about to meet the real power behind Kashani.

Finally, the door opened, and the bright light from the corridor blinded him for a moment. Kashani stepped in. "This way," he told Hayes. "There's someone you should see."

Hayes followed Kashani and two guards toward the underground garage. He wondered if they were moving him again or if the leader was there, in a safe room. A guard pushed open a heavy steel door.

Hayes peered inside. There was no chief here, only two soldiers sitting against the wall bound hand and foot. They wore *pakols* — round-topped wool caps — and loose-fitting robes in the local style, but their gear was clearly American special operations'.

Under the glaring fluorescent light over-head, Hayes could see blood trailing from the ear of one of the men, and judging from the cuts on his cheek, Hayes guessed he'd been injured by a grenade frag at just outside of the lethal range.

"Who are they?" Hayes asked.

"Some of your American killers. We found them closing in on the house. Good tactics. We wouldn't have seen them coming, but they triggered a slide of snow below the peak."

"They came to kill you?"

"We think they came to kill *you*."

Kashani took a handgun from a guard and entered the room. He kicked one man, knocking him over, then stepped on his neck, driving his face into the floor, and aimed the pistol at the back of his head.

Hayes followed him in, and the guards posted up in the corners.

"If you are what you say you are, surely you won't mind," Kashani said.

Hayes said nothing. He had expected a test of faith.

He recognized the American that Kashani was threatening with the gun, a man with a reddish-brown beard and a few minor cuts on his face. His name was Burke. Hayes had fought with him in Fallujah, back when

18

Burke was a SEAL, a kid on his second deployment; he had trained him in house-to-house fighting, and Burke had gone on to Green — the special operations shorthand for the unit commonly known as SEAL Team Six.

"Hayes?" Burke said. "Jesus. It's true. You son of a bitch." Hayes knew that if he tried to stop Kashani, the Pakistani would kill them all.

Kashani put his finger on the trigger.

"Wait," Hayes said. He stepped toward Kashani, who was smiling like a man who had called someone's bluff. The guards lifted their rifles.

Hayes gestured for the pistol. "How does the saying go? It's better that I kill my brother than a rival take him." It was a *tapa,* a two-line Pashtun poem often sung by soldiers or grieving wives.

"I've heard it," Kashani said. "Keep it in the family, you would say."

Hayes nodded. "Let me take care of this."

Kashani smiled and stepped back, then offered the pistol to Hayes. The guards kept their rifles at low ready, and Hayes traced the tendons standing tense along the backs of their hands.

Hayes stood over his former student. Burke arched back to look him in the eye as

19

Hayes lined up the shot.

"I never believed what they said about you. Until now. Go ahead. You'll burn for this."

Once, things had been simple for Hayes. There were commanders and rules of engagement, opposing forces and friendlies. But now he was on his own, and he understood the terrible weight of choice, of his own calculations of the greater evil, of trading lives like coins.

"You don't know me. What they put me through." He cracked Burke in the mouth with the slide of the pistol and put his foot on his back.

He wrapped his finger around the trigger and brought the gun before him, facing away from Kashani.

He raised it, and pulled the trigger.

The light blew out with a pop and a rain of glass. The room went black. But in his mind, Hayes could still see where each man stood. Kim's Game. He ducked to the left and aimed the pistol at the first guard.

Burke felt the hot glass scratch his neck as the lightbulb exploded, and he rolled onto his feet. The images came like strobes in the orange flash of Hayes's firing pistol: one guard flinching back, struck by gunfire, then the other. Hayes sidestepped left to right, and six shots flared in the dark. Kashani spun with a pistol and shot. The muzzle flame reached out toward empty space and lit up Hayes behind him, his knife out.

The dark returned. A body hit the ground. A flashlight cut through the room, then came the cinching and popping of the cords as someone cut Burke's hands free, drawing the knife a half inch from the skin on his wrist.

Hayes pulled the injured soldier's arm over his shoulder and helped him up. He was dazed.

"Burke," Hayes said. "Sorry about the jaw. I had to sell it. Are you good to walk?"

Burke fought back against the shock. "I think so," he said.

"I'm here undercover. I was trying to find out who he was working for, who wants those names."

Hayes aimed a flashlight that he'd pulled from one of the guards at the ceiling. "We've got to roll before they get backup."

Hayes grabbed Sanders's sniper rifle and rucksack, and Burke took his carbine. They exited into the garage. There were two Pinzgauer 6×6s parked along the back wall. A Swiss-built mountain truck, the Pinz was an ugly green box on six wheels that could climb a 100 percent slope. Hayes and Burke took the cockpit seats, and Sanders, conscious but still unsteady, got in the back.

Hayes gunned it up the ramp leading out of the underground garage. The vehicle rose high on its springs and was nearly airborne when it came off the ramp onto the long driveway.

Burke pointed to the passes to the east.

"We make it through there, and we're out of the badlands."

Hayes watched the mirrors while Burke cycled through the radio he'd pulled from the room.

"We could have killed you back there," Burke said.

"You couldn't have known. No one in the command knew I was here."

Burke looked at the house. He didn't see anyone coming.

"You have a QRF?" Hayes asked. A quick-reaction force: a team of soldiers ready to come in to back up the smaller special operations units.

"No. We have to get through the pass on our own," Burke said. "There's an extraction point ten kilometers out. But if we get there after twenty-one-hundred hours, we're done. They won't be back until tomorrow."

That was in an hour, and they wouldn't

survive if they were stuck here overnight. The notch in the mountains loomed closer and closer as Hayes fought the wheel. He looked through his side window. To call it a jeep track was generous; it was more like a goat path. It was so narrow, he couldn't see road, just his side panel hanging over a ravine that dropped away two hundred feet.

The snow grew thicker as they rose toward the pass, and the Pinz smeared through the turns, kicking debris off the cliffs.

"Almost there, Sanders," Burke said.

The pass opened high to their right as the path curved toward it. The black of the peak gave way to a blanket of stars to the north, but weather was moving in fast from the other direction. Sheets of white snow blew across Hayes's sight lines like static.

Over the grind of the Pinz's diesel, a deep rumble echoed through the pass. It loosed a curtain of snow high above them, and chunks of ice slammed into the side of the vehicle. Hayes forced the wheel toward the steep bank.

"Get out!" Hayes said.

"What?"

"Out! Now! Incoming!"

Only Hayes had identified the source of the noise, but it became clear a second later. A helicopter, banking hard, crossed the pass and disappeared behind the far peak.

"They're circling back."

It was a Bell Cobra, an older American-designed and -built attack helicopter with a 20-millimeter Gatling gun and a weapon pod on either side.

"We need to disperse and draw them in. Drop down the ridge ten or twenty feet. It's our only shot."

He grabbed the sniper rifle, opened his door. "Take the M4," Hayes told Burke. The carbine had a 40-millimeter grenade-launcher attachment under the barrel. "Hit the tail rotor or the pilots through the side glass. Wait for it to come over us. If they use the Gatling guns only, we might survive."

He left a blue light stick glowing in the cabin of the Pinz and climbed out. Burke and Sanders flailed down the snow on one side of the ridge. Hayes dropped six feet down the steep hill on the other and then cut wide across for cover. He dug in, the snow up to his waist, with a boulder between himself and the helo, then raised the rifle, snugged it hard against his cheek and shoulder, and took aim.

The chugging blades grew louder and louder. He watched the white snow blown by the rotor wash come at him like a band of storm clouds.

Hold . . . hold . . . hold.

The helicopter swept overhead, the rip of the Gatlings tearing the night in two as they shot up the Pinz. Hayes heard a low *pock* as Burke launched a grenade. The helo banked and flared to avoid it, and as it slowed, Hayes put one round, two, three, into the tail rotor. Fluid blew out in a spume, and from the other side of the ridge, Burke sent a hail of bullets through the Plexiglas into the cockpit.

It spun as it came over, out of control, losing precious altitude in that thin air. Hayes dove for cover. The ground shook, and he knew the helo was down.

He put his leg forward and postholed it in the deep snow. Another blast shook the hillside, and before he could even register relief at having taken the helicopter, the snow beneath his feet fell away. He dropped with it, clawed against it, but the whole hillside was liquid now, pouring into his mouth and down his shirt, tilting him over. The mountain peaks spun in his vision as he rag-dolled down, helpless.

High up, near the pass, a red light filled the night. A boom echoed along the range, but it was lost to him as blows came to his head and his body kept falling. He didn't know how long he tumbled, but it seemed like forever. And then he hit, and he was buried in a bank of snow.

His hands shot to his face and he clawed away the powder. Snow can melt and refreeze around the face, asphyxiating the avalanche victim in what's known as the mask of death. After he cleared the snow from around his head and shoulders, he started to dig himself out.

He hauled himself out of the bank, and after the dizziness passed, he was shocked to feel *okay*. His pack was six feet above him on the steep slope. The snow was too deep to walk in normally, so he crawled up, gaining only inches as he dragged the snow on top of him. He took time to pack down the powder and then tried to stand. His leg crumpled, and he fell to the side. He tested that leg again, putting weight on it, and it collapsed under him once more. Between the cold and the adrenaline, he felt no pain, only the queasy sense of his limb bending the wrong way. He'd torn something.

The driving snow scoured the exposed skin of his neck and cheek, becoming heavier and heavier until it was a whiteout. The flakes flew past him, down and to the left, a shimmering curtain so total that vertigo set in, and he couldn't fight the feeling that he was flying up and away, as if the snow were still and his body was in motion.

He shut his eyes, and the wind closed around him; snow drifted to his chin, spilled down his collar, filled his ear.

His first movements only dug him in deeper, but then he climbed deliberately, raising himself with his good leg and driving his bad knee into the steep snow to brace himself for another step. Remaining calm was the only way to survive. When he reached the pack, he pulled off part of the frame and two nylon straps and splinted his knee as best as he could.

Hayes had spent a lot of time in the mountains, and every fifteen minutes or so the blood flushed his face and hands — the hunter's response, an acquired physiological reflex to keep frostbite at bay.

He continued up the slope but knew he wasn't going fast enough to warm himself. And as the minutes turned to hours, the cold moved from outside in. The shivering began, crescendoed into a violent tremble, rattling his teeth in his skull. His muscles numbed and tightened, refused to obey. And even his brain slowed down, the thoughts of survival running in frantic, confused loops.

He didn't know how far he had traveled. The world was a white sphere. All he wanted was sleep. There was no ridge, no extraction point, no helicopter, only the fog of his breath turning into ice on his skin.

It didn't make any sense to work so hard when he could just sit down. He stopped and stared into the blizzard. He hadn't thought about how beautiful it was. He let his mind drift into the white.

And he was home in Virginia, in the foothills of the Blue Ridge Mountains. The night was a chorus of insects, and the room was drafty, but the comforter was white and thick with down. He pulled his wife, Lauren, to him in bed and held her tight. The stupor closed in. He welcomed it. The pain disappeared. His body disappeared, bit by bit. He felt warm . . . so warm . . . and he let the peace take him.

On the opposite side of the ridge from where Hayes had fallen, a U.S. Air Force pararescue jumper and a combat controller — members of the two elite specialties of that branch — had found Burke and Sanders.

They immobilized Burke's head and neck, strapped him to the backboard, and hauled him through the door of the helicopter. He had fallen far enough down the valley that they had been able to see his signal panel

— a square of fabric that shines like a beacon when viewed through infrared optics — from the extraction point.

"Turn on the lights," Burke said, staring at the interior of the helicopter. Pain stabbed through his skull. He had slammed his face on a boulder as he and Sanders slipped down the ridge after Kashani's helicopter exploded.

"Don't worry about the lights, Burke. We've got you."

"And Sanders?"

"We have him. He's alive. Was there anyone else?"

"Hayes — he went the other way. Might have fallen into the other valley. He could have made it."

Burke heard the radio chatter fill the helicopter. The voices, like the pain, seemed to be coming from a room at the end of a long hallway. They had given him something, probably morphine. He brought his hand near his face. His eyes were open. He just couldn't see anything.

I'm blind, he thought, then he heard the combat controller's voice: "This man is going to lose his sight, probably die if we don't pull out now."

"We have to go back," Burke said.

"The command wants us out of here. If

we're caught in this country, it'll cause an international crisis. We don't have stealth. And the visibility's going to zero. We'll all die if we don't pull up."

"Hayes is out there," Burke said. "We have to get him."

But no one answered. The engines revved up and drowned out every other noise.

Hayes drove his good leg down into the snow on the far side of the ridge, his brain barely functioning. One thought had broken him out of his trance: *They want the names.* The enemy was coming for Hayes's people at home, where they slept, where their families slept. He thought of his daughter, pictured her standing backlit at the end of the hall, needing him to do a last check under the bed. He had to go on, to warn them.

The world reduced to left foot, right foot. How many times had it come down to this, him exhausted past all reckoning and relying on simple will not to stop? In the end, he was a good soldier not because of any heroics, but because he refused to die and never stopped trudging toward his goal. And there was no pain anymore, even as he watched his knee twist strangely in the splint, the snow dragging him back a foot for every two he climbed.

He checked his watch. One minute until the extraction. The exposed skin on his wrist was red and waxy white with frostbite.

Left, right, left, right. He moved like a windup toy, like this was all he had done for his whole life, like it was all he would do forever.

Rotors echoed below him. He stepped toward the edge of the snowfield and realized he was at the lip of a cornice, hanging over a hundred-foot fall at the top of the ridge. He could see the helo moving through the blizzard below like a shadow.

He pulled an infrared panel he had taken from the pack, then dropped it. He put his hand down on it, but he couldn't close his fingers. The extremity was like a block of wood, and the wind hauled the panel down the cliff, turning it over like a falling leaf as Hayes shouted at the rising aircraft.

The helicopter spun and nosed down to the south, leaving Hayes in the snow and the dark. He was a black dot on a ridge, just a shadow against countless more mountain silhouettes extending back toward Afghanistan. And over the wind and diesel grind, of course no one could hear his voice.

CHAPTER 3

Samuel Cox sat behind a desk in a cramped West Wing basement office, signing a letter. Though a brigadier general, Cox almost never wore a uniform. He was Hayes's handler and a special adviser to the secretary of defense. He had no formal portfolio, and his real job wasn't on any org chart: he made problems go away. It was in that capacity that he had come to serve as the link between Hayes and the command.

He had borrowed this office, down the hall from the Situation Room, to help coordinate the rescue of Hayes and the other men. He had been working nonstop for twenty-four hours and was waiting for a callback from the CIA station chief in Islamabad.

He looked at the personnel photo of a smiling Army Ranger, twenty-four years old, who had died in North Africa the week before on a classified mission against human traffickers that Cox had helped run through the Joint Special Operations Command. He put the photo to the side, then took off his glasses and placed the signed letter in his outbox. It was addressed to the man's wife, the next of kin. Cox always wrote them himself. He could offer no details, only his grief, and he knew that wasn't worth much.

As he shut the file folder, a man with close-cropped silver hair stuck his head in the doorway. Cox stood.

"Any word on our guys, Sam?"

"We got the recon team out of Pakistan, sir. It's all deniable. Sanders is still in surgery. Burke will live. Probably never see again. Hayes is still missing."

Cox checked his watch. Hayes had been out there for nearly twenty-six hours. Most men would be dead from exposure after one night in those mountains.

"Have you called the family?"

"I know the wife. We gave her word that he'll be out longer than we expected. But she doesn't know anything about the mission. There's no sense in worrying her any further until we know if he's alive or dead."

"Whatever you decide. I'm going to the residence. Let me know if anything changes."

"I will, sir. Is Elizabeth back from school?"

"Yes. She's upstairs. Cramming for finals."

"Give her my best."

"Do you want to come up for dinner?"

Cox looked at the phone. He had work to do here.

"Of course." The visitor turned and started up the steps to the main hallway through the West Wing.

Cox could hear the Marine guard at the top of the stairs. "Good evening, Mr. President," echoed down the marble hall as Cox seated his glasses back on his nose and dialed up the regional Joint Special Operations commander for Afghanistan and Pakistan.

CHAPTER 4

Lauren Hayes, John Hayes's wife, raised the hammer and gave the nail a tap, then swung it back and drove the nail in its full length. *Tap-crack, tap-crack, tap-crack.* She finished laying in the trim on the second floor, letting the task fill her mind so she wouldn't look at her phone every five seconds. She had worked a twelve-hour shift at the hospital and would pick up Maggie from her aunt's house in the morning. But even after a day that long, she couldn't sleep, not until she heard her husband was safe. Something was wrong. She could tell, could read between the lines of the bullshit call they had made to her.

She and Hayes had started building this house together.

"I always come back," Hayes had said before he left.

He was two weeks late. This was going to be the first time he would be home for his daughter's birthday. It was in five days. And this wasn't like the other operations, when he was part of a special mission unit. There were no other wives holding vigil, stacking food high on counters and in the freezer. There was no chaplain on watch.

Hayes was working alone now. When he was here, the phone would ring, showing all zeros, and he would go meet with some shadows in suits who had come down from Washington.

Tap-crack. Tap-crack.

The phone rang and it shook her like a close blast. She missed the nail and split a long piece of molding.

She walked to the phone. The caller ID showed all zeros.

"Hello." The hammer hung down by her side.

"Lauren? This is Samuel Cox."

"Is he alive?"

CHAPTER 5

Hayes woke, and the past two days felt like a dream. He had been in and out of consciousness, and all he could remember was a doctor standing over him in scrubs and a few of the words he had spoken: "Warm and dead."

He tried to sit up, but he was strapped down. The skin of his hands and his toes and his face felt like it was on fire. He was in a hospital room. He looked to his left and saw two lines running out from the veins in his arm.

"Take it easy," a voice said, and Hayes turned his head to the right. A man in a wrinkled navy suit sat in a chair under the window. It was Samuel Cox.

"How are you feeling?" he asked.

"It's so hot. Is that the frostbite?"

"Probably. But it's also just hot. We're on Masirah."

Masirah was an island off the coast of

Oman in the Arabian Sea that classified units often staged out of. It had been the base from which they'd launched the doomed Iranian hostage-rescue mission in 1980. That disaster ultimately led to the creation of the Joint Special Operations Command — a secretive headquarters known as JSOC (pronounced "jay-sock") that controlled Team Six, Delta, and a host of other black units. It had been Hayes's employer for more than a decade.

"How are the other guys?"

"Sanders just came out of surgery. He and Burke are both stable. They told me about what you did to get them out of there, the shots you took on that tail rotor. I guess you're the right guy to bring a helicopter down."

Hayes was notorious for having crashed in every type of helicopter used by special operations. He thought that meant he was lucky, since he'd survived. But those who knew about it usually took the opposite view and a seat on a different helo than Hayes if they could.

"What the hell were you doing in Pakistan?" Cox went on. "You were just supposed to be gathering intelligence."

Years before, Hayes had been falsely accused of turning against his own soldiers while running a special operations team. He went into self-imposed exile overseas. He had survived two years on the run as an enemy of the United States and ultimately stopped the men who had framed him from launching an attack on Washington, DC.

After Hayes had cleared his name, the command didn't publicize his innocence or his return to special operations. That allowed him to go undercover using his old contacts from his time on the run, shielded by people's belief that he was still being hunted by the United States. He had started the operation that led to Kashani strictly to find out more information on the people who had sponsored the DC attack.

"That's all I had planned. But people were asking *me* questions. They wanted information on our spec ops teams, and not just the usual intelligence about where they were deployed and what informants they were using. The enemy was gathering names and photos. It sounded like they were putting together a kill list. I had to see who was behind it, so I dangled the information and set up a meeting."

"You didn't think to tell us?"

"The surveillance was too thick. There was no way without breaking cover. They're trying to find out about everyone who's in

Cold Harvest. Not just where they are working overseas. Where they live in the United States. Their homes."

Cox shut his eyes for a moment. It was everyone's worst fear.

"Kashani?"

"I had to kill him before we could find anything else out, but he wasn't the main guy. You know he's only interested in his own region. He was a cutout. There's someone above him. They're using our tricks against us, profiling the special operations community the way we would an enemy terror network." Hayes swallowed, his mouth suddenly dry as paper. Cox handed him the plastic tumbler of water and he drank.

"We have to get ahead of them," Hayes said. "They're after Cold Harvest. Double-down on the security of every name; protect our people. The covers. They can't find them."

"I'm on it. You need to rest."

Cox's eyes went to a machine beside his bed; it was the size of a hotel luggage cart and had multiple monitors above a collection of tubes and transparent pumps.

"What is that?" Hayes asked.

"It warmed up your blood."

He looked at his bandaged hands. "Did I

40

lose any fingers?"

"They think you can keep them all. You're lucky you froze."

Hayes touched his nose and winced. "This is lucky?"

"You can last a while longer when your core temp goes down. The docs say you're not officially dead until you're warm and dead."

"Does Lauren know I'm okay?"

"Yeah. You'll be back home in three days."

"Thanks, Cox. They want the names." Just a few minutes of talking had left Hayes exhausted. His eyes closed, and he leaned his head back. "Look out for our people."

"I will. You rest. I'm going to check on the others."

Cox walked down the hallway and looked in on another room. Burke lay in bed, his head and eyes covered in bandages. The head trauma had damaged the optic nerve.

He moved with a start.

"Who's there?"

"Samuel Cox. I'm from the Office of the Secretary of Defense."

"Oh, Jesus. Look, I didn't know that he was undercover. I didn't mean to crash his op."

"That's our fault. You're not in trouble.

41

Do you know the man who saved you?"

"John Hayes. He was attached to our team at First Fallujah."

"I need you to forget it. You never saw him. You're going to take the credit for this, for rescuing Sanders."

"No way. It was Hayes."

"Hayes was never there."

"Is it true? Was Hayes undercover? Did he stop the DC attack?"

Cox knew the rumors that circulated about Hayes. The noncommissioned officers' networks spread information faster than CNN. Some people even believed he had been responsible for the attack in Washington, DC, the one that he had, in fact, stopped. The darker legends about Hayes contributed to his strength, his ability to slip in and move among the enemy.

"What I'm telling you, you can't tell anyone. Understood?"

"Understood."

"It's true."

"Then let the poor bastard go. Why don't you tell everyone the truth and clear his name?"

"It's more valuable dirty."

"The guy's a hero. He's done his time."

"I agree," Cox said as his phone buzzed in

his pocket. "But it's more complicated than that."

CHAPTER 6

San Diego, Two Months Later
Burke fell onto his back on the bed, his eyes open wide, and took a long breath. He reached to the side and pulled Tara close. He had been home for five weeks and loved nothing more than being in this bungalow in Ocean Beach listening to the waves crash against the bluffs.

Her cheek rested against his.

"Hon, are you crying?"

"Yes." She laughed. "But it's good." She put her hand on his chest and looked into his eyes. "I didn't think you were going to make it home."

The sheets were in a tangled pile near their feet. Burke listened to the baby monitor — silence.

"God bless that kid." Their daughter was a sound sleeper, and their twin boys were staying over at a friend's house.

Tara sat up and gathered the sheets

44

around her. Burke stood and started to walk across the hardwood floor.

"Look out for my shoes," Tara said. But he had already stepped over them.

"You always leave them there." He headed toward the door, hand in front of him, moving quickly, confidently in the dark. The house was familiar, and for years he had fought in the night, so for him, not being able to see wasn't as odd as it might have been for someone else.

The baby's cry came from the monitor.

"I'll take care of her," Tara said.

"After that let's watch a movie."

"But —"

"Stay up with me. I'll go to the Redbox and get us something."

"You?"

"Yeah, me. Take care of June, and I'll be right back." His fingers glided over the wall, found the corner. He reached down and picked up the hiking stick he used instead of a white cane. The last thing he wanted was to look like a goddamn blind guy.

"You'll be careful."

"Always. For six years, I was doing things in the dark that were much sketchier than going to get a movie. Don't worry."

She said nothing.

"You can't hold my hand forever. Come

on. I'll get you a Kit Kat too."

"For a Kit Kat," she said, "sure." She was trying to make light of it, but he could hear the strain in her voice as she let him go.

The wood grain of the door passed under his fingertips. He found the knob, turned it, and felt the tip of his stick tapping on the concrete, then the open air. He stepped down, followed the front path to the sidewalk, and started toward the little downtown. Cars rushed by on Sunset Cliffs Boulevard ahead of him.

There was a man above Kashani, a man acquiring the identities of everyone in Cold Harvest. His name was Niko Hynd. He stood in the dark on the side of the road opposite Burke's house.

He was invisible on this quiet American street. Inside, the televisions threw dancing colors on the walls, and he watched people in their homes like they were animals in exhibits: daughters changing clothes, old men sleeping in their recliners, a young couple making love — Burke and his wife — only glimpsed in the cracks beside the blinds as she buried her face in his neck, trying to keep from waking the baby.

This didn't seem like a country at war, its soldiers on the other side of the world kicking down doors and tearing men and women from their families, raining death from above and killing in the dark.

No. What these people saw were American flags in car commercials. They were fat and happy. And why wouldn't they be? They didn't know the pain of wars unfolding in places they couldn't find on a map. It would never stop. They didn't see it. Didn't feel it. But that was about to change. It was only fair.

Hynd had lost a trusted associate when they'd killed Kashani. He and Kashani were both freelancers, small businessmen in the world of conflict. Hynd worked for hire and specialized in a particular kind of lethal operation: finding and finishing those whom no one else could locate. Kashani had been trying to acquire the names of Cold Harvest members on Hynd's behalf — for a price, of course — but he hadn't been careful enough.

Hynd had used the Pakistani as a middleman because he fit the Americans' narrow perception of a bad guy and would draw suspicion away from himself. They always feared the usual suspects and rarely considered the unexpected. That gave Hynd avenues to penetrate their defenses.

He couldn't afford any more mistakes, and

that's why he was here to do the work himself. He had enough names to keep going, and each death would yield more targets. Kashani's men had kept a photo of Burke, and Hynd had used publicly available online-image-matching software — the same technology that tagged faces in family photos posted on the web — to find an older photo of him, from before he went to the classified units, and then to trace him here.

The front door opened. A man emerged, feeling his way along with a stick. It was Burke. He had survived but lost his sight.

The wife and child were alone. Hynd checked the brass in the suppressed .22-caliber handgun and put it in the holster tight against his hip, then stepped out of the car and began tailing the man as he made his unsteady way down the street.

Burke stopped at the corner. Sounds had never seemed so clear. The cars' engines, as loud as the grind of Chinook helicopter blades, cut in and out as they passed, reflecting off the parked vehicles. He could hear the waves crashing in the distance.

He used to take a daily run here. He and Tara had walked along the old route a few times since he'd returned home, Tara burying her fingers in his forearm with fear every time he came near the edge of the cliffs. He took a deep breath, tasted the salt in the air.

A transformer buzzed to his right.

He listened, then took a step off the curb. The stick tapped along the ground. He tensed, anticipating hitting the opposite curb or a parked car's tire, but nothing came.

Did he have the angle wrong? He moved faster. Maybe he was in the middle of the intersection or had started up a cross street. He stopped and listened, lost.

A V-8 growled, throttle open, and grew louder. The sounds bounced off the buildings. Burke moved quickly to his left while the horn blared.

A rush of wind. The truck's engine note dropped in tone as it flew by.

Burke stumbled. The curb. Thank God. He had made it across the busiest road. He stepped up, felt the soft grass under his feet, and cursed.

It was only six blocks. "I just want to get a fucking movie for my wife," he said out loud. He put both hands on top of the stick and brought his head down for a moment, then straightened up. He listened for the ocean, oriented himself.

To hell with it. He'd figure it out. He

started off again, closer to the water now. Del Mar Avenue, heading toward Coronado. He had this. It was a straight shot down Bacon Street to the Redbox. He laughed about what a small thing it was, and how big, to be able to bring a movie back home.

A whimpering noise came from his left. He stopped. A man moaned, said something pleading, but Burke couldn't understand the words.

"Hello?"

"Help. Please!"

He walked toward the voice. "Are you okay?"

"No. I fell. Help!"

Hynd was crying for help. He watched as Burke moved quickly toward the railing beside the cliffs with more confidence than he'd had before. He must have forgotten to be afraid. These Americans believed in heroes and happy endings. That's what made them so easy to kill.

Hynd circled around quietly, the crash of waves covering his footsteps on the soft grass until he was behind Burke. The blind man placed his hand on the metal rail. Hynd stepped closer.

The handrail under Burke's palm was cold and wet. The ground shook as the waves crashed below. "Hello?" Burke said. "Are you okay?"

The pleading voice was gone. Burke reached into his pocket for his cell phone, a simple model with physical keys, not a touch-screen, that he could operate by feel. He ran his thumb over the plastic buttons, but then the phone jumped from his hand.

He reached for it, felt the railing press against his hip, and heard the plastic crack against the stone, farther and farther away, falling on the boulders at the base of the cliffs.

He heard footsteps behind him, pivoted, and swung his hand through the air. He was still fast. Whoever it was was on his other side now. He lunged in that direction but touched nothing, and as he came to the end of the blow, with all his weight on his forward foot, he felt the arms come in around his thighs. A quick wrestler's take-down from behind raised him in the air. He threw his elbow back, felt it crack against bone and heard the cry of pain, but by then it was too late. The railing hit his shins. His stomach went light, and the fall seemed so slow, so long.

Hynd walked down the worn concrete steps to the small boulder-strewn beach below the cliffs. Burke dragged himself along the sand, groaning in pain. His phone was only a foot away, but he was moving in the wrong direction. His legs were useless. Perhaps Burke had injured his spine near the waist in the fall. His arm was clearly broken.

"Who's there?" Burke growled.

"What does that matter now?"

"What do you want?"

"The names of two men in Cold Harvest. For that I'll let you live."

Hynd loved these moments. People spent their whole lives trusting in myths, abstractions like honor and sacrifice that the powerful feed to the weak-minded to control them.

Only when faced with death were they able to see what they really believed in, to cut through all the bullshit.

"What?"

"Two names. Give me men without families. You deserve to live, surely, after everything they took from you."

Hynd considered himself a student of human nature. It was his greatest weapon. If he could dissect his opponents' beliefs, their most deeply held fears, then he could predict their behavior, and if he could predict that, he could control them and kill them. This moment before death was his laboratory.

Honor or your life. That was the choice. It was a fate worse than death for many of the victims, to abandon their values and realize in the end that they were hypocrites.

Hynd watched Burke as he dragged himself closer.

"I'm going to kill you," Burke said.

Bluster. Typical. Hynd grabbed the man's collar and the sleeve of his good arm and pulled him along the sand. Even injured as he was, Burke fought back with the broken limb, and Hynd heard it grind. He hauled him into the shallow surf. It surged past them with each breaking wave. The moon was full, and the tide would rise six feet by morning.

Hynd leaned over and held him under the cool water while he struggled, fighting until the end.

It took four minutes.

Hynd climbed the stairs and returned to his car. His legs were still cold and damp with salt water. He drove off, and a moment later, he saw a flashlight bobbing four blocks from where Burke had fallen. It was the man's young wife with her baby cradled to her chest in a sling. Hynd doubted she would find the body before the sea claimed it.

A symphony played on the radio. He turned the volume up as the woodwinds picked up the melody from the strings. He pressed down on the gas and took a curving road over the hills of the peninsula toward the freeway.

He had the list of targets memorized, and in his mind he scratched out one name.

CHAPTER 7

The classified phone rang, a distinctive warble. Hayes put down his coping saw and trotted across the upstairs hall to his office. The pain radiated out from his knee, a manageable but insistent sting. He'd torn his medial collateral ligament. It hurt ten times more than tearing the ACL but it was a quicker rehab. He spent two hours a day on the exercises and was well ahead of the protocols.

"It's Cox." A pause. "Burke is dead."

Hayes let out a long breath as the coldness spread through him, that strange instant of numbness whenever he heard of a fellow teammate down.

"How?"

"Fell off the cliffs near his house."

"Foul play?"

"No clear evidence. He might have fallen, or he might've taken his life."

"I can't see him doing that."

Hayes and Burke were members of a small community of special operations soldiers. They had cross-trained with the CIA and acquired the intelligence tradecraft needed to perform operations undercover and alone.

The line between spy and fighter had blurred to the point where it disappeared. The CIA would borrow or hire the most experienced military shooters from the classified units for its direct-action branch, and spec ops would temporarily use CIA authority when it needed to go into nations where there was no state of war, a practice known as sheep-dipping. There were even cases where the legal authority was written so that teams could switch back and forth between military and CIA control as they moved across borders on a single mission.

Some of the best graduated to Cold Harvest, and they had no legal authority. Their only protection was their own tradecraft. There were no more than fifty.

Ever since Hayes had come home, it had bothered him, the number of Cold Harvest deaths over the past couple of years. Five that he knew about. One member had died from a heart attack, another in a motorcycle accident. The latter was depressingly common in the military. Motorcycles killed more good soldiers than enemy fire. But now Burke was gone, so soon after he had come across Kashani's plans.

"Was he involved with Cold Harvest?" Hayes asked.

"He worked with them on a few operations."

Maybe they had ID'd him somehow while he was in custody in Pakistan and traced him here.

"This wasn't an accident. I told you to protect those covers."

Hayes heard a scratching on the hardwood floor outside his office.

"We did everything we could," Cox said. "We don't know how they found him."

"But this isn't the first death."

"I know," Cox said.

"It can't be a coincidence. Do you think someone has gotten inside the classified programs, inside Cold Harvest? That our enemies have the names somehow?"

For a moment there was no response except for the sound of Cox's breathing, and then finally he said, "Yes."

Hayes's first instinct was to drop the phone, get his Mossberg shotgun, take Lauren and Maggie and put them in an interior room. But he had always been careful; he lived here at home with as much caution as he had abroad, undercover. He never stopped watching for surveillance.

No one but Cox and a few other friends he'd had for decades knew where he lived. Every time he went out to a base, he ran a countersurveillance route when he returned to make sure no one was tracking him to his home.

He had Lauren take precautions as well and taught her how to spot someone following her. He knew she resented it, the air of paranoia, as she should, but it was to protect them all. Even when Hayes left the war behind, the war never left him.

"I didn't want to call," Cox said.

"It didn't stop you. You want me on this?"

"I thought it should go to you first. A lot of these people came up under you. And . . ." He hesitated.

"I can think like a killer. You're not going to hurt my feelings." Hayes had never actually been part of the program, though he'd helped train its first members.

He heard rustling from the door.

"We need you on this. It's Black One." Code for the highest priority, from the president, although there was never any recorded link between the White House and Cold Harvest.

"This is ugly, Hayes. Someone might have

penetrated the program. I want you to have open eyes. If you take this job, you'll be a target as well."

The scratching grew louder.

"When is Burke's funeral?"

"Two days."

"I'll have an answer for you then."

He ended the call, went to the door, opened it, and quickly buttonhooked around the door frame. Old room-clearing instincts, drilled into him in the training facilities known as kill houses. A cardboard box sat in front of the door, shaking left to right and giggling.

Then his daughter jumped up and screamed, "Surprise!"

Hayes rubbed his forehead and took a few deep breaths. Lauren came up the stairs and stood at the end of the hallway, stifling a laugh.

"I had nothing to do with it. I swear."

He picked up his grinning daughter. "Did I scare you?" she asked.

"You sure did, sweetie."

Nothing better for a man with poorly managed low-grade PTSD than a preschooler who loved surprises.

Hayes lowered her to her feet. "Why don't you go pick out a story."

She ran down the hall.

"Work?" Lauren asked.

"Yes."

"You're going back?"

"I haven't decided."

Half his toes were still black, the skin continuing to come off in pieces. He had just taken off the knee brace.

"I won't tell you what to do. That was never our arrangement."

She knew what it meant to him, to protect the people he worked alongside. They were as close to him as brothers and sisters.

Maggie came out with a Dr. Seuss book. "Daddy!"

Black One. The highest priority.

Hayes lifted his daughter.

No, not the highest.

CHAPTER 8

Hayes knelt in front of the casket. It looked like Burke. They had done a good job, all in all, but there was something off about the hands, like they were two wooden paddles. They never got the hands right. Hayes had buried a lot of his boys. He hated funerals, hated the way the dead men's faces always looked old and tranquil, at peace. He'd never seen Burke rest easy. Even asleep, he'd been like a coiled spring.

Hayes rose from the kneeler. The funeral would take place at Arlington later that day. Burke's father and grandfather were buried there. This was an early visitation being held for classified personnel at Fort Belvoir, a base on the Potomac south of DC with a long history of black army intelligence work. Lauren and Maggie were in the sitting room just outside. As Hayes waited to speak to Burke's widow, he saw an old teammate, a man named Drew Ochoa. He had come up to Team Six through the navy's explosive-ordnance disposal programs, and he and Hayes had worked together hunting down high-value targets and chemical weapons in Syria.

"Good to see you," Drew said, then he took Hayes's hand and wrapped his arm around him. When Drew stepped back, Hayes glanced down at the man's fingers. Drew flexed them and smiled slightly.

Drew had been taken by the enemy while on a patrol in the eastern deserts, and Hayes had pulled him half dead out of an al-Nusra cell, literally a metal cage, twelve days later. His captors had bound his wrists so tight with battery wire, they'd nearly cut the radial nerve on one hand. The medic thought he might never be able to use it again. Hayes hadn't run into him since, so he was glad to see it was working.

"Thanks," Drew said.

"Of course." Hayes reached up and squeezed his shoulder.

That was it. They didn't do much talking about the past. Drew dipped his head toward Burke's wife, Tara, who sat at the end of the front row of chairs on the far side of the coffin. It was Hayes's turn to offer his condolences. He walked to her.

"I'm John Hayes. I worked with Connor.

I'm so sorry for your loss."

"Thank you for coming," she said, and then she looked at him more closely. "You were with him . . ." She raised her hand to her eyes.

"I was."

"You were one of the men he saved."

"Yes. I'll never be able to repay him."

Her gaze drifted toward the casket. Hayes looked at the last few mourners behind him, waiting. But Tara reached out and touched his arm, raised her face to his. There was something about Hayes that made people trust him.

"People are saying that he jumped," she said.

"That doesn't sound like Connor."

"Then why would he go near those cliffs?"

"I don't know. But he never gave up and never backed down from anything."

Five other men had been killed. Burke had been murdered too. He wanted to tell her that he would hunt down whoever had done this. But there was nothing Hayes could say. He had sworn, and sharing these secrets was dangerous.

Hayes hated the evasions, hated holding information back from Lauren, disappearing, waking covered in sweat and not being able to talk about the memories that stalked his sleep. The men he had killed, the men who had left him to die. Deceiving the ones he loved seemed colder than the violence he faced downrange. He could never get used to it.

Tara Burke's eyes narrowed and she looked at Hayes with something like disdain.

"I know that face. What aren't you telling me?" She shook her head and looked at his wedding ring. "You men and your lies. Honor isn't going to raise my kids. You were supposed to protect him. Get out now. Be with your family. The rest is just —"

She buried her face in her hands and took four long breaths.

"I'm sorry," she said. "I don't know what I'm saying."

Hayes laid his hand on her shoulder. "It's okay."

"He was a good guy," she said.

"The best." Hayes put his arm around her and she cried quietly for a moment, then straightened up.

"Thank you for coming," she said in a flat tone. She was bottling everything up, pushing him away.

Hayes left her with the next mourner. In the entry hall, outside the viewing room, one of Burke's boys was playing with Hayes's daughter. He slipped his arm out of the sleeve of his small blazer and then started turning in circles, trying to get it back in.

"How many kids does she have?" Lauren asked Hayes when he joined her.

"Three."

She shook her head slowly.

"I know. The team wives will take care of her out there, though she might come back to the East Coast to be closer to her family."

"It doesn't make sense," Lauren said. She had been to too many funerals, seen too many young widows. "What's happening, John?"

He took her to the side.

"Someone is hunting us down. The command wants me to come back," he said. "To find out who's behind this, to stop them."

Hayes had been in exile when his daughter was born. He didn't see her until she was two, when he was finally able to return home. It took him months to break through with her, for her to stop hiding behind her mother's legs when he came into the room.

He knew the risks; he didn't want to leave his wife a widow, like Tara and the others. But he couldn't stay at home and wait for another silent kill. What if they came for his family? He'd lost the closest thing he had to a father to the network behind the DC attack, and they had threatened his wife and daughter.

Now the enemy was inside the United States. Hayes couldn't protect his family by sitting on his hands at home. He could protect them by closing on whoever was behind this and putting him in the ground. He knew it would make him a target, that the killers might never stop coming after him. So be it.

His wife was strong. She had family not too far away. She and Maggie had been okay without him. He might not get to see Maggie grow up, but he was willing to pay that price to keep her safe.

"I'm going after them," he said.

She pressed her lips together tightly and, after a moment, nodded. "All right. I get it. I've been to too many of these things, seen too many of these girls wearing black. I can handle it . . ."

She trailed off, but he knew. She could handle the family solo — for now, forever — if it meant that no more of these young women would have to go through this. Her strength was his.

"Do what you do, John. They need you."

His daughter walked toward him, and he took her hand. He saw Tara, Burke's widow, through the open doors as they left.

In the parking lot, Lauren and Maggie went to the car while Hayes hung back. He watched Lauren lift Maggie into the car seat as he took out his phone.

Cox answered on the fourth ring.

"It's Hayes. I'm in."

The morning sun was still low in the sky. As Hayes spoke, there was no way he could see the man in the woods on the far side of the highway, watching him and his family through a long lens. He worked for Niko Hynd.

CHAPTER 9

Killing is drudgery. Hours of scouting, of learning patterns.

Hynd stepped silently down the hall. Carpet. That was good. A patch of moonlight from the living-room window angled across him. Water ran at the end of the corridor. A toilet flushed. He heard her spit out toothpaste.

She wasn't ready for him. Soon. A few more minutes. She was a widow, and this was unfinished business. The key to Cold Harvest lay with this woman.

He eased the door open in silence and examined the third bedroom. It was set up as a guest room and home office. Dust swirled in the light edging around the blinds and settled on the desk, a photographer's workspace. Racks of hard drives, cameras, and lenses in Pelican cases stacked against the wall. He looked over the photos; there was one of a man fly-fishing in a river under aspen trees and another of a group on touring skis making their way across the top of a snow-covered cliff. The room was empty. It had sat untouched for a long time. He stepped out.

Light leaked from under the door of the master bedroom, then disappeared. He heard the creak of springs. He lingered in the hallway.

The house was an L-shaped ranch set back in the woods off a country road that snaked through the mountains outside Charlottesville. The nearest neighbor down the street went to bed at 11:35, after the nightly news. The newspaper was delivered by a man in a rusted-out Mercury wagon at 5:30 a.m. There were no late-night guests, no sexual partners. She slept alone in a home built for a family. He had bugged her phone, a process as simple as clipping into the telephone wires on the outside of the house.

He opened the door to the second bedroom. It would have been good for a child. They'd wanted roots here, had never planned to leave.

Did she know how her husband had died? Did she suspect the truth? Did she hope, in these long nights alone, to join him?

He checked his watch and returned to the

hallway. Toe, heel, toe, heel. He stepped carefully, keeping the weight on the trailing leg, slowly applying it to the front, almost like a toddler's walk, in order to remain silent. Awkward, but he had grown used to it, could do it quickly. He stood outside her door, listening to her breathe, waiting however long was necessary for her to fall fully asleep.

Hynd had others helping him. An operation this complex required many hands. Most were already inside this country. He had backup nearby, but he and his team were still working through stealth, disguising the murders, and stealth was easiest with one man.

Killing was his profession, and this job was simple: eliminate everyone in Cold Harvest. But he was more than a gun for hire. This cause was personal, and there was nothing he enjoyed more than the flush of adrenaline in his veins.

After so many hours of surveillance, he would begin to feel invincible: The woman down the street would walk the dog, the trash trucks would trundle by, the lights of the other houses in the valley would go on and off, all by his cue, and all the work would be rewarded. He would know the secret script of this environment, and soon he would feel like he was summoning it all, controlling it all himself.

Until this moment.

Because at some point, you have to put yourself in danger.

It was time. He twisted the knob and stepped into the room where she slept. The hardwood floor flexed gently as he shifted his weight to his forward foot. He leaned back, tried a spot a few inches over, and proceeded in silence.

When he came around, he could see her face, the mouth tight as if in anger. This was his next target, Carol Duncan, an executive recruiter. Her hands rested near the pillow, and she lay on her side. Her chest rose and fell, rose and fell, beneath the covers — deep sleep.

He took a breath in and could smell her: a clean, lotion-y fragrance. He put his hands on the foot of the bed. She turned slightly, more on her back, her face toward him.

There were easier ways to kill than this approach.

When you first teach soldiers to shoot, you make the target an abstraction. It's not hard to fire at someone from a distance, to aim at a man or woman who might as well be a paper target.

When fighters get up close, the instinctive

human revulsion at killing paralyzes most of them. They won't take the shot even if their own lives are in danger. But the intimate work was his specialty. It took decades to unlearn every moral instinct.

This was the moment he loved, after all the silent watching. To get so close to that time where there was no script, only danger, only death, breathing the same air.

His shadow moved up the bare skin of her arm, toward her chest and neck.

He knew her now as well as anyone. He'd been watching her for days and had seen patterns she might not recognize herself. He'd gotten close to her, so close that he knew her mind, her reactions.

That was the hardest thing. You had to open yourself to the targets, to understand them at the most intimate, human level; in a way, to love them.

And then you had to kill them without hesitation or remorse and stare into their eyes while their lives drained away.

He felt the latex glove, clammy against his skin, as he closed his fingers around the barrel of the syringe. She whimpered and rolled onto her back, and then he reached out toward her.

CHAPTER 10

In the bed, Carol Duncan was dreaming of the cop in town again, a deputy sheriff named Tim. She imagined them together in this room as he lifted her, laid her on the bed, and kissed her. But as she lay back, she saw her husband's photo on the nightstand.

She'd had similar dreams before. They always turned into nightmares about the car fire that killed her husband. She tried to wake herself but couldn't. The scene blurred and she was in the smoking rubble with him, crawling through collapsed concrete blocks and joists with barely enough room for her shoulders. The rough debris tore at the skin on her knees as she pushed in farther. Sweat dripped down her forehead and stung her eyes. And she could hear the cries — her husband, shouting in pain somewhere ahead.

Smoke poured through the broken stone. The hot fumes scorched her lungs. No room now. She dragged herself forward on her belly. There was a crack ahead. She pushed her head and arm in. The ground pressed against her cheek. She tried to force her way through, to get smaller, emptying her lungs, as her husband called her name.

The wreckage pressed in. Her lungs couldn't fill. She couldn't back up, couldn't go farther, couldn't see anything in the blackness.

The shouting grew faint. She heard her name one last time, and then his voice was gone.

Carol jerked upright in bed and took a long gasping breath. The clock read 5:30 a.m. She pressed her hands to her face and felt the sweat on her cheeks.

She lived alone, but every time she shut her eyes to sleep, she was sure there was someone else in the house watching, hovering over her.

Carol hadn't been right since her husband died. She kept his semiautomatic pistol in a drawer in the nightstand. She found it in the dark now, entered the lockbox code by feel, and lifted up the gun, taking care to keep her finger out of the trigger guard. She patted the nightstand where she usually put her glasses. They were gone.

There was a rustling noise from deep in the house.

The pistol felt heavy, and the grip was too big for her hands. But the weight reassured her as she walked blindly in the dark, navigating the room by memory.

What would her clients think, she wondered, of a woman scaring herself awake with bad dreams, and taking a twenty-year-old loaded .45 with the safety off to go to the bathroom in the middle of the night?

She hit the lights and flinched to the side when she saw a figure.

But as her eyes adjusted, she realized it was just her bathrobe hanging from a hook behind the door. She found her glasses on the sink, and, with her heart pounding, she checked inside the shower.

Next, she started up the hallway, telling herself this was ridiculous but not believing it. The rest of the house was clear, but she had saved Paul's office for last.

She wrapped her fingers around the cold knob and opened the door. She never came in here anymore. She looked over the strange bottles of liquor labeled in languages she couldn't understand — from Luanda and Baku and God knew where else. The photos looked down through a layer of dust: her husband at Camp 4 in the Yosemite Valley, the mecca for rock climbing; fishing in Paradise Valley; skiing in the San Juan Mountains of southwest Colorado.

She stopped next to one. Paul was wearing body armor and a helmet, PRESS written on his chest, riding a mule through a bombed-out mountain pass. His saddle was slipping to the side as the mule reached for some high grass on the trail, and he was laughing, arms thrown out, trying to keep his balance. He was a freelance photographer and did mostly nature shots and some combat work.

She could hear him laugh as clearly as if he were in the room. Her legs froze, and she felt like her throat was swelling shut. She pressed her thumbs into the corners of her eyes and swallowed, and then walked quickly back into the hall.

She couldn't stay in there. Not yet. She touched the ring on her finger. She hadn't taken it off. Hadn't moved it to the right hand, though she had started wondering what was the decent interval. She pulled the door shut, walked back to her bedroom, entered the bathroom, and put down the pistol.

Carol dropped her pajama bottoms to the floor and started the shower. As the steam clouded the mirrors, she remembered the gun, took it off the counter, and walked back to the nightstand.

The edge had gone off the fear, and she looked at that lethal hunk of metal, shining with its light coat of oil. "A weapon you won't use is less than worthless," Paul had said once. *Would I be able to pull the trigger if I found someone there, hiding behind the door? Or would he just take the gun from me while I stood paralyzed by fear?*

She left it on the bed and returned to the shower. The water ran hot, almost scalding her skin until the heat was all she could feel, washing that sticky-sour smell of panic off her body. By the time she was finished, she could hear the birds calling outside. Dawn wouldn't be too far behind. She stretched her hand out the shower door, grabbed her towel, and laughed at the bathrobe hanging off the door like a specter.

Crack and squeal, then silence. Crack and squeal. She knew the noise; it was the gate in the backyard. It was cheap, and the wind pried it open. It was still dark, and there was no way she was going out there.

In the foggy mirror, she looked at the lines around her eyes and beside her lips, and she touched the skin of her neck. A hard year since Paul had died, but it showed only in the circles under her eyes and in the set of her jaw. She didn't look as bad as she felt, and she could see the men in town casually glancing at the ring, waiting for it to disappear.

A quarter mile away, on a steep side street, Hynd slipped into the passenger seat of a sedan and laid the syringe on his leg. A woman sat behind the wheel, her black hair pulled into a tight bun. Her strength was evident even in the loose-fitting clothes she was wearing. She was Vera Choriev, one of Hynd's two deputies on this operation. Her mixed European and Asian features gave her a stark beauty, though few who saw her would come away with that as their first impression. They were left only with coldness.

"Is it done?"

"No," he said. "She woke. It would have been messy, would have left too much evidence in her home."

They waited, watching the house, until an eight-year-old BMW rolled down the driveway and turned onto the two-lane road through the valley; Carol's car. Vera called to their backup vehicle on an encrypted radio. "She's heading south. Pick up the tail."

She brought the car around and raced after.

Chapter 11

The dawn broke, and Carol stopped at a traffic light on the way to her little town. She had started answering e-mails at the kitchen table with a cup of yogurt and a loaded gun next to the laptop and then thought, *What the hell am I doing? I have to get out of this house.* She decided to head to the bakery on Main Street. The pastries would be fresh, and she liked to catch up over coffee with the woman who ran the shop.

She didn't notice the Toyota pickup that pulled out behind her BMW. She saw Tim, the cop from her dream, stepping out of the mini-mart attached to the Exxon station with a cup of coffee in his hand.

He gave her a wave. He was one of the guys who would check, when he thought she wasn't looking, to see if the ring had been taken off her finger. She didn't mind. It was nice to be noticed by a decent man, not to feel so alone. She felt the color rise in her cheeks as she thought about the night before, the dream.

Pollen drifted through the slanting morning light, and a line of black clouds over the mountain promised a break in the heat.

There was construction on the highway, so she went on the back roads. It was a longer route, little used, but she liked to drive it, twisting through a hollow with hills banking up on both sides. Forest roads branched off into the woods. She came to a Y intersection and pulled up to the stop sign.

Metal crunched. Her car jumped forward, and her skull snapped against the headrest. She looked in the rearview. A Toyota truck loomed behind her. It had rear-ended her. She couldn't see the driver. He had stepped out and was behind the door.

She opened hers, put one foot on the asphalt, and then saw the gun barrel leveled at her face between the cab and the open driver door of the Toyota. She leaped back in the car as her window glass blew out, tinkling across the country road.

She threw the shifter into first, punched the gas, and dropped the clutch. She stayed low as the acceleration slammed her door shut.

Another shot. The rear window exploded. Glass cut into the skin of her neck. Fat drops of rain plunked against the roof.

Her eyes were just barely above the wheel as she turned right at a fork. Time seemed to slow, like in a dream, as her rear tires screeched, kicking gravel out as they veered off the road and a yellow traction-control light flashed on her dashboard. She was still reeling from the collision. The Toyota pulled up closer.

Blood dripped down her neck, soaked into her collar.

The movements seemed to come automatically as she watched the tachometer drift toward the red line and slightly past with each gear shift. As the first curve came, she drifted wide, then cut the corner as closely as she could, branches scraping her window, and exited wide again. The Toyota shrank in her rearview and disappeared around the curve. She didn't know this road. It narrowed, and the broken-up asphalt shook the car, cracked her teeth together over the washboard surface.

The truck had the advantage with its high clearance and four-wheel drive. It would catch her soon. There was no time to think. Fighting the wheel took all her attention. It was a long, sweeping curve. A rise sent the car weightless, giving her a sick feeling in her stomach for a moment until the front end crashed down and her head whipped forward and the car slid sideways and threatened to roll into the ditch. She could hear the Toyota's engine in the hills behind her.

There was no time. She saw a forest road ahead, leading back toward town. She came into it at speed, a ninety-degree turn, and slowed the car. As she turned the wheel, she stabbed the clutch and the gas and dropped the stick into second gear. The rear tires came loose as the car began to spin, and all she could see through the windshield were the second-growth trees twelve feet in front of her. She palmed her wheel into the skid. The rear tires bit just as the car ended up pointed down the unpaved side road, and she shot off over the rough surface.

She kept on, hoping the man in the Toyota would continue past on the main road. Her phone showed no signal. Rain showered down. For a moment there was quiet, then something rumbled low behind her.

She checked the rearview. No. He was coming. As she took the first curve, the tires smeared through the mud, and she brought the wheel around, fighting the skid. The road curved away from town, up the mountain. In the mirror, she could see the Toyota's headlights, its grille growing larger and larger. She didn't have a chance. Her BMW dipped into a rut. Brown water splashed on the windshield and for a second her tires spun uselessly as the car slipped toward the high dirt walls laced with branches.

The truck's lights knifed through the woods behind her. She pulled her husband's gun from the glove box, stumbled out, and clambered up the bank on her hands and knees. The rain soaked her hair, her clothes, dripped down the small of her back. She ran. The brambles tore at her shins, and a vine dragged thorns along her neck. It was an ugly forest here, overgrown and immature, and she could barely manage more than a walking pace despite all her exertions.

A door opened and slammed shut behind her. She cut to the left, thinking in a half a dozen directions at once. He would guess she'd run away, so maybe she could get around him, circle back to her car.

The mud filled her shoes, sucked them down. She reached her hand in to free her foot and stumbled another twenty yards, then stood behind a wide oak and rested her head against its bark. Her breath came fast and ragged. Wet hair was pasted to her cheek. She looked back the way she had come and saw it: broken branches, huge smears of footprints through the red clay, mud streaked over the downed trees she had jumped over.

The trail was so obvious. He would find her.

"Come out and I won't hurt you!" The voice sounded like it was just on the other side of the tree. It was a man's voice, loud and calm, accustomed to being obeyed.

Footsteps slopping through the mud, closer now.

"I just want to talk to you. Come on out."

Even closer. Off to her left. He would see her any second. She pressed against the tree, wished she could shrink down to nothing.

She ducked down and saw him. He was tall and thin, wearing a simple dark blue suit, striding through the torrent in the woods like it was the most normal thing in the world. A short rifle hung from his shoulder, and as his eyes fixed on her, he brought it forward.

You're going to fucking die! the voice screamed in her head. *Run! Use the gun!* It hung at the end of her trembling arm, but her hands were numb, bloodless from the fear. Her legs felt like concrete, planted there in the ground.

A weapon you won't use is less than worthless.

She fell to one knee on the red clay, and he took aim.

Four gunshots cracked the air.

CHAPTER 12

When you're weak, play strong, and when you're strong, play weak. Hayes had taught her that a long time ago, when he was training her for Cold Harvest. If you're undercover in a hostile city and someone follows you and corners you, don't draw and then ask questions. That's for the movies.

Shoot him in the face and exit the situation.

Her name wasn't Carol Duncan, it was Claire Rhodes. And she was a headhunter, but she didn't recruit executives. Long ago she'd learned that the only way to sell a lie is to believe it in your bones, to live it as the truth, to inhabit the persona, because you never know who's watching.

She'd worked for Cold Harvest until a year ago, when her husband was killed, and the teammates closest to her started dying, and the commanders that had turned her into this machine cut her loose.

She sat back over her right heel with her left leg slightly in front of her, her left knee bracing the pistol in the most accurate kneeling firing position. The pungent smell of burned propellant drifted from the .45 and tingled in her nose.

She had fired all four shots.

The target dropped into the undergrowth. She moved quickly, flanking left, following her pistol, and jumped over a downed tree. The carbine had fallen to the man's side. She dragged it away with her foot by the sling as she stepped over him and patted him down for hidden weapons.

"Who are you?" she said.

Two bullets had hit him in the eye, destroying the socket. He lay on his side.

Claire shook her head. Rusty. The first two shots had missed. In another situation that would have cost her her life.

She pressed her fingertips to the side of his neck. The pulse was barely palpable. His chest was still. His remaining eye fixed on her desperately as he clung to the last seconds of life. Sirens cried deep in the woods behind her: the police.

Even if he could talk, there was no time for intel. The authorities would be here any second.

"It's okay," she said. "It's over."

She aimed the gun at him, turned her head away to avoid the spray, and fired, destroying his brain stem. She scanned the woods for any accomplices, then ducked down and searched his pockets. The sirens were closer now. She had only minutes, but she needed any clue she could find about who had sent this man to kill her.

She pulled a wallet from his chest pocket and opened it. There was a badge with a five-pointed star on one side and an ID on the other.

"Department of Justice. James Grier. Deputy U.S. Marshal."

She muttered a curse. She had just killed a federal agent. The FBI had watched her for a while after Paul was killed. She knew they suspected her. But why now? Why like this? Why not announce themselves?

Panic rose in her; her thinking became disordered.

"Carol! Carol!"

She looked back to the roadway. A police cruiser had stopped behind the Toyota. It was Tim's patrol car. She saw him walking through the woods, his sidearm out.

Just turn around, Tim. This game is too dangerous for you. It goes too high.

But he strode on, coming to save her.

She picked up the carbine and crouched

beside the lifeless body. Blood ran through the red mud, swirled over the leaves. She pulled back the charging handle, checked that there was a round in the chamber, then dropped the magazine and felt its weight in her hand. Plenty of ammo. She slammed it back in, rested the barrel on the downed tree, and looked through the sight.

Tim moved closer, glanced down, and saw the tracks through the mud.

"Carol! Are you okay?"

He kept the pistol at a low ready. It had been his father's in Vietnam. He'd never used it on duty, only at the range. She remembered him talking about it at the bakery, talking about his father.

She pressed her cheek against the stock and placed the crosshairs on his heart, moving with him as the trees passed like shadows between them. She'd just shot a federal agent, and now she might have to shoot Tim to get away.

"Carol!"

Turn around, Tim. Please. I don't want to kill anymore.

He stepped closer. He'd always been kind to her, could see when she was hurting and was there, not demanding, but ready for whenever she wanted to talk, whenever she needed someone to listen. She never did.

This is why she had to live the lie. Because when people found out the truth about her, they ended up dead.

Her finger curled around the trigger, and she tracked him as he moved closer. She'd shoot when he stopped.

"Carol!" He turned and looked directly over her head.

Good-bye, Tim. I'm sorry.

CHAPTER 13

Black tips. That's what saved his life. When she had checked the rounds in the rifle's magazine, she saw they had black tips. M995 ammunition. The bullet was made of lead wrapped around a large ultra-hard tungsten carbide penetrator, good for punching through a bulletproof vest or killing someone inside an armored car. It was illegal in the United States, and the only Feds who used it were special teams guarding nuclear materials in transit.

It took her a moment to put it together. There was no way a marshal would use it in a duty weapon. They used jacketed soft points so the rounds wouldn't penetrate walls and hurt bystanders. Nothing would stop this bullet. It was rare and difficult to acquire, an assassin's round.

No U.S. Marshal would have bumped her car, stalked her in her house, shot at her without warning, no matter how dangerous people thought she was. There *were* units that might, like her former employer. But the dead man had been an impostor; he wasn't a Fed, so there was no need for her to shoot her way out of this.

She ditched the gun, and her face changed as she began to cry quietly, forced a tremble in her hands, and let Tim find her. The dab of black on that bullet had saved his life.

"Carol! Back away!" He stalked toward the body. She had nearly killed him when it was obvious that she hadn't needed to. Too much killing — her answer to every puzzle. The old ways.

"Are there others?"

"No," she said.

He put his arm around her shoulders.

"Is he dead?" she asked.

"He's gone. You're safe."

Forty-five minutes later, she sat in the back of the ambulance, covered in a foil blanket, with a bandage tugging on the skin of her neck, a blood pressure cuff on her arm, and a pulse oximeter on her finger.

Like she was the one who'd been shot.

Tim stepped into the back door.

"Can I come up?"

"Sure."

"You mind if I sit?"

"Course not."

He was asking questions, seeking permission, making her feel in control; proper victim management. He was a good cop.

"How are you feeling?"

"I can't believe this happened to me." That's what victims always said, over and over.

"Take your time with it. You're safe now. Carol?"

He ran his fingers over the leather cover of his notebook, kneading it, worried.

"Yes."

"Is there anything else you want to tell me?"

"I think that was it. Thank God you came along. Why?"

"Bill Drummond was up on the ridge. He heard the shots and called it in. He saw some of the chase, too."

She watched him, waited it out.

"Where did you learn to drive like that?"

"I was scared. I tried to keep it under control as best I could."

"Drifting a corner?"

"Turn into the skid. Isn't that what you're supposed to do?"

"Yes," he said, and he looked down.

"What is it?" she asked.

He looked at the monitor that showed her

pulse rate; she guessed he was checking to see if she could handle the questions.

"You shot him twice in the eye, through the same hole."

"God." She raised her hand to her mouth.

"Even professionals can't do that. Your brass was twenty-five yards away from his body. That's U.S. Army Marksmanship Unit stuff."

She fixed her eyes on him, forcing him to bully her, using his decency against him, but she was doing him a favor. The truth would only hurt him.

"Is there anything you want to tell me, Carol? Are you in some kind of trouble?"

She put her hand on his and squeezed it gently.

"Can I go home?" She gave him a soft look. "Please."

"Of course. I'm glad you're okay, Carol."

You too.

"Thanks," she said.

Tim dropped her at home. "Do you want me to stay?" he asked. "Until you get settled? Or I can take you to the station or some family nearby?"

"I just want to lie down."

"Sure."

He walked her to the door, and she

95

opened it and then wrapped her arms around him.

"It's best if you stay close to home until we get this settled," he said. "I'm sure it will check out, but we might need to interview you again."

She had a clean truck in a garage twenty minutes away with two prepaid phones, an M4 rifle, and a Glock 26 in the trunk. Everything she needed to run.

"I'm not going anywhere," she said. "Thank you, Tim."

She shut the door.

There were four cover identities ready to go. The passports were hidden with the guns in the truck, but she knew the faces. She remembered the photos, taken when she was a couple of years younger. She stood in front of the mirror in the master bedroom and watched her face change as she recalled the false personas available to her.

She would become Sasha Behrend, privileged, ridden with social anxiety, hiding behind her scarves and glasses. Her cheeks went hollow. Her eyes narrowed. Her posture straightened. She had a dancer's carriage. Her neck seemed to grow, and her feet turned out slightly.

Music helped. Carol Duncan was plain-spoken, salt of the earth, unpretentious. She liked Patty Griffin and Diana Krall. Sasha Behrend was classical, difficult; Schoenberg, Debussy. Oboes played in her head as she studied her reflection.

"Hello. I'm Sasha Behrend. What gate is flight four ninety-six?" The words came fast; she was rushing through the exchange. She tried it a few more times. Carol was gone. Sasha looked back at her. She felt different.

She wasn't Carol. She wasn't Sasha. She wasn't any of them. And she was. She'd been living this way so long that these names and faces were all she had left. Whoever she'd been when she'd started was dead, destroyed like burned paper.

Because you have to live the lie, forget the past, the truth, yourself. Or else people get hurt. They see the way you drive. They notice two bullets through one hole. They ask questions. The answers are fatal.

She remembered the last days with her husband.

"Is there anything you want to tell me?" Paul had asked. She had wanted to tell him everything. She had wanted all the killing to end so she could remember the person she had been before all this.

Her husband asked questions. He was the last person to find out who she really was,

97

and in short order he was dead.

The reflection stared back at her, and she didn't recognize the woman in the glass as she opened her mouth and began to speak.

"I did not kill my husband." She said it with utter conviction. She believed it in her bones.

There was only one way out. All the suspicions, the paranoia, the midnight fears — they were all well founded. Someone had come to execute her — a former enemy, a former boss, perhaps a former friend. And he would be back to finish the job.

Unless she got him first. She stopped outside Paul's office, listened to the silence for a moment, and then moved to the rear of the house and put her hand on the screen door.

This had been her home for five years. For five years she had lived as Carol Duncan; she had married Paul under that name. But he was gone, and she would most likely never return to this home. Carol Duncan was dead too.

She slipped out the back door, eyes on the patrol car parked down the street, then sprinted for the edge of the woods.

CHAPTER 14

Niko Hynd stood outside the sedan with the door open, looking over the rounded valleys of Claire Rhodes's adopted town. Her home was far below him to the left. There were still police lights flashing in the woods near the ridgeline where the man disguised as a U.S. Marshal had been killed. He'd been working for Hynd. The police wouldn't find any trace of his true identity.

Vera sat behind the wheel with the window open.

He had warned the man in the truck to follow Claire only, not to engage. He couldn't handle her. Few could.

"I told him to wait," he said.

"He thought he had her," Vera replied. "She's on the move now. Do we take her?"

There was providence in this, and Hynd was glad he hadn't killed her at the house.

"Let her go."

"What?" Vera asked.

He thought of what he knew about Claire, how anger drove her to violence, short-circuited any self-control.

"She may not understand how, but she's on our side. Let's go."

The real work was just starting. And the men who paid Hynd wanted results.

CHAPTER 15

Hayes and Cox had eaten lunch at an Afghan hole-in-the-wall in Alexandria, Virginia, a historic city just across the Potomac from DC. The owner had come to the U.S. in the 1970s. The two men had talked to him in Pashto for a while and he'd shared a few of his favorite *tapas,* the two-line poems. It was nice to hear the ones about love and hometowns for a change.

From there they went to Fort Belvoir, about twenty-five minutes south along the Potomac. JSOC and the CIA Special Activities Division sometimes used its airfield because it was a convenient staging area near Washington. Cox was headed out with another compartmented task force.

Hayes had visited this base often and spent a lot of time at the CIA's two classified facilities — Camp Peary, near Williamsburg, and Harvey Point, in North Carolina — as well as at the Joint Special Operations

Command's headquarters at Fort Bragg. He trained a select group of men and women who knew the full story of his return, passing on what he had learned about the enemy and about deep-cover missions during his time in exile.

Hayes and Cox walked alongside a hangar. "How'd it work out with the Pakistanis?" Hayes asked.

"They denied knowing anything about Kashani. We denied having anything to do with a downed helicopter or having any personnel in their country. The usual: drinking tea together with both sides lying through their teeth."

"Thank God for allies," Hayes said. When they reached the edge of the tarmac, Cox stopped and turned to him.

"Are you sure about taking this on, Hayes? Everyone who gets involved in Cold Harvest has a target on his back."

"I told you my answer. I'm going to find whoever is killing our people. I don't have time for a heart-to-heart."

"Good," Cox said, and he patted him on the shoulder. "I'm going to be offline for the next ten days — in the field, no contact — so I won't be able to step in."

"Who's in charge of the program? Tom Gray?" He was the former CIA officer who had run Cold Harvest from the beginning. He and Hayes had worked closely together, and Hayes had helped select and train a lot of the early Cold Harvest crew.

"No. Gray retired; he's somewhere on the Chesapeake with his family."

"He deserves a break."

Cold Harvest had been a huge risk. It was technically illegal. There was no presidential finding to authorize it, and it was organized as a corporation, a contractor operating outside the government. It did the United States' bidding, but if it was ever discovered, its members would be prosecuted as a group of criminals who had set up their own private kill teams.

Service was voluntary. The Cold Harvest personnel knew the dangers and understood that they were risking arrest, conviction, execution. But they did it because they knew it needed to be done.

That was how it had started, a human sequel to the successful CIA drone-killing programs. Despite the popular misconception of the CIA as a bunch of freewheeling James Bonds, the primary mission of its officers was to gather intelligence and report on situations as they were, not to launch operations or change facts on the ground. The institution was temperamentally risk-averse and had been for fifty years. It only reluctantly embraced lethal missions with drones.

Thomas Gray, the man behind Cold Harvest, had come up in a much bolder CIA, the wild years of the 1960s and early '70s, before the Senate investigated the excesses in the intelligence community and reined them in. He'd raised the question in a meeting: If we can kill bad guys with drones in Yemen, why can't we shoot them in the face in Paris?

There were no good answers, and one of the political bosses jokingly asked, "And who will pull the trigger?"

"I will," Gray had said, and after more than a year of navigating legal loopholes and setting up shell companies, he stood up Cold Harvest. He'd been willing to risk a thirty-year career, his pension, and his life to take out the enemies that couldn't be reached any other way.

Hayes and Cox paused their conversation as a helicopter roared overhead and rose into the sky. In a hangar to their right, a ground crew loaded unmarked crates onto a Black Hawk.

"Who's running Cold Harvest now?" Hayes asked.

"Kathryn Morgan is handling the staff

side of things," Cox said as the noise subsided. Hayes knew her. She was a former army helicopter pilot who'd lost her leg in a crash in Iraq. People tended to underestimate her, but she was hard as nails. He liked her.

"I need everything they've got, the names of everyone who was part of the program and any of them who've died."

"Morgan will set you up," Cox said, and he checked his watch. A Suburban cruised along the access road. Morgan was sending a car to take Hayes to the Cold Harvest headquarters.

"That must be her ride."

The SUV parked at the far end of the field.

"You coming?" Hayes asked.

"No. I can't get near Cold Harvest. I'm too close to the president, and that program is —"

"The dark side?"

"I didn't say that," Cox said. "I didn't say anything."

"Course not."

Cox shook his hand. "Keep your eyes open, Hayes."

"Will do." He turned and walked alone toward the SUV. Two men stepped out. He remembered the last time he'd climbed into

the back of a truck. It hadn't worked out so
well.

CHAPTER 16

Kathryn Morgan dropped her cigarette butt into an empty plastic water bottle on her desk. She was technically in charge of Cold Harvest, a duty she needed to pass off to someone else as quickly as possible. Smoking indoors was one of the few upsides of running an illegal program. The room smelled like an ashtray, but she no longer noticed.

She checked her watch. Her next appointment was running ten minutes late.

Finally, her phone buzzed. She walked to the back stairs and found national security adviser Kenneth Tucker looking winded. He had a half-empty plastic to-go cup with what looked like the remains of a green smoothie in it. He wore a warm-up suit that read COLBY LACROSSE on the chest. His hair, usually perfect, was a mess. She guessed he wasn't used to running surveillance-detection routes. He'd changed cars twice on the way here, coming through the underground garages at Tysons Corner.

But Tucker wasn't running from foreign surveillance or a kill team. He was hiding from the press. He had helped authorize Cold Harvest but couldn't be seen having anything to do with it, especially not now that the program was in crisis. If they played this wrong, they would both go down with it. No one could know about this meeting.

Tucker had a lock on his party's nomination for president and was four points behind his opponent and closing fast. The election was four months off. But he didn't look confident.

"Come on in," she said.

He followed without a word. The back corridor was empty. At her office door, she slid a plastic card into the lock, then logged in with a six-digit PIN. The lock retracted.

Tucker looked like a news anchor, which had led many to dismiss him as another walking haircut, but Morgan knew better. He was a rich, spoiled prick, no doubt — the entitled son of Westchester lawyers — but that made people underestimate his ruthlessness.

His wife and young son had died in a car crash in 1992, which softened his profile and won him a lot of sympathy during his political career. It had happened on the same night his primary opponent had dropped out of his first House race. Tucker had been on his way to the victory party when he received a phone call from the police in Darien, Connecticut, telling him that his wife and son had been killed by a drunk driver.

Morgan remembered the first time she'd heard him tell the story of that night. She remembered the second time she'd heard it, and the third, and the fourth. Each beat was the same, with minor variations, and she'd realized that this was an act, that he had sat somewhere and practiced it, used their deaths as a tool to advance his career.

Some might have been disgusted, and she was, but she had learned the hard way in Washington that when it came to the truly ambitious — and Tucker was without peer in that arena, a sort of self-promotion savant — you could either get in their way and be rolled over, or get behind them and roll along easily.

When Tucker was on the House Intelligence Committee, he had secretly given Thomas Gray authorization to set up Cold Harvest. It wasn't because Tucker believed in the program, really, but because the premise appealed to him. He was a political climber, and the operations were deniable, so the triumphs but not the risks would accrue to him.

Cold Harvest shooters racked up a string of successes — nuclear transfers stopped, terrorists killed, kidnapped Americans freed — all without receiving a word of recognition. Tucker quietly took credit for their achievements among the upper echelons of the political, military, and intelligence establishments, building his reputation on his way to becoming the national security adviser and a presidential candidate.

But it was a dangerous game to run, and Tucker didn't have the stomach to run it. He'd always wanted to be able to deny any association with Cold Harvest if anything went wrong and had given Gray free rein. But Gray had started to suffer from early-onset Alzheimer's just when the killings of the Cold Harvest members began.

He was out. And now Tucker and his deputy Morgan were left with the mess. They had met when she was a military liaison to the House. She was the only one he trusted to help him get ahead of this disaster.

As she moved behind the desk, Morgan's left-lower-limb prosthesis emitted a quiet mechanical whine with every other step.

Born in Queens to Jamaican parents, she had striking hazel eyes and a light spray of freckles across the bridge of her nose. While some people found religion after an accident like a helicopter crash, she found that she simply didn't give a fuck about anything anymore except rising to a position where idiots above her could no longer nearly get her killed, as they had on the night they'd ordered her to fly her Chinook straight into what turned out to be an enemy stronghold.

Politics revolted her, so she found the best approach was to draft off political animals like Tucker. He had the connections she needed. If he won this election and she kept Cold Harvest under control, he would set her up in a position where she would never have to answer to anyone again.

Tucker ran his hand through his hair and stared into empty space for a half a second, then took a sip of his drink.

"Jesus Christ," he said. "That was awful. I've got twenty reporters camped outside my condo. I've got opposition researchers filming me every moment I'm outdoors. I've got Secret Service up my ass. You're not recording anything?"

"No," she said.

"Good," he said. "I only have about a half hour. They think I'm exercising. What the hell is going on in Virginia? I hear Claire Rhodes is on the loose, and we have a dead body and local cops involved."

"Yes. I'm taking care of it."

"I'm asking people for million-dollar checks. I can't have this come back on me now. There is too much at stake."

"It's under control."

"Really? Because it sounds like a shit-show. We had a firefight on American soil, and Rhodes is running around like a five-foot-five time bomb. I just need it to go away."

Morgan had been at the meeting where they'd first conceived of Cold Harvest, seated against the wall while the principals ringed the conference table. Tucker was the one who had jokingly asked Gray who would pull the trigger. Gray put himself on the line, and Tucker had profited hand-somely from the arrangement, but now the free ride was over.

"This is why we should only kill with drones," Tucker said. "People are messy. You can scrap a drone. It doesn't go to the *New York Times.* It doesn't come to your house and try to kill you."

"Calm down, Ken. I have a plan."

"You had better."

Nothing would be easier than shutting it

down. Half the bad guys in the world would line up to kill the people in Cold Harvest. If they knew their names.

"Understood," Morgan said.

She knew who she needed to stop this, to get the program back under control: John Hayes. Because he was the best they had, and because his name had never been cleared. If this all went south, there would be no one better to take the fall.

She'd already sent two of her security team to get him. He was on his way.

CHAPTER 17

Hayes sat in the back of the Suburban as they drove in silence through the choked highways of Northern Virginia.

He could see the towers, hundreds of them, springing up like kudzu along Route 66. Buildings with easily forgotten names. Little more than initials. The military-industrial complex was over, and this was the new iteration: the contractor renaissance. Satellites, bodyguards, interrogations. For a long time, the joke was that they had outsourced everything in war but the shooting. But then they outsourced that too.

The driver cruised through an office park, pulled into a garage under a nondescript beige-and-glass tower, and parked beside the stairwell. Hayes and the two men entered an elevator, and the taller guard swiped a key card.

They exited onto the seventh floor and crossed an empty lobby toward a door on the far side.

The first guard placed his hand on a palm rest, and the lock chunked open. There was another door three feet in: a mantrap. The guard stepped into the small space, and Hayes watched the floor depress slightly — to check weight and make sure only one person passed at a time.

The door closed, and the palm rest turned green, indicating it was ready for another entrant.

"Go ahead," the guard said.

Hayes laid his hand on the cold glass. It glowed red while it scanned. The lock clicked open.

They had his biometrics. No one was supposed to have that info.

The doors slid back. His eyes went to the corners — doors with numbers but no name plaques. There was an open floor-plan office to his left, with young men and women at desks.

This was supposed to be a one-on-one meet-up with Morgan, and he'd thought he was coming to a brass plate — intelligence shorthand for a cover office, typically empty or manned by a single communications officer. There were too many people here, too many seeing his face. Hayes was well aware there could be a leak from inside the pro-

115

gram. This could mark him as a target.

A woman with her hair back in a loose bun approached him, the catch in her stride from the lower-leg prosthesis barely noticeable. It was Kathryn Morgan. He caught the scent of cigarettes from twelve feet out.

Hayes's eyes didn't move, but he saw two men rise to his right and then flank him on either side.

Morgan stopped at the end of the row. "Derek, Will. What the hell are you doing?"

They were flexed in an active stance. Derek's hand hovered near his jacket.

"Sit down," she said.

"Do you know who that is?" one of them asked.

"That's your new boss. Meet John Hayes."

"But he —"

"That was a cover."

Hayes's nostrils flared. He was barely able to hold down the anger at hearing his real name and the cover he had killed and almost died for being given away like a stick of gum.

"I'm sorry, sir."

The young man bowed his head, and Hayes appraised him: West Point or Annapolis, former jock. Morgan looked at him.

"And that is why you're in a cubicle in Fairfax. You'll learn," she said.

She led Hayes to an office marked 671. It was a corner suite with two windows, a desk, and a small seating area. By government-executive standards, it was practically Xanadu.

Hayes walked to the far corner and put his back to the wall. He had a view of the door and the windows, a command of the room.

"Is this your office?" Hayes asked.

"It was Gray's. Now it's yours. We can get you some different furniture and a computer later."

Hayes's eyes swept the room. They wanted his name and face all over this program.

"No."

"Sorry?"

A staff, an office, clout, and, above all, a budget. These were the marks of power in Washington. Hayes had spent years among killers. He could handle himself there. But politics put him on edge.

"I'm sorry, Morgan. That's the only way this works. The target is out there, and to do my job I need to be a ghost."

"Hayes. These people are all intelligence professionals. They can keep a secret. It's fine if they know who you are."

"If I run into Derek two years from now on an operation, undercover, and he gives me a second look, we're dead or shooting our way out."

It had happened before. Morgan surveyed the office, and her hand touched her pocket. She was anxious. She wanted another cigarette.

"I get it. What do you need?"

"Ten grand and clean papers."

"Of course."

"And two FASCIA techs at the National Security Agency who are on my call and cleared to work stateside."

FASCIA was a surveillance database. He was going to track the cell phones of all the members of Cold Harvest and find anyone who was following their movements.

"But bulk collection of American phone records —"

He cut her off with a *Don't bullshit me* look.

"Try to get a warrant from the surveillance court. If it was ever justified, it's for this. I need the names. Everyone in the program. Living and dead."

Morgan began to protest.

"If someone got their hands on that —"

"It would be a road map for the killers. I know. That's how I'm going to find them."

"Hayes —" She looked at Gray's safe. Hayes knew what she was afraid of. Cold

Harvest had become indispensable, a magic bullet to take down the most dangerous threats. If they lost those operators, there would be nothing between the U.S. and chaos.

"The names have already leaked, Kathryn. Our people are getting murdered."

"The deaths can't all be murders."

Hayes thought through them: a carbon monoxide leak, a fall on the California coast, a motorcycle crash . . .

"Yes, they can."

Hayes knew exactly how. He'd spent a long time killing, and sometimes it meant leaving no trace.

She walked over to the wall safe and twisted the dial, hiding what she was doing with her body. Hayes heard the dial reverse four times, and the bolt retracted.

She pulled out a sheaf of papers with a red and black cover sheet: SPECIAL ACCESS REQUIRED — COLD HARVEST.

"You think it's one of us?"

Hayes took it. "Very few others could pull off kills like this."

She reached in and grabbed a pile of used U.S. currency, twenties and fifties, and counted out ten thousand dollars. She placed it in his hand, a surprisingly small stack, and then looked up at him.

"Claire Rhodes killed a man this morning, a mile from her home, and disappeared."

It came out like a confession.

"Did she know the others who died?"

"Yes. She was the common denominator."

"Who did she kill?"

"A cleanskin" — someone with no trace in the databases — "we have no idea who. She's gone."

Hayes knew Claire. He had trained her in surviving capture and torture and in operating undercover solo. They were close, though Hayes had always worried about her dark side. She looked like a very proper preppie girl from Connecticut, but when things went kinetic, she was capable of close-range, extreme violence. He'd seen her put an Army Ranger in the hospital. There was a deep anger there. Hayes didn't trust emotion in tactics, but she seemed to be able to control it, to put it to good use. *Seemed to,* anyway.

"You suspect her?" he asked.

"She was the common link to the operators who died, and her husband was killed in a building fire a year ago. A fuel-oil tank let go in the garage at his office. It appeared to be an accident, leaking vapors ignited by his car starting up."

"You think she had something to do with it?"

"Maybe they were aiming for her and mistakenly killed him, or maybe she was up to something and she killed him by accident or because he discovered something he shouldn't have. We never found any evidence of foul play. But afterward, the Cold Harvest deaths stopped."

"Until now."

"That's how it seems. She's dangerous, Hayes. She can convince people of anything, convince *herself* of anything."

"Who's tracking her down now?"

"The FBI."

"And where's this body?" It was the most recent kill, a place to start.

"The local medical examiner's office. Where are you based? Home? I can have a courier bring some more background info later today."

"I'll take what you have now."

He looked through the glass at the open-floor-plan office. There was no way he was going to give them the place where his family slept.

He thought of Claire as she'd been during the last phase of her selection, a week of hell meant to weed out the weak. He remembered her smiling at him after she'd finished a forty-eight-hour ruck march with a fifty-five-pound pack and a boot full of blood and saying, "All good, sir. What's next?"

She'd killed a man this morning, a man with no trace of an identity. She was at the center of this, though he didn't yet know at which end of the gun.

CHAPTER 18

Thunderheads rolled in low over the Chesapeake. Thomas Gray watched them come across the silvery water and stack over Smith Point Light. He loved the Northern Neck, a long peninsula on the Virginia side of the bay. It was rural, and people kept to themselves, nothing like the scene of retired Washingtonians over in Maryland around St. Michaels. He liked the emptiness, the woods, the old churches. Being out here in nature was the only way he'd found to take his mind off all the ugliness he had seen.

Small waves hushed against the rocks, and he heard something behind him. He pivoted around, steeled himself. It was an osprey.

It was hard to lose the old habits.

He walked toward the house. Children and grandchildren, husbands and wives, college friends. He could see them through the window sitting around the big farm table.

So many names and faces. Gray couldn't

remember them all. He would stare blankly at a woman while she smiled over sadness. His son would whisper that she was his daughter-in-law. For a moment he had forgotten who she was. It was a common smile these days, patronizing but well-meaning, torture for the man, not old really, just sixty-two, who prided himself on his brain. It was his weapon.

He opened the double doors that led from the garden to his library. A hi-fi from the 1970s sat on the cabinets. He had bought it in Japan when he was stationed there. He tilted a record sleeve, placed the vinyl on the turntable, then walked over to the pool table and put out a rack for nine-ball.

A fanfare, then a soaring contralto. Mahler, a song about being forgotten by the world.

Gray shook his head and smiled.

It's why he liked country music too. Listening to something so irredeemably sad, he always found it harder to feel sorry for himself.

"Do you still listen to him, Claire?"

He didn't look back as he spoke. He tapped the edge of his glasses. "It's darker in front of me than it is behind," he said. "I caught your reflection." In the corner of his glasses, he could see a mirrored image of his former student, the suppressed pistol at her side. He held his arms out and turned slowly.

"The things I remember, and the things I forget. It doesn't make any sense."

"There," Claire said, and she pointed to a low-backed chair.

He sat while Claire circled around to the desk, rummaged through the drawers, and came out with an M1911 pistol, a gun that GIs had carried since the First World War and that was still favored by many for its stopping power. She slipped it into her waistband.

"I'm glad they sent someone I know. Do me a favor, don't let my kids find the body. The water is right there."

"That's not what I'm here for, Gray."

He pointed to the gun. "Is that a house-warming present, then?"

"I need to know what happened to my husband. It wasn't an accident. Someone tried to kill me this morning. I don't know who to go to, who to trust."

"They came for you?" He turned his head to the side and examined the cuts on her neck.

"Did you kill my husband, Gray?"

He kneaded his temple, as if trying to recall. "Claire, Claire, Claire," he muttered, then he lifted his head up straight as if he had just remembered something.

"Didn't you?" he asked.

He watched her knuckles turn white as her fist closed on the grip of the gun. She was broken; that's why they had picked her, for that rage that had no bottom.

During her training, another Cold Harvest candidate, an Army Ranger, had tried to haze her. She was a natural target, the only remaining woman. It was near the end of the diving phase, and sometimes the trainees would lock a newcomer in a storage trunk with an air tank and a regulator but no mask and then drop the trunk into the deep end of the pool for fifteen minutes.

Gray talked to the man afterward, in the hospital. As the Ranger had come for her, she kept saying, "Please, don't. Please," with her fists balled at her sides. He'd thought she was begging for her own sake, but it was for his.

She broke his nose and left him with both eyes swollen shut; she might have killed him if two others hadn't pulled her off. She was like an animal, they said.

Gray stared at her now, her jaw set, her eyes narrowed. As he watched the gun rise and the barrel aim square at his face, he thought maybe Hayes had been right. He'd always said it was too risky, trying to tame anger like that. Gray looked at her over the iron sights of the pistol and wondered, *Did you ever find peace, Claire? Did you ever get control?*

CHAPTER 19

Claire eased her grip on the pistol and took long, deep breaths.

"Are you trying to provoke me?"

Gray couldn't help but laugh. "I know that's a losing bet. I'm asking you, honestly, did you kill him? Didn't I warn you back then? About not getting involved with that man?"

"You did."

He had cautioned her against attachments when he'd first heard about Paul. Relationships with civilians usually ended badly. He encouraged operators to get together with people inside the teams.

For all the silence directed to outsiders, there was openness with those in the brotherhood. Intelligence professionals bonded deeply and quickly. It was like putting your thumb over a hose: All that built-up pressure from not being able to talk to most people made relationships with those you could confide in all the more intense.

But Claire hated the bubble, the same small circle of lies, of fake names in the same bars in the same war-torn towns, the same circuit of contractors and black units in their flannel shirts, beards, and ball caps.

Cold Harvest had brought out the most dangerous parts of her, and living that life both at home and at work was too much. She had met Paul while using her cover in Turkey. That was all he knew of her: Carol, the innocent. He and that fake life were her escape from the killing.

But Gray had warned her: "You can't tell him who you are. It's too dangerous. He's a reporter."

"He's a photographer."

She had understood, even then. His life was about exposing the truth. Hers was about hiding it. "Come on, Claire," Gray had said.

It didn't take a genius to see the logic: That getting involved with Paul was a suicidal impulse. That it meant she wanted to expose herself, let the sunlight in. Kill everything that grew in the dark. She had nothing to be afraid of. She would stand up and answer for the death of every terrorist, arms trafficker, and dictator she had put in the ground.

"Does Paul check out?" she had asked him then.

Of course Gray had done the background workup. He ran checks on his pool cleaner.

"Does he?"

"He does. Are you going to get married as Carol? Live as a cover?"

That had been her plan: The lie would become the real life, and the person she had been before would become an odd variation, locked away in her work. It sounded wrong to say yes back then. But the more she thought about it, the more she liked it.

"Who could imagine?" she'd said. "A woman getting married and losing her name."

"Those bonds are dangerous, Claire. People can exploit them. They give the enemy a way in."

"I can take care of myself."

"I know. But what about him?"

She hadn't had an answer for him then. But he had been right. And now her husband was dead.

CHAPTER 20

Claire brought the gun down to her side and took two steps across the library toward Gray. "Why did you freeze me out after Paul died? Do you remember?"

"We went to the memorial. I remember that."

"That was bullshit. You knew what was going on and you and the rest of them cut me off."

"Every death in Cold Harvest. Do you know what they had in common?" Gray asked.

"They were made to look like accidents."

"You. You were the common factor. You worked with them. You saw their reports. We did a network analysis and all the signs pointed to you. And there was no indication of foul play."

"Because it was done by professionals."

"You're one of how many who can do a job like that? A half a dozen in the world.

Maybe it was you, or maybe they were just accidents."

She'd never understood why they'd dropped her. She had access to some of the national security intranets. Stealing passwords was an old habit of hers, and she still had a few working credentials she had lifted from the intelligence staffers. But they gave her only low-level permissions, glimpses of calendars and meetings, some travel plans, nothing of use. The real secrets were much more closely held or not recorded at all.

"But why would I kill my husband?"

He let out a long, pained exhale. "You want the headlines? You sure?"

"I've been torturing myself not knowing for a year. Anything's better than doubt."

"Doubt is all we had. The deaths stopped after Paul died. Let's say you were the one targeting our people. Maybe an incendiary device went off at the wrong time and killed him. Or Paul found out who you really were and threatened to expose you."

She remembered that morning, the first time she'd told her husband her real name. And she remembered wondering what she would do if it came down to a choice between him and the job.

In the room with Gray, she felt her throat working, acid at the base of her tongue, like she was going to be sick.

"Claire? Are you okay?"

"Fine. That was it? I killed him deliberately or accidentally? Then why would you let me walk?"

"You know I give the bad news first. Maybe it was whoever was killing our people. They came for you and missed. Paul was in your car. Or maybe it was actually an accident."

No. That was the first thing he had taught her. Accidents don't happen. Every coincidence is suspect.

"Why didn't you come to me, Gray?"

"There was no evidence. The explosive tests came back negative. These were all just theories. With nothing firm, why would I tell you that, directly or indirectly, you might have harmed your family? Tucker and the politicians wanted it to go away. Think of the optics. Bystanders killed on American soil. Blowback from an unsanctioned program. It could have exposed the whole thing. So it went away."

"Best for everyone," she sneered.

"You know the game."

"How badly did they want to keep the program a secret?"

"What did you do to keep it a secret?"

She killed people. And once, with a loaded

gun in her car, she'd sat watching her husband and thinking through how she would take him down if he threatened the work.

"Are they cleaning house, Gray? Are they killing us all?"

"It would be easy, wouldn't it? No one knows who we really are. Unrelated deaths, anonymous civilians, scattered around the country, around the world. And after we're gone, the only ones who could connect the dots would be the killers themselves."

"Who put an end to the investigation of Paul's death?"

He reached into his pocket.

She raised the gun, and their eyes met along the sights. He looked down, unfazed, as he brought a pill bottle from his pocket. He shook two out and swallowed them dry. She lowered the gun slightly.

"Kathryn Morgan. Right before they shoved me out."

"Jesus."

"The wilderness of mirrors."

The music had ended, and the needle spun in the empty space at the end of the record, giving a soft pop with every turn.

He pointed to the suppressor. "Is that wet?"

"Wire-pulling gel."

"Good stuff. You think they'd hear it?"

"No." Filling a silencer with a liquid or gel made it vastly more effective.

"I think you're right." He seemed sharper now; canny, dangerous. The master she remembered. He was the father of the program. And even with him cornered, she could feel a trace of the fear she'd had when he was her teacher, evaluating, judging. She and the other candidates had been so desperate to earn his approval.

Was he still working with Morgan? Luring her into a trap?

"Why would you start talking to me now?"

"Margaret's dead, you know." His wife. "We had a deal. I would give my life to the Agency for thirty-five years, and then she would be waiting. There would be time for everything. I put in my papers, and we bought this place, and she died."

"I know, Tom. I sent flowers."

"When was it?"

"What?"

"How long ago?"

"What do you mean? It was last year."

He looked down. She scanned the room and saw the stacks of paper, the empty pill bottles on the shelves, the used coffee cups. Gray had always been so precise.

"Are you okay, Gray? Are you sick?"

"I feel fine, but I'm . . . I'm disappearing. A little at a time."

He shut his eyes and cleared his throat. Claire wanted to extend her hand, to comfort him, but the training wouldn't allow her to let him within ten feet of her gun. She had seen him put on better deceptions. He had taught her how.

He opened his eyes, and they went to the pistol. "The worst part is, I can't remember the good things. My wife's face is fading. But the bad — every shit town and every dead body — they won't leave. I gave everything to the job. I'm paid up."

"You trust me?"

"No." He coughed, a deep rattle in his chest. "But you get tired of the mirrors. Of thinking everything is a lie. Everyone is carrying a knife. I'm too old for these games. Sometimes you just want to believe in someone, even if you think it's a mistake. It's either you or these telemarketers."

He smiled, and Claire looked at him, tried to measure the truth in the smile, and for a second it looked as fake as a mall Santa's.

All Gray had to do was keep up his ally act, get through this moment, get her out of there, and make a call, and she would be dead.

Unless he couldn't warn them. Unless she

used that gun. She took a step toward him, then lifted the pistol.

His face fell, and he shut his eyes. She studied the gray stubble on his chin, the old-man hairs of his ears and nose.

She took his pistol from her waistband and laid it on the table beside her.

"I'm not going to hurt you, Gray."

"Poor girl. It wasn't you who killed them, was it?"

"No," she said. "Were you going to let me shoot you to find that out?"

"I didn't have much say in the matter. I've worried about you, Claire. I've picked up the phone. I haven't called. At least for those few seconds, I would have known."

"So you believe me? Anything you want to add?"

"I wish I had gone to the memorial for Paul."

"You did, Tom."

Anger and frustration came across his face. Footsteps drummed in the hall. Claire stepped to the side. The doorknob turned, and the hinges creaked. Gray's pistol was on the table, out of reach. She jumped behind the door as it opened, and held her silenced handgun down by her leg.

"Dad, are you okay? I thought I heard you talking."

He smiled at whoever was at the door. His gun lay on the table, in plain view if the visitor looked to her right.

"Just doddering. I'm fine. What are you all doing?"

"Playing Catch Phrase. Do you want to join?"

"I'll slow you down. I can't remember the names of anything anymore."

"Come sit with us. You can't stay in here by yourself all night."

"I will. In a moment."

"Okay. It's just us, Matthew and Scott and me."

"Thank you."

She shut the door. Claire stepped forward.

"I'm sorry, Gray. This is your house. Your family." It was the ultimate violation: to bring the violence home. It had happened to her, and now she had brought it to him. She put his pistol back in the desk drawer.

"Claire. When did you —"

She looked at him for a moment.

He glanced at her gun. "I'm fine. I remember now. I'm fine."

"I have to go."

She could see the concentration on his face as he tried to hold on to the thread of what was happening.

She put her hand on the French doors.

"Thank you, Gray."

Voices rose from deeper in the house. Laughter echoed down the halls.

"You're welcome."

She slipped out and shut the doors behind her. And as she crossed the yard, she looked back and saw him standing over the pool table, holding his head in his hands.

She couldn't bring him into this. He had done his time, and she wasn't sure if she could trust him, or those memories of his. This could get ugly, and she couldn't have someone holding her back.

But what he'd said about Morgan rang true. Morgan and Tucker. They had never trusted Cold Harvest, were always ready to cut it off. She didn't know if or why they would go so far as killing its members, but she was going to find out.

Claire clambered over a rock wall. Cool air hit her with the brine smell of the channel as she moved unseen around the back of the house.

In the library, Gray drove the cue into the white ball. A run. The game absorbed him, the angles. He lined up the last shot on the nine ball.

A faint shadow crossed the table. He turned. A figure stood before him. Good

139

tactics, moving from dark to light. Only the glow of the desk lamp had given the gunman away, and by then it was too late.

Gray looked up from the suppressed pistol to the face. Gray shook his head, like a man finally let it on the joke.

The intruder remained silent.

"She's in on it," Gray said.

"Drop the cue."

Gray rested it against the table, leaned back against the carved oak.

"Was that all stagecraft, Claire's tortured act?" Gray asked. Despite the fear tightening up his spine, he had to admire his pupil. She was the best student he'd ever had, and he was proud of her. He'd known that one day she would surpass him, leave him behind like a kid going off to college.

The man gestured with the gun for Gray to move away from the table. Gray obliged and watched the man study him, fix on the chalk in his hands. He stood next to the corner pocket and picked up the nine ball with his free hand.

"Come out with it. What do you want? Talk to me," Gray said. "You know the game."

"The game is over."

Gray understood and lunged for the desk drawer where he kept his gun. The other

140

man drove the ball in his hand down on top of another. The crack filled the room and covered the report of the pistol.

Crack-crack.

He put the ball back, and it rolled, tapped softly against a cushion, and came to rest.

After he shot Gray, Niko Hynd left the property, and walked through the woods near the inlet. He had been right. Claire had done her job, led him to another target. She would be so valuable. Killing Gray was crucial. If Hynd played it right, he could draw all of Cold Harvest into his trap. He heard sirens in the distance and moved faster.

By nightfall the normally quiet peninsula was a carnival of police and emergency response vehicles. Patrol boats circled, hunting over the rocks with million-candlepower floodlights.

But Hynd and Claire were both long gone.

CHAPTER 21

Hayes had come home for his assault kit. If he was going after these killers, he had to be ready for a fight at any moment. He usually carried a Glock 19 pistol and kept the rest of his gear in a concrete outbuilding at the edge of the property. He had paperwork in his office that technically declared it a remote JSOC facility, because possessing this stuff in the United States would land someone in prison for several lifetimes.

His basic load-out was a rifle, pistol, ammo, and knife, along with grenades — fragmentation, smoke, and flash-bang — and some basic door-breaching explosives. His night optics had been wrecked on an op— an eighty-thousand-dollar piece of gear — and he was waiting on the replacement.

The military was generally not allowed to operate within the U.S. because of the Posse Comitatus Act, but exemptions were routinely made for the classified units to assist on critical cases and presidential security. Cox had a legal finding that exempted Hayes while on the job. "Congratulations, you're a walking war zone," he had said, but now that he was part of Cold Harvest, Hayes didn't know if that protection still applied.

He finished packing his gear, then locked the outbuilding door with the bag inside and went back to the house. His daughter, Maggie, was looking at the floor, miserable. They'd just come back from soccer.

"She all right?" Hayes asked Lauren.

"She had to take a time-out. She knocked over another kid."

Hayes waited for the whole story.

"He wouldn't let anyone else play. He was a year older."

Hayes put his hands on his hips and looked at Maggie as Lauren went back out to the car. Then Hayes crouched so he was eye to eye with his daughter.

"Nice work," Hayes whispered. "Someone has to stand up to those guys."

Upstairs in his office, he spread the files out across the table. They were Cold Harvest operators, but they were also mothers and fathers, friends and former students of his.

They stared back at him from the pages.

The killers were moving fast. Hayes couldn't find them from the body of the man Claire had killed any better than the FBI could, and he wasn't going to outdo a law enforcement manhunt solo. He'd already told Morgan to set up security on the Cold Harvest people and to warn them. They were their own best defense. The higher-ups had been in denial about the Cold Harvest murders and hadn't taken the necessary steps until now.

He hoped for a hit from the signals surveillance. He had spent a half hour on the phone with an NSA tech named Jonathan Baer. FASCIA was a database that collected location information on millions of mobile phones and it was never "intentionally" set to collect Americans' information. But in fact the NSA used it to scoop up whatever the hell it wanted.

The NSA could use that information to locate phones or any other communications devices that were traveling together. Normally, it was deployed to track groups of bad guys, but if the bad guys were following Cold Harvest members, Hayes assumed it could pick them up too.

Hayes knew the NSA and its capabilities. He'd spent years evading it, and it was so odd to think of their lethal ever-present gaze and then go meet the computer kids — comic-book and fantasy geeks at Fort Meade — who wielded all that power but were so wrapped up in the technical details they didn't understand the gravity of what they were doing.

Given the complexity and speed of the operation, the killers would have to be using real-time communications, but given the sophistication, they would be dumping phones every day. He wouldn't be able to get their present fix through Jonathan, but he could find patterns. If he knew which Cold Harvest members they were targeting, he could at least warn the target and hopefully use that information to draw out and kill his bad guys.

There was another piece of the operation he needed to get rolling on: Claire. The killers were on to her, or she was the killer. He could find her because he had trained her. He doubted she was anywhere near her home.

"Movement is life." It was a motto of his old unit, one he taught his students. Never stop. From the time he had spent training Cold Harvest members, he knew some of their old communications and escape-and-evasion plans — instructions on how to reestablish contact with an operator stuck behind enemy lines.

Alone, hungry, and hunted; Hayes had been where she was, and he didn't figure her for the killer, although his own biases worried him. He opened his laptop, went on eBay, and started writing up a listing for a vintage pack of playing cards. It was a coded emergency signal to Claire.

When he had first been trained to find an agent in hostile terrain, the technique was to broadcast a wide radio signal. It was an emergency instruction, encrypted, so that only the recipient could understand it. The enemy would know that someone was carpeting their territory with messages but they wouldn't know the contents.

Back then, replying was what got the agent killed. Even if he used a burst transmitter, the enemy would be listening and could zero in on the source and then circle and kill the sender. Hayes remembered the hours spent waiting in silence for a message that never came, never knowing what happened to the agent, never knowing how much had been compromised.

Now they used the Internet, secret signals that anyone could see, like this eBay listing. He added a photo from a vintage deck of cards: the queen of hearts; the boys had nicknamed Claire the Red Queen because she was so good with the knife. He entered a few exact coded phrases in the eBay description to confirm his identity, then posted it.

Both eBay and craigslist had become so popular for coded comms that the Mossad had a team dedicated to hunting down hidden terrorist messages on the sites. A respondent could reply with a different code in a different posting. The messages never went point to point, never connected the senders. Each had its own hidden meaning: *I'm safe* or *I need extraction* or whatever.

"Come on, Claire," he said. He knew how the command could lash out when it panicked, how easily it could kill the wrong operator. He wanted to find her first.

He wanted to get those steps in motion, and it was the next task that he wished he could avoid.

He looked back at the faces on the desk. He needed to connect a string of murders that weren't murders. He needed the pattern to find these bastards. That was the only way to get ahead of them.

For every death he had to ask himself, *How would I have killed this man?* And for every living operator, he had to ask, *Who would I kill next and how?*

147

He had to hunt them down, the people he loved most in the world beside his family, in order to save them. He buried himself in the work, and in his mind he stalked them. As he read through the medical examiners' reports, he imagined himself downstairs in a house in Colorado loosening a hose clamp on the furnace that would flood the home with carbon monoxide or holding the mobile defibrillator to someone's chest, a traceless way to stop a heart.

Because there were times he had been given a kill-or-capture mission but he'd known there was only one choice. A death would start a regional war, rally terrorists. He knew how to kill without leaving a trace.

"Daddy!" his daughter called up the stairs.

The dead stared back at him from the pages. They had been found by their wives and kids.

He looked at the dossiers on the living. There would be more deaths soon if he didn't see it.

He put his daughter down for her nap, and when she finally fell asleep, he shut the book. Then he sat there for a few seconds, watching her chest rise and fall.

He tried to take her in, to fill his mind completely, a focus he had only ever found in combat. He had to go, but he gave himself this moment.

He stayed there like that for some time, but soon the mission crept in again, unbidden, and he was back in that basement, back in the killer's mind.

Not here, not now.

But the work called.

He had made it back in time to see her blow out three candles on a cupcake. He'd never thought he would get to do that. She had been frightened of him for the first few months, watching, saying little, then one night she'd come out into the living room after they had put her to bed. Lauren leaned forward, but she went to Hayes.

"What's up, honey?"

"Monsters."

Lauren gave him an amused look. Hayes was definitely the man for that. His daughter took his hand and led him down the dark hallway.

He still never really slept, still woke in the middle of the night reaching for a weapon or shivering cold back on that ridge in Pakistan. They had hunted him for so long. Some part of him had never come back from exile. He couldn't look at a man without weighing the threat he posed and deciding how he would take him down.

"Don't worry," Lauren would say. "You'll get over it. It takes time."

And Hayes could never tell her this: He didn't want to lose those instincts. They kept him and his family and his people alive.

He heard the phone in his office ringing and slipped away from his daughter. Cox had set up the line. If anyone traced it, it would show up as a Pentagon location.

Hayes lifted the handset.

"Is this secure?" the caller asked.

"Yes. Go ahead."

"It's Jonathan." The analyst from the NSA. "We have preliminary results." Hayes listened for a moment. The techs had been able to use Claire's number and location and pattern-matching software to pick up the path of phones that had been following her and a couple others that they had called.

"When's the most recent fix?"

"Twenty-four hours. That's as close we can get in this case."

"Give me what you have," Hayes said, and he mapped out the locations. They centered on a town about two hours from Hayes's home.

"There's no record of any of your targets there, though." Jonathan was referring to the target cell phones belonging to Cold

150

Harvest members.

Hayes knew that town. He remembered Drew Ochoa talking about it when they were deployed. He'd grown up there. He ran through the files, looking for a way to call Drew, to warn him. He found a landline number on a personnel file, but it was twelve years old.

"Thanks, Jonathan. Can you get me a number for a guy in that town named Drew Ochoa? Might be under an alias, Martin Pruitt."

"Hang on," he said, and a minute later he came back. "Forty years old? Born there?"

"That's about right."

Jonathan read out the numbers.

"Appreciate it. Hit me with anything else that comes up."

"This pattern doesn't seem to be active anymore, but I will."

Hayes dialed Drew's number, but no one answered. A machine picked up. Hayes recognized his old teammate's voice.

Hayes hung up and stepped out of his office. Lauren was at the kitchen table reading a medical journal.

"You're heading out?"

"Yeah. It's work. Love you."

He kissed her on the top of her head and she put her arm around him. "You too."

He grabbed his assault gear on his way to his truck, threw it in the back, and took off.

Chapter 22

In the mountains a hundred miles away, Ruben Olivares kept his rifle close to his chest as he picked his way through the gnarled roots of the hillsides leading down to the lake and his target.

Million-dollar vacation houses surrounded the serpentine body of water, formed when a river had been dammed and flooded the valley behind it. An old village lay drowned somewhere at the bottom.

He pulled his Mets cap down low, took a knee beside a tree, and slid a stick of spearmint gum from a pack.

He offered one to his second in command, but the man declined.

Olivares had had no trouble making his way through the woods. He'd lived in the jungle for months on end while in the Honduran special forces, the TIGRES. He and the man beside him had been indicted for killing four villagers outside an airstrip near La Ceiba while secretly on the payroll of a local drug trafficker. They'd fled.

They were employed by Hynd, one of the few who would give them work and who even seemed pleased by their performance in Central America. The job was dangerous, but Ruben and his team asked no questions. It paid well enough that after this operation he could retire to a four-bedroom house in Chula Vista and buy the BMW M5 he had always wanted.

Olivares couldn't believe how cheap the cars were here. In Honduras, the prices were jacked up, and in any case, a nice ride only made you a target.

He stopped and cast an appraising look at the vehicles in the driveway of the house below, then borrowed the rifle of his number two. It had the magnifying optic. He settled the crosshairs on the face of a young boy on a sofa, then another at a kitchen table, and finally he saw his target: Drew Ochoa, sorting through a tackle box at the kitchen island.

"That's him," he said and passed the rifle back.

They had first identified him at the Burke funeral and tracked him in the days after in order to understand his patterns of life well enough to kill him quietly.

He was one of two targets picked up at Burke's funeral. The other was a man with a slight limp, the one who had killed Kashani. They'd seen him with his family, a wife and daughter.

He would come next, but for now, they closed on the lake house with Ochoa in it, crossing silently through the trees.

CHAPTER 23

Hynd walked between the steel tanks towering overhead. The site had once been a brewery, but it had been abandoned for almost thirty years. He reached the main floor of the warehouse. Slabs of marble and fifty-five-gallon drums were laid out before him, along with the chassis of a truck trailer.

The shooting near Claire's house, the dead body on the Northern Neck. This operation was attracting too much attention for it to stay hidden much longer. His strategy of silence and close kills was coming to an end. Fair enough. He was getting tired of sneaking around. He had trouble letting go of control, but there was no way to be in two places at once.

"The Hondurans?" he asked Vera.

"In place. Ready to go whenever they see the chance."

He had two deputies, Vera and her brother, Timur Choriev, who was working the torch on the warehouse floor, helping a younger man reinforce the springs on the truck trailer to conceal its load. The siblings were the only ones given Hynd's full confidence.

Timur's eyes and skin were tinged yellow. He looked skeletal, his cheeks hollow. It always surprised Hynd how much strength remained in him.

His wife had left him long ago and took his children. He hadn't seen them in sixteen years. Had given his life to the cause, and there wasn't much life left.

He had cancer of the stomach. Hynd would give his money to his children. Hynd was good at that sort of thing. Seychelles limited-liability companies and Guernsey bank accounts and *hawala* transfers.

For a decade they had sought to infiltrate and destroy the inner ring of American operatives and, at its heart, Cold Harvest.

Timur and Vera were both from the Fergana Valley, a lush region in Central Asia that for decades had been a war-torn crossroads known to few Westerners. It was a hotbed of radicalism and terror groups, but given the place's lack of strategic importance, most powers just let it burn, the way they had once ignored Afghanistan.

As the operation grew, Hynd brought on contract shooters, former military from the elite units of the Caucasus, the Balkans, Latin America, and Southeast Asia. They did work for hire, as simple as that. He took great care in recruiting, but there were plenty of applicants.

Americans never fully appreciated how much they were resented around the world. When they left their little bubble of the United States and Europe and a few vacation spots, they were always surprised to find that much of the world hated the U.S. and considered the nation a bully. Most Americans were barely aware of the long history of ill-conceived foreign interventions that their government had orchestrated, going all the way back to the CIA-sponsored coups in Iran and Guatemala in the 1950s.

The U.S. had put itself in charge of the world. There were states and groups that tried to resist its rule, tried to move weapons and money and people in defiance of its sanctions, to build their own nuclear arsenals, to project power through armed proxies. But all too often their attempts failed. The U.S. was too powerful. Its opponents had seen their men killed, shot dead by a superpower that could see in the dark. The Americans weren't warriors — they were cowards, technological sucker-punchers.

Again and again those opposed to the

United States' dominance were branded terrorists and stopped at will by this tiny cadre called Cold Harvest. By Hynd's estimate, there were thirty-six men and women in it, perhaps a few more he didn't know of. Such a small number.

There were plenty of groups and governments that wanted to draw American blood, but they were too afraid of the consequences. That was Hynd's niche. He collected bounties from all of them to finance a mission to kill off Cold Harvest.

He knew the weakness, the arrogance of strength. The Americans believed they were invulnerable. Even while they battered down the doors of homes around the world, they believed their own homes were safe.

Hynd watched Timur's torch throw a rainbow of red sparks across the floor.

"Trouble," Vera said.

"What is it?"

"The team on Drew Ochoa. They might have company. Someone called his house. Do you want to pull them out now?"

"No. Tell them to get ready to take it."

"But it will be ugly. The family's there."

The time for stealth was over.

"That's fine."

CHAPTER 24

Hayes felt the tires drift slightly as he rounded the corner and watched the speedometer rise: 80, 90, 100.

His phone was pressed to his ear, connecting him to Jonathan. He had asked the tech for Drew's mobile number and a location fifteen minutes ago.

"Where is the number?" he asked again.

"I'm working on it, but he wasn't on the list."

Drew was a friend of Tom Gray's. He might have worked for Cold Harvest without any record. Hip pocket, they called it.

People always talked about what you owe to someone who's saved your life, and that was true enough. But as Hayes thought back to the moment when he'd pulled Drew — rail-thin, his back covered in cigarette burns — off the floor of that cage in Syria, he knew it worked both ways. You never let go of the ones you save. Once someone trusts you with his life, you always feel responsible for it.

"Okay, okay," the tech said. "I have it. You ready?"

"Go."

Jonathan read out the cell phone number and gave him Drew's last location.

"He's at the lake?" Hayes said.

"Yes."

Traveling away from familiar ground and resources. That's where they would take him. Hayes ended the call and voice-dialed the number. One ring, two.

"Come on, Drew. Come on."

The needle climbed toward 110 miles per hour, and the wheel shook in his hand. Still no answer.

CHAPTER 25

The hand closed on Drew's shoulder, and he sat forward with a start, then looked up at the man beside him. It was the other father on this trip, a short vacation for the Fourth of July. They would be at the lake through the weekend.

Drew relaxed.

"Sure I can't get you a scotch or a beer or anything?"

"I'm fine, thanks," Drew said. The kids were in the basement theater room. Their wives were in town. Drew barely knew the other man, Greg Talley, though their wives were close. Drew was restless, had never been very good at sitting around doing nothing.

"Check this out," the other man said. He took a seat next to Drew and pulled out his phone. It was a shot of him kneeling next to the carcass of a black bear.

"That was up in British Columbia. Top-

of-the-line everything. Private chefs. It's a
long day. Up at dawn. Sitting in the blind,
waiting. Hard work." He gave Drew an
elbow and a wink. "But they make sure you
don't miss. Baits, you know. You do a lot of
hunting?"

"Some," Drew said.

"When you see an animal like that, that
could tear you apart, and you line up the
shot and . . . *bang!*"

He looked for some reaction from Drew,
who remained calm. Greg stroked his own
forearm. "It still gives me chills. It's hard to
explain the feeling."

"Sounds pretty unbelievable," Drew said.
"Excuse me."

He stood and walked to the top of the
stairs, called, "Michael!"

Greg liked to spend money. This place was
too expensive, everything a cabin shouldn't
be — huge and full of electronic distrac-
tions. But Drew would do anything to have
time with his kid, so he'd gladly chipped in
his half.

"What sort of work did you say you did
again?" the other man asked, standing up
from the sofa.

"Personnel systems analyst," Drew said.

"I looked you up, didn't really see much
on LinkedIn."

Long-range reconnaissance, undercover time in arms trafficking, close-in lethal jobs. It wasn't the kind of stuff you put on a résumé.

"It's all about building a personal brand," Greg went on. "Putting yourself out there. Promoting yourself isn't a bad thing. It's saying, *Hey, I'm great, I'm passionate about what I do. I want to tell you about me.*"

"I'll look into that. My brand could use some work."

Drew had once stood in a hangar at Bragg with the rest of his team and two CIA operators. They had killed the acting commander of al-Shabaab, and the president came down to congratulate them personally on the success of the mission. When he asked who'd fired the shot that killed the chief, Drew and the others remained stone-faced.

The head of JSOC told the president, "The team did, sir." They didn't talk like that, didn't seek out or take individual credit for successes.

He was working in the local fire and rescue now that he had left Cold Harvest, but he still said "personnel systems analyst" when anyone asked him about his job because he didn't like to talk about what he did — an ingrained habit — and that tended to bring the work conversation to a close.

He was sick of killing and of being away from his family. He liked the straightforwardness of working in public safety. He came from a long line of cops and firemen. But money was tight. His wife had needed thyroid surgery the year before. There were plenty of jobs for a guy like him, security contractor work, but he was tired of telling his kid he would see him in a couple of weeks and not knowing if he was telling the truth.

He was one of the lucky ones, though. He could still walk, still see his son play football.

"I've been doing a lot of public speaking, actually —"

Drew ignored Greg, walked downstairs, and saw his son, Michael, sitting on the couch next to Greg's son, Daniel. Michael barely looked up from the TV. His long hair hung over his eyes. He was playing a video game, a military shooter, running and hip-firing without cover, like a jihadi. *Inshallah* shots, they called them, which meant God-willing shots, because they prayed they would hit something. It was almost hard for Drew not to say something about the tactics.

"I'm going to get a little exercise before dinner," Drew said. "Then I'll get some pizza."

"Uh, okay," Michael replied. "But I'm off cheese."

"Since when?"

"Since forever."

"All right," Drew said, and he ran his hand through Michael's hair while his son twisted away.

Drew changed into a pair of board shorts, then walked past his truck and through the trees to the edge of the lake. The sun was setting. He slipped into the cold water and felt his skin contract. It was about sixty degrees, but he would be fine if he kept the pace up. He slid through the water.

That conversation was progress. For a long time, Michael would barely talk to him, and Drew couldn't blame him. He'd been gone for most of his life, popping in for two or three weeks like an uncle from another coast.

Drew's wife would tell him about the bad dreams and the angry speeches: *Where is he? Why is he always leaving us behind? What if we need him?*

Michael pretended not to care about anything, but Drew saw otherwise on the football field, saw Michael's red face and trembling hands after all-out sprints at practice. He'd seen a picture his son texted to his friends, a photo of the two of them fishing together, with Michael holding up a thirty-inch striper.

It was a start.

He slipped through the black water, going twenty feet under the surface at a time.

On the shore, folded in his towel beside his sweatshirt, Drew's phone rang and rang. Thirty miles away, Hayes hit redial and pressed the damp glass of his phone to his cheek.

CHAPTER 26

Hynd watched the metal glow red beside the torch.

"Olivares is set outside the house," Vera said.

"Good. Send them in."

"What's the cover?"

Working in the U.S. was dangerous, but it had one advantage: the flood of guns and everyday violence. Drug addiction and petty theft were rife in these mountains. As long as you took a few innocents along with your target, it was possible to blend in.

"Home invasion," Hynd said. "Raid the medicine chests, the valuables."

It was a thin cover, but it was all they needed to buy time with the local police before someone figured out that the victim wasn't some suburban dad.

"Rules of engagement?"

This was the first move toward open war. The one-at-a-time murders had only been a prelude. The real violence was just beginning.

"Kill everyone in the house."

Chapter 27

In the basement of the vacation house, Michael Ochoa, Drew's son, moved his thumb just slightly to the left on the game controller and stared at the sixty-inch TV. The surround-sound speakers pumped the rattle of automatic gunfire and the hiss of bullets through the room, while the screen showed the first-person perspective down a Remington combat shotgun as Michael sneaked up on a man on-screen.

He blew his head off in a red cloud, and the boy beside Michael on the couch punched him in the arm and cried out, "Sick!"

The sliding glass door to the right shattered into the room. Michael dropped the controller and froze as two men ran inside, looking down the sights of submachine guns. They checked the corners closest to the doors, then the lead man sprinted toward Michael and drove his elbow into the boy's temple.

The room turned into a red flash as the pain overwhelmed him, and they threw him onto his stomach and cinched his hands behind his back.

"What are you doing!" he yelled, but there was no reply. They moved so quickly, so calmly, as they dragged him and Daniel up the stairs, his feet thudding over the steps. His slipper fell off, and he watched the tiles of the kitchen floor move by.

In the living room, he heard more men shouting. They must have broken in through another door. Mr. Talley tried to calm them down, but then Michael heard him cry out in pain.

They brought Michael upstairs, into the master bedroom, and threw him down on the bed. The bindings cut into his wrists, and he felt a small trickle of blood working its way through his hair. They dragged Mr. Talley and Daniel in next.

One man aimed a pistol at Mr. Talley. The others were arguing in Spanish, and for the first time they seemed panicked.

"Drew Ochoa. Where is he?" the lead man asked the father as he pointed the gun at Daniel's face.

Michael shook his head over and over in disbelief. Where was his dad? *He left us here,*

Michael thought. *He's gone. He's always gone.*

CHAPTER 28

Drew held his hands, fingers laced, over his head as he caught his breath. The cold water and night air caused his skin to goose-pimple, but he had burned off some of the restlessness.

As he walked toward his towel, he heard his phone ringing. He pulled it out and put on his sweatshirt as he picked his way through the stones.

He saw there were half a dozen missed calls.

Drew answered the phone. "Go ahead," he said.

"It's Hayes. Are you okay?"

"Yeah, I — what's happening?"

"We think someone's going after Cold Harvest personnel in the States."

"Burke's death?"

"Yes. That was them. We tracked a couple phones that might be connected and they were near your house."

173

"No one's there. I'm up at the lake."

"I know. I'm five minutes out. You have any contact?"

"No —" He looked at the house and saw the blinds pulled upstairs, every light out.

"I have to go, Hayes. I'll —"

Another call came in. It was Greg Talley's number.

"Hang on," he said to Hayes and switched to the incoming call. "Is everything okay in the house, Greg? Have you seen anybody watching the place?"

"Drew, where are you? Are you okay?"

"Yes. I'm outside. What's —"

"Jesus, Drew, these guys busted in. They've got me and the kids."

"Stay calm. All right. Put me on the phone with them."

A loud crack came from the earpiece. Drew leaned his head away. "Greg? Greg!"

There was yelling in the background, and then someone screaming.

"Greg!" Drew shouted.

Nothing. Four deep breaths in, four out; he tried to steady his hammering pulse.

"Hello!"

He heard someone breathing on the line. "We have your son and the other boy and his father. We only want you. Come to the house and give yourself up and they will live." The voice was calm. The speaker had done this before.

"If you so much as —"

"I explained the situation. The doors are rigged with explosives. If there is any attempt to assault the building, they will all die."

There was a rustling on the phone.

"Dad?"

"Michael. Thank God. Are you okay?"

"Dad. There are guys here with guns and they hurt Mr. Talley. Where are you?"

"I'm coming, Michael. I'm close. It'll be okay. Is your mother there?" He didn't see her car.

"No." He heard a rustling at the end of the phone, then a slap and a cry.

"You have two minutes," the first speaker said. "We have two kilos of PETN in the room. It will blow if you or anyone else attempts a rescue."

The English was fluent, but Drew picked up a trace of an accent, Mexican or Central American.

PETN was one of the most powerful plastic explosives known. Two kilos would take off the top story of that house. They'd said it would blow if anyone attempted a rescue. That might mean a dead man switch.

It was a type of detonator that worked

similarly to a grenade after the pin was pulled. If the bomber let the device go, either intentionally or because he was injured or killed, it would set off the explosive.

"Come to the front door. Hands on your head. Try anything and they die. We only want you. We'll let them go. Do you understand?"

"I understand. If you tell me —"

The call ended.

"Hayes?" Drew said after his phone switched back to the initial call.

"I'm here."

"They have my boy in the house, along with two other hostages. They want me inside in exchange for them. They say they have the entrances wired with explosives, and there's a charge in the room with the kids that will blow if we try anything."

"Did they give you a deadline?"

"Two minutes. Do you have a team?"

"I called it in, but that'll take at least a half hour. It's just me."

"I'm going in."

"Drew. They're not going to let them go. I have my breaching kit and frags. We can take them. I'm coming up the street now."

"No, Hayes. We don't know enough. They want me."

176

"The MO of these guys is bad. They've been making these murders seem like accidents. They'll kill all of you to avoid having it look like a targeted assassination."

"We don't have time or men for an assault. It's my son, John. I was never around for him. I can't leave him in there. Even if they kill me."

"Don't do it, Drew."

"I can give you ears inside. I'll keep the phone call live as I go in. That's the best I can do."

Drew held the phone away from him and went to the settings. There were options for visually impaired people to change the brightness and contrast of the screen, and with those he could also disable the screen completely. He'd used it before to turn a phone into an ad hoc listening device.

"You still there?" Hayes asked.

"Yes. I have the screen off and the call running. Mute your phone."

"Drew. Wait."

"I can't. I'll see if I can give you some info from the inside. When —"

Three shots shattered the quiet of the empty valley. From a high window, a man's body fell; it landed on the roof below and slid down a foot.

"I'm going in," Drew said. "Mute it."

"Okay," Hayes replied.

Drew put the phone in the pocket of his sweatshirt.

"I'll give you as much as I can," Drew said. "Don't come for the kids unless you have them one hundred percent." He repeated it, slowly. "One hundred percent."

Hayes brought the truck to a stop, then jumped out, slinging his bag on his shoulder as the vehicle rocked on its springs. The bug was working. Through the earbud attached to his phone, he could hear the rustling of wind and Drew's breath as he approached the house.

Hayes slipped through the woods and took cover at the tree line. He could see a figure moving toward the house. It was Drew.

"Approaching the doors," Drew said. "The south windows look clear. That's a good entrance, but wait for my word."

There was silence, then Hayes heard the creak of the front door opening.

"Keep your hands up," Hayes heard someone say.

"You seem like a good man," Drew replied. "Where are the rest of them?"

"Quiet!"

Hayes concentrated on the voices in his ear. Drew was signaling information to him.

You seem like a good man. Where are the rest of them? There was only one guard on the ground floor. There should have been at least two on watch and two handling Drew. These men were unprepared. This was on the fly.

Hayes heard footsteps, muffled. He sprinted for the bushes along a low wall, noting where the power and telephone lines entered the house. He looked at the window, which was secured with only a sash lock.

He saw shadows moving past the window at the rear of the house and heard the tempo of the steps double; the guard was taking Drew upstairs. Someone shouted, "Dad!" And then the voices all joined together until someone barked them down.

"Please," Drew said. "Take me. Let them go. Like you said."

There was no response. Hayes's muscles tensed and it was all he could do not to go in. He hated standing still, losing initiative. *Movement is life.*

But it wasn't his call. It wasn't his kid.

"Ayúdame a cubrirlo." Help me cover him. He heard them talk back and forth in Spanish. Drew was six two and 220 pounds. They needed a man downstairs but also another to cover him. They were short-handed.

179

"What about the trigger?" another asked in Spanish, and then Hayes heard shouting: "Stay still!"

"Fine," Drew said. "You're in charge. One hundred percent. One hundred percent."

Hayes rose up. That was all he needed, a coded green light. Drew had warned him that the room might blow if a rescue was attempted, but either that had been a bluff or Drew thought he could handle the explosives. There was no one Hayes trusted more on demolition.

Or it was the worst case: Drew had concluded that the gunmen were going to kill them all anyway.

Hayes drove his knife between the two window rails and levered them apart until the lock disengaged. He eased the window up, then slashed the screen along the bottom and side, put his hands on the sill, and pulled himself through.

As he came down in a crouch, he drew his pistol, covering the close corner and then the room. He moved down the main hall toward the back stairs.

Hayes heard footsteps above him, one of the men coming back down to post security. He ducked under the stairs, holstered his gun, pulled his knife from its chest sheath, and waited. Someone banged down the treads just above his head. The man reached the floor and turned around the end of the banister; Hayes could see his boots. He held still for an instant in the dark, then launched at him, covered his mouth, stabbed him in the side, and dragged him under the stairs.

He took the man's radio and climbed to the second floor. He heard more shouting in Spanish, and then Drew's voice.

"Please, I'm begging you — all three of you seem like honorable men. Take me and let the kids go."

Three of them.

"Do you want them to see you die? Or do you want to watch them?"

"No. Just take me in the closet, away from the children."

The closet was clear, a point of entry.

Hayes looked in the open doors along the hallway as he advanced. He could hear the muffled shouting and then caught it a half a second later with the delay in his earpiece.

He stopped fifteen feet from the door Drew and the boys were behind and looked into the next room, a bathroom. It was shaped like an L, a long rectangle of tile and then the shower on the left. The space for the shower projected into what Hayes assumed must be the master bedroom, where the shooters were, probably leaving an area in that room for a large closet.

Entering a hostage situation through the only door, alone, was a suicidal move. Doors were known as fatal funnels, because they were where the enemy concentrated fire. The best bet was to make your own entry, known as a mousehole in close-quarters combat.

Hayes stepped into the bathroom and from his bag pulled a length of detonation cord. It was high explosive wrapped in a cover and it looked like clothesline. The blast ran along the cord at four miles per second and was powerful enough on its own to cut through most interior walls.

"Please, just take me," Drew said.

"You don't have the stomach to watch, do you?" There was screaming in the background.

"No, just me. Please. I'm the one you want."

Hayes slapped a length of cord against the wall in a long upside-down U about his height and wide enough for him to go through, then secured it with duct tape.

"This one is your son?"

"No!"

"Stand him up!"

Hayes could hear the voice coming muffled through the wall.

He tightened his primer at the end of the cord and ran out the thin wire that led to the detonator in his left hand.

"This is your father. He is a murderer and a coward. And he lied to you your whole life. This is his fault."

As Hayes took cover just outside the shower stall, he heard someone cry out. He triggered the det cord. The overpressure hit him like a baseball bat, but he sprinted despite the disorientation, first taking a long breath before entering the hot, choking smoke. Hayes threw himself through the gap, tearing a piece of wiring, and flew through the breach into an empty closet.

The blast dazed the others. Hayes kept going into the room as a short man in a Mets cap stumbled and clasped an adolescent boy to his chest.

Hayes fell back on his training, ignoring the noise and smoke and cuing on every weapon, every hostage and threat, calculating his course through the room as if by instinct. He saw the primed charge of plastic explosive but there was no trigger in view.

Out of the corner of his eye, Hayes watched as Drew rolled on his back, tucked his knees to his chest, and brought the flex cuffs from behind him to his front. He held his palms together as if in prayer and then slammed them back against his chest, using his ribs as a wedge to drive his forearms apart and snap the flex cuffs.

At the same time, Hayes put the front sight on the head of the man in the cap and pulled the trigger twice, sending a bullet within inches of the boy's face and dropping his captor.

He turned to the other man and scanned his hands for a detonator but saw only a gun barrel swinging toward him. He put two bullets in his heart and, tracking him as he fell, one in his head. He turned back to see Drew was already in motion; his old teammate seized a coffee mug off the low table, snapped it against the wall, shattering the ceramic, then launched himself at the last man as he dove behind the bed.

As Hayes was coming around the bed and closing on them, a flash blinded him and he heard Drew grunt in pain. Moving forward despite the shots, Drew drove the sharp edge of the mug into the man's chest where it met his arm, at the brachial plexus, severing multiple nerves. The man's arm dropped, and as Drew collapsed to the side, Hayes fired into the man's forehead and eye. He slumped down, releasing the detonator from his limp fingers. Hayes braced for the blast, but there was none. He picked up the trigger, then went to the explosives and pulled out the primer, disabling the charge.

Hayes took a knee next to Drew, tore open his shirt, and saw the entrance wound in his upper chest, near the collarbone. Blood spilled out, soaking into the carpet.

"Any more?" Drew gasped.

"I don't think so," Hayes said, and he pulled a compress from his first-aid kit. "Sit tight."

The whole thing had taken fifteen seconds.

Michael came around the bed in a slow shuffling step, his hand on the mattress to steady himself.

"Dad. Dad. Are you okay?"

Hayes shifted the light away from the blood.

"I'm good, Michael. Are you? How's Danny?"

"He can't talk. He's just staring straight ahead. I don't want to look at them anymore. At the men."

"That's okay, Michael."

"My hands won't stop shaking."

"That was just your body getting ready for the fight. You did great."

"Okay."

"Sit down, bud. You did good."

Drew opened his eyes wide twice, like a

man fighting to stay awake, and then his head fell back.

"Is he okay?" the son asked Hayes.

"He'll be all right."

Michael looked at the broken mug and the dead body. "How did he know how to do all that?"

"That's his job. He saves people."

"He never told me."

"It's not something you talk about, you understand? It's safer that way."

Michael nodded, shut his eyes, and went quiet.

CHAPTER 29

Tucker sprinted on the treadmill. Sweat dripped down his face. His secure Black-Berry buzzed in the cup holder, but he ignored it until the third message.

He lifted it up and read the text: *Call me back. Another attack. John Hayes stopped it, killed four men in Virginia.*

Tucker mashed the button on the panel until the treadmill maxed out at fifteen miles an hour at a 15 percent grade. He ran all out until he was panting and it felt like his lungs had crumpled down to the size of walnuts.

After ninety seconds, he stumbled, grabbed the handrails, and put his feet to the side.

He stepped off the treadmill and wiped his face with the towel. He was in his condo in Georgetown during a rare respite from campaigning. He had an hour until the car would come for his next flight.

The desk in his office was littered with binders and vitamin bottles. Tucker read the messages coming in about the lake-house shootings. A father, a civilian named Talley, had been killed. He waited a minute for his breath to even out and then lifted his phone.

When Morgan picked up, Tucker wanted to know only one thing: "Is there press?"

"Yes. But we've told them it was a home invasion."

"I can't be in the news. You told me you had this."

"I do."

"A firefight in the middle of the fucking Blue Ridge. You do not. I need Hayes under control."

"I'm on it."

"No more mistakes."

Morgan put her phone down, unlocked the door to the hospital conference room she'd commandeered, and walked down the hall-way.

Hayes sat in a worn upholstered chair at the far end of the hospital wing with a saline drip in his arm. Some of the frag had cut him behind the jawline. He hadn't noticed until he arrived at the hospital behind the ambulance for Drew and a nurse pointed it out; one of the doctors sewed it up.

Morgan came down the hall.

"How is he?" she asked.

"Stable enough to airlift to Bethesda." That was the military's main regional medical center now that the Walter Reed campus in DC had been shut down.

"And you?"

"Fine."

"You're home, John; this isn't North Africa. A firefight in a house surrounded by civilians. We can't have a war on the street."

"We already do. I'm trying to stop it. Four dead killers is a start. They're getting more violent. Less concerned about stealth. They're building to something. Any ID on those bodies?"

"None yet."

"They were pros, Kathryn. They'll hit us again."

The detonator was a custom fabrication with two modes. It had been set to work as a normal trigger at the lake house, but it could also have been armed as a dead man switch. Only a sophisticated group could make or acquire that kind of hardware.

She looked at the tiles. "Someone shot Gray last night."

Hayes slammed his left hand against the wall.

"At home?" he asked.

"Yes. His family was okay. They found him. No suspects. I'm going to add some protection for you."

Hayes shook his head and laughed grimly. "No, thanks."

They'd failed these people and their families. Hayes had already called over to the Special Activities Division base at Camp Peary to set up security for Lauren and Maggie. There were a couple of lifers over there he had come up under when they were master sergeants. He trusted them absolutely, and now they were retired, working protective service and always looking for overtime.

They called themselves the High-36 Hunting Club, an in-joke about how the military calculated pensions. They'd cut their teeth in Beirut and Central America. Hayes had assured the watch lead that he would work out the budgeting, and the man told him not to worry about it.

Morgan raised her hands. "We're trying here, John. Drew wasn't on the list or we would have had people on him. I had two men detailed over from the FBI who will watch your back. They'll be here in five minutes."

"No," Hayes said. He wasn't going to give Morgan the address of where his family slept. Not until he figured out how the killers were finding their victims and if there was a leak.

"It's not a suggestion. They're downstairs."

Her phone rang. She raised one finger and stepped away. Hayes waited for her to clear the corner, then pulled the IV from his arm and started down the hallway.

A drop of blood ran down his wrist as he entered the elevator. When the doors closed, he felt his phone vibrate in his pocket. He lifted his phone and saw the message. *A question about your eBay item.*

Claire. He scrolled down to the text.

Remember where you killed me? Come alone, 0200 hours. Don't trust the bosses.

He trotted out of the hospital and saw the unmarked Dodge Charger coming from the other end of the parking lot. FBI. They weren't the best with fluid situations and coloring outside the lines, and Hayes didn't have time to deal with them. He hugged the side of the building and ran a long buttonhook to his truck, going behind them as they parked.

191

The men got out of the Charger, one of them with a radio to his ear. Hayes started the engine and drove over the curbs and grass. His tires chirped as he took off on the road.

He saw them in his rearview, sprinting back toward their car, but he moved into a grid of residential streets. Three highways ran nearby. There were too many outlets for them to cover this quickly.

He pulled onto a two-lane blacktop and checked his mirrors. Nothing. Claire was moving fast, using direct communications instead of the old protocol of hidden signals. She had no time for codes or subterfuge. They could trace the IP address of whatever computer she had used, but she likely would have run it through a proxy. Even if they could find it, she would be long gone by the time they got there.

Remember where you killed me? It was a concrete ruin in a West Virginia no-man's-land, an abandoned World War 1 munitions plant. He remembered it well, remembered aiming the gun at her heart and pulling the trigger.

Two a.m. He might just make it. He turned northwest toward the mountains that ran like dark wavering lines across the sky.

It seemed strange that a few hours away from these strip malls and tract houses, there was that old factory. But America still had its hidden corners, its wild places.

It might be a trap. Or it might be the answer he was looking for. He hoped she wasn't trying to get him, for her sake as much as his own.

Hayes had few fears. But one always haunted him: that at some point he would have to kill one of his own.

He punched the gas.

CHAPTER 30

Claire heard the skitter of paws coming from somewhere above her. The roof of the mobile home had collapsed near the far corner. On top of one of the exposed trusses, two eyes flashed at her like blue coins in the night: a raccoon. It froze, then disappeared. She swept leaves and a quarter inch of dust from a folding chair and sat down.

This base in the highlands was where they had been selected and trained for Cold Harvest. She looked out the window and could see the concrete pilings sticking out of the forest like strange Mayan ruins — twelve-foot-tall cylinders interspersed among the trees. The government had manufactured ordnance up here for the First World War, and there were ruins hidden in among the limestone cliffs and red spruce.

The camp was a set of run-down trailers

and Quonset huts and rarely used. It was meant to send out a forsaken vibe to the trainees. The only light in the room was the faint blue glow of her camping stove under a pot of water on the card table. She had a foil pouch of dehydrated vegetable lasagna open and ready to go.

Her pistol lay beside it. She had different search alerts set up to notify her if anyone used any of her old emergency codes. She knew it was crazy, her hope that even after they'd cut her off, someone would call her up with an old signal like she was a super-hero.

And then she'd received the message from Hayes. Maybe he was in trouble. Maybe they had come for him too. She'd never trusted anyone in the program the way she trusted him, although he had been there only for her training. She needed his help, and he needed hers. Maybe together they could stop this. He might know more about what the politicians were up to. Why they were interested in covering up the deaths.

Her stolen passwords for the intelligence intranets were practically useless. Anything that might shed light on what was really happening was in the special access files.

There was a chance, of course, that this was a trap, that Hayes was involved. It was her training: trust no one. She ran her thumb over the grip of the gun. She was ready for him.

She watched the first bubbles rise in the pot of water. Sitting in the dark, waiting to kill or be killed. She'd been here before, so many times.

She knew Hayes was back with his family. He was trying to live both lives — violence and peace — and keep them separate. She'd tried that for years. And it was odd that she had learned it before her mentors: You can't have both. You have to choose. Or else the people you love end up dead.

Paris. That was the beginning of the end. It had been two years before. She'd been sent to kill a sixty-year-old terrorist logistics chief, code-named Tempest, who provisioned self-radicalized locals in France and Belgium.

His shooters were local kids, petty gangsters who knew more about Grand Theft Auto video games than the Koran, but they were killing dozens of innocent civilians, taking advantage of Europe's lowered guard and weak intelligence apparatus. Tempest was old-guard radical left. He had been letting other people fight his wars since the days of the Red Brigades, Action Directe, and the Baader-Meinhof group.

They'd called her in for the trigger. No one was better at the up-close work. She knew how the other guys talked about her — she was the angel of death, the queen of hearts, standing over a man and savoring the sight of his life draining from him.

But that wasn't what she was doing. Even the worst targets, when they died, looked so afraid and so alone and called out, often for their mothers. She stood by every kill, looked cold-eyed at every death. But it creeped out her teammates, who often shrank from the gravity of what they did by joking around, distancing themselves. She wanted to see and face the consequences of her actions. She never wanted it to be easy. That's when you made mistakes. Killing should be hard.

That night in Paris, it was crucial to stay there, because they were using a drug to kill Tempest, and she had to feel the absent pulse.

The locks to his town house on the Avenue des Gobelins had already been impressioned and a duplicate key made by the advance team. They were using a skeleton crew for this job. The French intelligence services and gendarmerie couldn't know they were here. Tempest had a family, but he was usually in Paris alone. He liked to whore among the African girls on rue Saint-Denis, would pay extra to make them degrade themselves and each other. He didn't take his security detail with him. His behavior in Paris didn't quite fit with his brand as a tech-savvy old-guard friend to the Islamists.

It was a stay-behind job. Claire entered while his security was out, forced the doors on the elevator, and rode on top of it for four hours until he returned. His security swept the house and then left.

She pulled the doors open, settled the night optics over her eyes, and walked through his apartment like an invited guest. She entered his suite and stood there, perfectly still, in the hall leading to the master bathroom while he fussed in bed.

For an hour and forty-five minutes, she was in that room with him, studying his breathing as it slowed and slowed and then, finally, picked up again. He'd entered REM sleep, the period of dreams, when the body's muscles go slack — muscle atonia — so as not to act out the brain's visions.

It was time. She slid toward him and sprayed a small canister, like a perfume tester, up his nose. It partially paralyzed him, piggybacking on his own deep-muscle inhibition. His eyes opened. He could still see and hear everything. He tried to move, and she could see terror in his face as his body failed to respond. Maybe he thought he was dreaming.

She pulled the sheets back and took one sock off, then removed a small syringe, normally used in microsurgery, from a zippered kit on her vest. She slid it under the nail on his largest toe and dropped the plunger. Then she stood beside the bed and watched as his face turned red, the veins in his neck became engorged, and his eyes scanned the room, lids fluttering in panic.

When she touched his neck with her latex-gloved hand, she could feel the pulse going thready. He was almost gone when she saw lights cross the ceiling. Cars. Voices at the door. She glanced down to the street. Her secondary exit was blocked.

The ground-floor door opened and slammed. Heavy footfalls reverberated through the house.

Light spilled under the doorway into the room. There was only one chance, the master bathroom. Hide or attack? A woman's voice came muffled through the door.

The knob turned. Claire leaped behind the door as it opened and stood there in the narrow space between it and the wall. She pulled her knife with her left hand, a thin special operations dagger. It was designed to be used like an ice pick, and she slipped her index finger through the ring at the end of the handle so she could retain it no matter what. She held her silenced Ruger 22 in her right hand and waited.

The guard whispered from the door to the dying man on the bed: *"Êtes-vous éveillé?"*

No answer. The guard paused on the other side of the door. Eight inches away from Claire. She could smell cheap musk and cigarettes. He didn't do anything.

A minute passed, and then two. The guard's weight moved from foot to foot; hesitation. He had his orders to protect this man, to check on him, but he didn't want to piss him off.

He called back into the living room, "He's sleeping." The other man responded with something she couldn't fully make out, but she did pick up one word: *réveille.* Wake.

She'd been waiting three minutes. It was too long, enough time for her to overthink, for the reflexes to rot, for worry to find leaks in her resolve.

The silenced .22 she carried wouldn't have much stopping power against two guards. She favored the knife, for stealth. A gunshot might draw God knows how many other guys. The guard crossed the room toward the bed. She was in plain sight. One glance and it was over.

She moved toward him, knife out in her left hand, and drew killing-close before he heard anything and turned, spooked that she was already almost beside him. He raised his gun, but she clamped her left hand down on that wrist, retaining the knife pressed flat against his skin. She yanked him to the side as she swung her right hand back just above his trapped arm and slammed the butt of the pistol into his trachea like she was driving a nail.

His tongue shot out and he made a noise like a frog. She was slightly behind and to his left now, both of them facing the same direction. She kicked the back of his left leg; he was already off balance, and he fell to his knees, opening his chest toward the ceiling. She dropped his gun hand, let the knife come back into the ice-pick grip in her left, and drove it between his ribs and into his aorta.

The pain paralyzed him and he dropped the gun. She swept it away with her foot. The man tried to stand, running on anger and shock, but he had only seconds left as the blood flooded out into his thoracic cavity. He took a stumbling step, bounced off the edge of the bed, and hit the floor.

She resheathed her knife on the webbing of her vest and stepped through the door into the main room, checked the corner to her immediate right. There was a figure to her left, raising a gun at her. She braced her pistol and fired three rounds, two into his heart and one into his cheek, and he fell to one knee. Rather than keeping her eyes there, she scanned for other threats. It was the fairness principle of clearing a room: every bad guy gets at least two shots before you finish any of them.

A figure appeared, and she aimed at the head, her front gun sight in focus, the target slightly blurred, but she could see it was a woman, and could hear the strangled cry — real fear. She lunged toward her, arm-checked her hard into the wall, and saw her flail, her hands empty. There wasn't a lot of room under the clothes for a concealed weapon. Claire turned back to the first man she'd shot, a more pressing threat.

She took a step toward him and saw he was dead. Just as she was starting for the dark hall, a searing pain tore through her middle, and a flash blinded her.

Ungrateful bitch, Claire thought, and she took a knee, letting the pain move over her in waves. She'd been shot in the stomach.

She forced herself to stand, then walked back to the hall. The woman had fled. And that hall led to a nest of rooms.

The target was dead. The mission was in full clusterfuck. She didn't have the time or ability to clear this place solo.

She shoved through the front door and started half trotting, half stumbling toward the stairs, her hand clamped over the bloody hole in her lower abdomen.

The rear door banged open, and she hit the street, let the cold air brace her, keep her from falling as she ran, stars in her eyes, edge of blackout, to the next corner, then she turned and ambled, suddenly changed, a woman out for a thoughtful walk, never mind the warmth soaking her shirt and dripping over her belt.

"Urgent medical, urgent medical," she called into her backup radio.

Gut shots hurt like no other kind, and they were messy with infection, but they weren't usually immediately lethal unless a major artery was clipped, and she wouldn't have been able to walk if that had happened.

The pain radiated out and shut down her muscles, but she forced herself to keep going. She pictured the hurt moving out, turning her to stone, to black, as she walked toward the Seine and her backup.

The thirteenth arrondissement was a strange mix of 1960s high-rises and classical stone buildings, and she could see the Bibliothèque nationale de France ahead, four towers looming over a vast and empty plaza like some alien monument. To her left was the Pitié-Salpêtrière. Once a seventeenth-century gunpowder factory and then an asylum where Paris deposited prostitutes and madmen, it was now a world-class hospital, but not for her.

She heard the squeak of car tires and stumbled down the steps to the quai. A shadow came toward her, growing longer, crossing over her, and she raised her pistol.

The Seine lapped against its banks. Yellow light painted the stones. This wouldn't be a bad place to die, she thought. She'd always dreamed of going to Paris when she was a girl. She wondered what lie they would tell Paul as she aimed dead center at the figure.

One street lamp seemed to grow brighter and brighter, like a giant sun, until it was all she could see.

She came to in a safe house in Neuilly. It looked like a two-star hotel, generic furniture and paintings, except for plastic sheeting taped to the ceiling to transform it into an impromptu operating room. She recognized it. Her backup team must have brought her here.

She lay on a table with an IV in her arm. A doctor leaned down and examined her abdomen. There was a tray of scalpels and clamps and scissors on a stand beside her. Her mind was hazy. They had injected her with something for the pain.

She thought of the woman who shot her. Why hadn't Claire killed her on first look? Soft; she was getting soft, worried about bystanders, spouses, innocents.

The doctor put a syringe into her IV line. "Count backward from a hundred."

Even with the drugs, Claire could feel the tear through her stomach. Paul would know a scar from a gunshot wound. He'd seen plenty.

"Wait," she croaked. "It can't be a gunshot. Cut it wide, so it looks like a surgery."

The doctor nodded, and she started counting down. The last thing she saw was him picking up the scalpel.

She would tell her husband it had been a ruptured appendix when she returned to the States.

It was a good joke, in the end, because as soon as she made it home, Paul took one look at the mess of blood and black stitches and puckered skin and surrounding trauma and understood that she was lying about an appendectomy.

She knew deception. She could see it in his face, a reaction halfway between sympathy and distrust. That was when she knew she had to make a choice. The lie was over, but the truth might kill him.

In the trailer now, she ran her finger along the hard scar tissue across her abdomen and then heard a rustle through the window. Someone was coming.

CHAPTER 31

Hayes could see patches of stars through the forest canopy overhead. It was hard to imagine he was only three and a half hours from DC. He lifted his watch, left the light off and used only the faint glow of the hands: 0150. He started trotting.

Grays and blacks were all he could see as the branches slapped at him. There were no trails this deep in the wilderness, and he had circled from the forest road to make sure there wasn't an ambush.

He kept the compass out in his left hand, guiding himself with its tritium needle. He knew his pace bushwhacking at this grade and could dead reckon. He rarely had a chance to use the compass like this, the kind of night hikes and land navigation that he had cut his teeth on in the unit.

All the fighting was in cities now, and he was as likely to be in a skyscraper in a suit as he was to be in a swamp wearing jungle boots.

He hit the ridge and checked his watch. A half a minute off, not bad, given his knee. The joint was crying out, but it felt stable. He took a deep breath and looked over the plateau below.

Strange country. It was known as Dolly Sods. Dolly, an old ranger had told him, was a family name, and *sods* the Scotch-Irish for these high meadows and balds. The area seemed more like Yukon taiga or Alaskan subalpine than West Virginia hills. The front side had become popular with hikers in the past decade or so, but back here was still off-limits and wild.

A cold wind picked up, and light hail started bouncing down from the leaves overhead.

The task at hand filled his mind: Making sense of the blackness ahead of him, feeling the contours of the ridge with every step, guiding himself across the topographic lines. He would have enjoyed it all if death weren't so close. His, maybe, or Claire's.

He hadn't told Morgan he was coming, hadn't told anyone. He thought of that shooting near Claire's house. Maybe the killer had come for her, and she'd responded to Hayes's call because she needed help.

If it was true what they said about her, he could be walking into the arms of his executioner. But it didn't make sense that she was responsible for the murders.

He wasn't sure what the politicians would do if they found her. They were panicked. He'd seen them kill rather than admit their mistakes. He had been hunted too, been falsely accused. He wanted to get to her first. He owed her that much.

But he knew sympathy was dangerous. And if she was involved in those deaths, if this was an ambush, Hayes trusted in his training. He thought of one of the Pashtun poems: "It's better that I kill my brother . . ."

He could see the trailer now, and made out a pale blue light, like gas burning. He'd come along the best ambush routes and seen no signs of others, although given that he was alone with no night optics, that didn't prove much.

He picked his way through the undergrowth. The trailer's screen door rattled in the wind. It was a single-wide, rotting plywood and vinyl, nothing charming like rough-hewn pine or piled stone. It looked like a meth house and smelled like dead raccoons.

But it had the high ground, and anyone with a current-generation night-vision headset would be able to see the enemy coming.

"Claire!" he shouted, but the wind took any reply.

He stepped onto the chipped concrete stoop. His hand went to his pistol, but he didn't want to send the wrong message.

The blue glow wavered on the trailer walls.

"How are you doing, Hayes?" she said. "Come on in."

He entered. His eyes went to her hips, her ankles, her chest, ticking off the weapons: handgun in a hip holster, concealed dagger on her chest.

She stood over a card table in the center of the room and twisted the valve on a camping stove. The smell of naphtha filled the cabin and reminded him of every shithole outpost he'd ever slept at. An empty foil pouch was rolled up on the table.

"Hungry?" she asked.

"I'm all right."

"Tea? I have chamomile."

The flames pooled and danced, blue and white under the little camping pot.

"Perfect," Hayes said.

She sat down and placed a tea bag in each of two enameled mugs with chips around the rims. Hayes hesitated. This close together, neither one would have the reaction time to stop a fatal shot. Whoever moved first would get the kill.

He remembered her, in this room, six years ago. So young. He hadn't had a chance to reach out to her after her husband died. It was when he was in exile. Identification, sympathy; he thought carefully about his emotional reactions to her. He had seen her use them as weapons before, luring in men who took her for a victim, an easy kill.

The openness might be an act. She could be playing him in order to draw him in, to get more names. He was more valuable fooled than dead. That would be the worst outcome. That, in his weakness, he would aid the enemy.

The CIA guys were always tapping out these endless wires back to their stations: numbered paragraphs in all caps running through the suspicions and counter-suspicions. The wilderness of mirrors. Hayes hated it. Gray was the old master of espionage, and Claire was the best student Gray had ever had. This was their world, and Hayes was an interloper. He preferred direct action, combat, where, for all the open sewers and squalid violence, you generally knew who was trying to kill you.

He sat. She poured the hot water into the mugs and slid one to him. The blue light glimmered over the surface as he hesitated, and she killed the stove.

"Do you want to switch?" she said, and she pushed her mug an inch toward him.

"No," he said, and he laughed in spite of himself and dunked the bag. They'd run a lot of shooting drills up here, and hostage-rescue scenarios with live rounds. In one of the final exercises, he and Claire had stood on the range wearing body armor to do a drill Hayes had picked up from the Russian special forces he'd worked with in Chechnya.

Hayes had a paper target mounted behind him, over his shoulder. Claire would turn and draw, and he would shoot her in the ceramic plate on her chest. Then she would have to fire back and hit the target over Hayes's shoulder. Another shot to the chest, one more to the target. Back and forth for seven shots until her fear of that gun going off in her face and bullets smacking into her chest didn't interfere with her targeting and the slow, even squeeze of the trigger.

"How did you know I was there for your interrogations?" Hayes asked. Claire had said to meet him where he'd killed her, and he knew she was referring to the stress phases of her training at this camp. But she had been blind — wearing blacked-out ski goggles — during the most intense sessions.

"It was you and Gray, right?"

"But we didn't talk."

"No, you didn't."

In her last weeks, they ran a mock-kidnapping and POW scenario. The trainee was told nothing when he or she was hauled out of the back of a car, blindfolded, and brought to these godforsaken cabins. At some point after a few weeks of sleep deprivation, starvation, and mind games, the candidate would begin to wonder, *Is this for real?*

In the back of this trailer, Claire, blindfolded and with her hands and ankles bound, had been laid out on an old door that was set at an incline, her head at the bottom. Gray sealed her mouth with Saran Wrap, so she could breathe only through her nose, and poured a plastic pitcher of water over her nostrils, slowly.

Hayes hated to see it, but he wanted to be here to make sure nothing went wrong.

Three taps, a doctor they kept on call would tell her. *Three taps and it's over. All you have to do is tell us the names of your people.*

She tried not to breathe. They always did, but usually at around twelve seconds or so they'd inhale, and the water would start to

213

fill their sinuses. She'd bucked on that door as the water ran up her nose, and Hayes watched her fingers, waiting for the taps.

It felt like drowning — he knew; he'd been through it half a dozen times — felt like an execution, but there was air trapped in the lungs. She wouldn't die, not for a long time.

She held on. *Twenty seconds.*

He knew from her gagging it was heading down her trachea toward her lungs.

"Just tell us who you are and who you work for and we will stop. Just tap."

But she didn't move. The water kept flowing onto her face.

Twenty-five seconds.

She stayed calm.

Thirty.

That's when Hayes had quit. But she held on.

Thirty-five.

Her body tone disappeared. She blacked out. Hayes hauled her off the board while they pulled the Saran Wrap off, then tilted her head forward. Water poured from her mouth and nose. So much water. He checked her pulse as the doctor stepped in with a bag-valve mask and started the rescue breathing.

Hayes watched her chest; when the doctor stopped bagging her briefly, it didn't move.

Then finally the breath came, gurgling through all the water in her airway. After she finished throwing up water, she lifted her head up, still wearing the goggles, and asked if she had given up.

"No," the doctor said.

Claire sipped her tea. "I knew it was Gray because of the smell. That shaving soap he used. Harris Windsor."

Hayes nodded. Gray had come up old-school army infantry and was a prick about grooming standards.

"You remember Korea?" Hayes asked, smiling at the memory of Gray in a bitterly cold tent on the side of a mountain in Korea trying to shave with a frozen badger brush. He'd held it against his cheek, hoping it would thaw.

"And how did you know I was there?"

"No way you'd let them do that without looking out for me."

Hayes nodded. It was true. He had a soft spot for her. He hadn't thought they should use her because of the way anger fueled her. He'd read her psych profile. He had watched the footage from her screening interviews, when a psychologist spent hours probing the most sensitive parts of her history. Often the questioner had to do an

215

elaborate dance to draw out the details from a candidate, but as soon as the shrink began asking about her family's past, Claire saw where he was going. She looked straight at him, cut through all the psychological games, and told the story.

Her father had been an oil executive for Shell. He was a drinker, and abusive. He'd beaten her mother to death one early morning in the house they were renting in Singapore when Claire was eight. She had heard her mother cry for help from behind the closed bedroom door but felt too paralyzed to do anything. The authorities weren't interested in making any trouble for the wealthy American.

She related the whole incident in a calm, even voice and then stared at the camera in the interview room as if to say, *That's who I am. Can you use it or not?*

Claire was a bullet in search of a target, driven by anger and that frustrated desire to protect the innocent. She was just what they needed for Cold Harvest.

Hayes knew how they used the profiles to control their people. It was the same for him. He grew up never knowing where he'd come from, always looking for a home, a place to belong. That's how he blended in so easily behind enemy lines.

"Do you need help, Claire? Who's after you? You don't have to do this alone."

"You shouldn't be involved in this, John. They've taken plenty from you. You should be with your family."

"You can talk to me."

"You can't have two lives, Hayes. Eventually they touch, and then it all burns. The people closest to you get hurt. How can you work for them after everything this country did to you, after they hunted you down like a criminal?"

Rage. He felt it every day while he was in exile. She thought that the only way to deal with it was to give it some outlet, bend it toward justice. But Hayes had never given in to it, never turned on his country, never sought revenge. Then he'd have been no better than the enemy. He'd seen that anger hollow out some of his teammates. They didn't make it. They never should have used her trauma as a tool. It was too toxic, too hard to control.

She chewed her lower lip. She was withholding. God, did she think he might be involved with the deaths?

"I saw Gray last night," she said.

Hayes focused on his breath to dull any reaction. At the same time, he was thinking through the draw, the first shot, anticipating her news. What was this? Confession? An invitation to join her?

Careful, John, he told himself. All the signs pointed to her. Why shouldn't he just take her out now and end this?

"Gray is dead, Claire."

"What?"

"Last night. Someone shot him."

She looked into the empty corner.

"Claire. Did you kill him?"

He didn't want to shoot her. He watched the shock work through her and saw the muscles around her mouth tighten like a snare. Hayes always looked for that reflex. It was involuntary, a sure sign of a coming reaction.

There were ways to conceal lies, defeat the polygraphs, clench your ass at the right times, but they were cheap, and an expert could detect them in the baselines. But Claire went a step beyond. She was the best they'd seen. Whatever emotion was needed, she could bring it to bear, because she believed it herself.

"No. Christ. It's happening."

"What's happening?"

"Gray warned me. They're killing us all to hide the truth. It's someone inside the program. Morgan called off the investigation into my husband's death, John. Who told you about Gray?"

It was Morgan, but he wasn't ready to tell her that. Claire seemed able to read his reaction, though.

"Morgan is behind this, Hayes. Wait. You met with her. Are you working for her?"

"Not like that."

Her hand twitched on the table. "That's why they never cleared your name. They're holding it over your head; they're forcing you."

Hayes couldn't understand, if her doubts about him were this strong, why she hadn't tried to kill him already. It was only their past that was keeping them from moving, and that wouldn't last. "Claire, I'm here to help."

She stared back at him, her face pale. "You killed the others."

CHAPTER 32

Hayes heard it first, the softest crunch of gravel. His eyes went to one side. Someone was coming. No one but Claire knew they were here.

An ambush? Then what the hell was this whole performance? A mind game? An attempt to get information out of him?

His eyes met Claire's. He saw them narrow, saw her shoulders tense. She was going for the gun.

He launched forward, driving the table into her arm as she drew. The pistol discharged into the floor, and the table's edge struck her in the bottom of the jaw. She fell back in the chair, and Hayes reached her as she hit the ground. He stepped on her arm with the toe of his boot, then kicked her pistol out of her fingers with his other foot. He stood over her, his gun aimed at her head.

"How could you, John?" she asked.

The glass blew out to his right. The cheap vinyl-over-gypsum siding exploded in clouds of white. He saw flares of red outside, through the window. Shooters were closing in from the north and east.

He ducked, turned, and started to sprint. He had to assume they were covering the door. He had to hit it fast.

He dropped his shoulder and charged the front door near the knob. The frame splintered out and he kept moving. It was a kill funnel but at the speed he was going, it would take anyone outside a second to target him.

He brought his leg forward, stumbling slightly after the impact with the door, and felt bone slam into bone as he crashed into someone just outside. The two of them tumbled, and as Hayes put his hand down to brace the fall, a powerful grip seized his wrist and chicken-winged his arm behind his back. His wrist was bent backward, and the ligaments in his shoulder sang out in pain. He tried to rise, but the armlock drove him forward. The man was behind him and slightly to his left.

Hayes saw movement ahead, another shooter, closing in at fifty yards. He had held on to the gun with his right hand, and now he stood tall, ignoring the pain. He brought the pistol across his body, as if hugging himself, to shoot the man wrenching his arm.

Click. Christ. He might have knocked the slide during the tumble and unseated the round in the chamber. He was wide open as the other gunman closed for an easy shot.

The reaction to get his gun working was almost instinct: Tap. Rack. Bang. You hit the magazine to make sure it's all the way in, racked the slide back to eject the misfed round, and then pulled the trigger and fired. It was the standard drill for clearing a malfunction in a pistol. Easy enough with two hands.

Hayes slammed the grip of the pistol against his thigh, then hooked his rear sights on his belt and shoved it down, cycling the slide. The unseated round spun glinting through the air as Hayes, leaning forward, brought the pistol back across his body, aimed up, and fired two bullets into the upper belly and sternum of the man on his back.

The grip on his wrist relaxed as the rounds blew through the man's chest, and he stumbled back. Hayes moved at the other shooter now, coming around a tree. The gun barked twice in Hayes's hand as he dropped the man with a double-tap.

Hayes sidestepped to the corner of the trailer, searching out other gunmen. As he rounded the door, he saw that Claire was gone.

Two shots blew out the corner, and splinters scratched the side of his face. He saw red flare out from behind one of the pillars near the wood line.

Claire.

Hayes fired back but heard only the zip of bullets on stone. He took cover next to the foundation, then circled the trailer and came out on the far side. The night had cleared, and moonlight cast long shadows. Beside one of the pillars, the air wavered like smoke.

It was the hot vapors leaving a gun barrel just out of view behind the pillar. He crossed closer, then saw the black silhouette of the shooter, unsuspecting, looking for him where he had first taken cover. He centered his sights on the figure's head and eased the trigger back twice.

Crack-crack.

The figure dropped like a puppet with its strings cut, and he heard it thud against the ground.

Hayes closed on the position, sprinting now. He moved through the gap between the pillars and saw the small hand, the gun.

The face wasn't something he particularly wanted to see, but he had to be sure.

It was a young man, maybe eighteen or nineteen.

A two-stroke ripped through the night. A dirt bike, up the ridge. He heard it tear toward the deeper forest.

He started running straight to his truck, but even then he knew. There were ten thousand routes out of those woods. She was gone.

CHAPTER 33

Hynd paced across the warehouse floor with the phone pressed to his ear, waiting for an update from his hit team in the mountains.

His footsteps echoed between the tanks of the old brewery. He had sent three men to follow Claire to the wilderness where she had met with someone from Cold Harvest. His team had identified him as the same man they had spotted at Burke's funeral: John Hayes.

When they had asked what to do, Hynd took his time answering. "Kill him," he said finally, "and let the woman live."

That was thirty minutes ago, and all he had gotten since was a panicked emergency message from the youngest shooter: Claire had escaped, and Hynd's other two men were dead. He hadn't heard anything further from that man and could only assume that Hayes had taken him down as well.

Vera came toward him, carrying a laptop

with a map of the Northeast and Mid-Atlantic states open on the screen.

"I think they're all dead," Hynd said.

"And the targets?"

"The Cold Harvest man escaped, and so did Claire."

"We have a signal. We're tracking her."

"Good," Hynd said.

There had been so much violence in such a short period, barely more than a day. Even the most willfully blind politicians wouldn't be able to deny it.

He had studied the Americans for a long time, probed them at their most honest moments, in the face of death, to understand how the others would react, where they would go, how their beliefs would move them.

They would probably at least shut down Cold Harvest. That was the history of American interventions. The slightest real pain and they fled home and hid.

That would be a victory, of course. He was paid to eliminate the program. The Americans had become too reliant on it.

The armed groups and intelligence services who'd hired him had been frustrated for years. With Cold Harvest gone, they would be able to proceed with their plans. There were dozens of plots waiting for Cold

Harvest to go down before they could be launched. It would be a time of freedom.

But Hynd knew he could do more than simply close down the program. He knew these people better than they knew themselves. The men in Cold Harvest thought they were individuals. It was one of the great myths of this country. Maybe they would stay out in the field as singletons, and he would hunt them one by one.

But he didn't think so. They were sheep. And in danger, they would herd together, and then he could take them all at once. He had hoped for this, planned for this. It's why he had shot Gray, the father of the program. By killing their master, he hoped to draw them all into one place.

He had started with a few names from inside the program, and the funerals had led him to more. It was slow, painstaking work, and he knew it couldn't last. At some point, the fight would move into open war. If the Americans were on guard, he would need a vastly more powerful weapon to overcome their defenses: explosives.

He had studied all the Homeland Security guidelines, all the building manuals. It was all public. He knew the formulas. There were regulation standoff distances to keep secure buildings safe.

But there was no way to be safe in an open society. The first calculations after 9/11 suggested that the four blocks around the White House should be shut down, like a giant hole punched in downtown DC. There was no will, so they just closed off Pennsylvania Ave. and then seemed to forget. It happened everywhere, a brief clear-eyed view of the threat and then a lot of talking and little action.

There were so many exotic plots out there, the underwear and shoe bombs, but there was nothing more proven and more lethal than a truck bomb. Nothing fancy, just ammonium nitrate — fertilizer — and fuel, easy to make in bulk, the same explosive Timothy McVeigh used. That attack on a federal building in Oklahoma City was put together by just two men, killed a hundred and sixty-eight, and leveled three downtown blocks.

Yet the Americans still refused to acknowledge their vulnerability. The standoff guidelines went only so high, and then they fell back on prayer and willful blindness. He would simply go higher.

As they drove back to the brewery that afternoon, he had seen the firework stands on the side of the highway getting ready for the Fourth of July. It brought a smile to his face. His plan was so American in a way. There was no subtlety to it; he would just go bigger and bigger. Eventually no target would be safe. There was nowhere they could hide.

The truck was ready, but they still needed more explosive. He had a source in mind. He wished he had more time to perfect his plans, but he knew his one chance to take them all out was coming, and he had to be ready.

"Where's the cargo?" Hynd asked.

Vera scrolled on the laptop's trackpad and then pointed to the screen. "The target truck stopped for the night. Timur is following him about a half mile back."

The United States had few facilities for parking dangerous loads overnight along the highway. It was a known flaw, but nothing had been done about it.

"Take it now," Hynd said.

CHAPTER 34

The tractor-trailer was parked along the side of a two-lane Pennsylvania highway. Its driver, a man named Colin Raynaud, woke up drenched in sweat on top of a sleeping bag. He lay on an air mattress on the floor of the truck's cab in a cramped area behind the seats.

The mayflies were humming like a boat engine outside. It sounded way too loud. Usually the air conditioner's fan and compressor drowned them out.

He felt above his head near the vent. Nothing. The AC was dead. The soft glow of lights in the cab was gone. Moonlight filtered around the curtains. He sat up.

The electrical must have gone out. He cursed and wiped the sweat from the back of his neck, the drenched, close-cropped hair.

He stood up, slipped his bare feet into his boots, and tied them loosely around the ankles. The truck was holding up well, especially considering he'd been on the road six weeks. He liked to listen to lectures and audiobooks and had gone through three college courses this month. He was in the middle of one on the American Revolution.

Condensation clung to the windows. It was like a hot bath in there. He needed some air. He stepped outside, down onto the broken-up asphalt. He was the only truck in the small lot. The moonlight reflected and arced along his silver trailer. He kept it spotless.

A creek wandered through the tall grass to his right. He couldn't see any lights in the countryside ahead. He liked working hazmat rides because they kept to these rural routes. No cities. No schools. They were strict on the sleep requirements. He had a folder full of credentials and clearances and could drive the nastiest loads out to the mining and demolition companies.

There was a yellow square with a four in it on his hazmat diamond: *readily capable of detonation or explosive reaction at normal temperatures and pressures.* Not just anyone could haul that.

He liked sticking to the boondocks, the old two-lanes that had been abandoned for the interstates. The quiet soothed him.

It reminded him of early mornings in Natchitoches Parish, camping with his father before the hunt. His father would still be sleeping away, sawing logs from the moment he shut his eyes, and Colin never understood how he could make it that long. Colin would always have to go to the bathroom at some point, would have to find his shoes and glasses and stumble, freezing, in his underwear and his loose boots through the silvery night. Another planet. Ghosts everywhere. Animals on the move. Magic.

He craned his head back and traced the Big Dipper and a few other constellations he couldn't remember the names of. They'd stopped hunting once he was eleven. His dad's body wasn't up for it. And they just fell out of the habit.

Hopefully it was only the battery. He took a last look over the fields, then stepped toward the truck and noticed the glint of copper. The wires were cut. He went to inspect them, but then he heard the rustling behind him and turned.

A young man clamped his hand over Raynaud's mouth and slid a knife into his lower back, then dragged him into the moon shadow beside the truck.

The pain paralyzed him, and Timur looked

on as the man put Raynaud on his face in the dirt and handcuffed his wrists, taking care to keep the back of the hands together, thumbs pointed to the sky. Blood flowed freely, pooling and dripping from his white T-shirt, but it wasn't the pump of an arterial wound. Timur rolled a bandage around his finger, put it through the tear in the shirt, and felt around until he could drive it into the cut in Raynaud's back. The clotting agent in the gauze stopped the blood flow. The young man gagged him, bound his ankles, and dragged him into the cab of the truck.

It took a moment for Timur to find Raynaud's papers, the clearances that allowed him to haul high explosives and toxic inhalation hazards.

They would notice the missing shipment at some point, of course, even after Timur spoofed the GPS, but by then he would be long gone, and the truck would be swapped out and its cargo taken. Companies were always reluctant to report missing explosives because it might cost them their licenses. The full response would take almost a week to begin, if it got going at all.

CHAPTER 35

Raynaud came to in a tiled room. He shouted for help several times, louder and louder, but the only response was his own voice echoing back. He felt weak and groggy, and as he tried to stand he could hear his restraints jingling behind his back. He was chained to the rail that ran along the gang shower. He couldn't feel his hands.

The door opened. A man entered and sat on the bench across from him. He looked like he was in his forties, but there was something youthful about him. He was smiling, an expression so out of place in the midst of this terror that it didn't seem real.

"What's going on?" Raynaud said. "Just let me go."

"It's okay," Hynd said in a soothing voice. "It's okay."

"Please, just —"

"Be quiet," Hynd said with a sudden bite in his voice.

Raynaud stopped talking.

"You want me to let you go?"

"Yes."

"You want another day alive? Another look at the sun?"

"Yes, man. Please. What's going on? I'm not going to tell anyone anything. Just let me go —"

"So yes."

"Yes, I do."

"You know why someone would steal your truck?"

"No. I don't know anything about you or what's up." He looked at the ground. "Please, man. I've got a kid."

"I know. Don't be stupid. Were those your tapes? In the truck? The lectures? The courses?"

"Yes."

"That's good. Those are good things to learn about. You're smart. You know what we're doing, why we would take your cargo."

"I won't call it in."

"I'll make you a deal," Hynd said. "Help us."

"I don't want anything to do with it, but you let me go, and I won't say anything."

"Help us and you'll live one more day. It's your choice."

"I don't want any trouble."

"You won't say anything?"

"No."

"You know we're going to kill people with your cargo? You'll let us do that?"

"I won't talk."

"If they're going to die anyway, why not help us? People you don't know. Would never meet. You would never even be able to tell they're gone. In your life, they don't exist anyway. And then you get to see your daughter again. How many would you kill for that? What's it worth to you?"

Raynaud began to cry and dropped his head. Hynd crouched near him and looked in his eyes.

"Would you kill one man? Twelve?"

"I don't want to kill anyone."

Hynd stood and put his hand on his shoulder. "You're a good man. That's the right answer."

Hynd held his hand out to the side and Timur passed him a knife with the blade carefully pinched between his fingers so Hynd could take the handle. It was long and thin and double-edged.

"Wait!" Raynaud said. "Wait. What do you want me to do!"

Hynd watched him beg. The man hadn't known he was a killer. No one does. Not until he has to make the choice.

Hynd nodded to Timur, who held Raynaud still by the shoulders against the wall. Then Hynd put the tip of the blade to his chest and slid it home.

CHAPTER 36

Hynd ran the cleaning solution over his palms and then washed away the last traces of red. His hands smelled faintly of bleach. They might call him a terrorist, but that was bullshit. He was finishing what the Americans and Israelis had started, a war he'd been caught in the middle of from the day he was born. He'd seen them kill firsthand as a child. His father had been a German engineer who went to work for the Egyptians on their nuclear program.

The Mossad led the kill teams that took down his father, and the Americans gave them their tacit approval. He knew how the Israeli assassins did their work. They believed there was a certain mercy in terror. They would first try to frighten the scientists into quitting. It began with threatening notes and calls, and then an empty car would explode.

Hynd had found one of the first notes

when he was ten, a letter on the front door of their house in Cairo along with photos of himself, his father, and his mother that had been taken with a telephoto lens. His father was a proud man, and he ignored the threats. He wouldn't be coerced by violence. He had fled his homeland rather than bend to the Fascists' will.

"You give in to these people, bullies — *schikanieren* — and they only get stronger."

His father was defiant. He continued the work. Nuclear power. Nuclear defense. The Americans did nothing after Israel acquired the atomic bomb, but if anyone else should try to get it, the U.S. would stand by as men of science were assassinated in their homes. It took Hynd years to realize that the Americans were the root evil, and by then they had fielded their own kill teams in Cold Harvest.

The West didn't obey their own laws. They tortured and killed. And when another nation tried to defend itself, to arm itself against threats, they came in and murdered everyone involved. They didn't scare his father. He'd never backed down.

He died on a Sunday. Hynd was in his room, reading, when the boom shook the floor. He went to the window and saw the flames rising from his family's Lada sedan.

It was so strange, how his father loved all those finely tooled gears and pistons, would spend hours going over the mechanical drawings for the lab, and in the end it was machinery that tore him apart. They buried him in a closed casket.

Hynd wasn't like the other children. He never cried, never laughed. Beliefs fascinated him. Belief had gotten his father killed, so he himself held none. He would study others, to understand how they behaved, what motivated them, to pretend he was like them, to make them do what he wanted, to get control. He'd been studying people ever since, and he'd found it so useful against the Americans.

His work of killing began long ago as a personal vendetta against the men who'd murdered his father, and it led him to the great powers who were ultimately behind that act. It became his calling and his profession. America had many enemies, open and secret, and he drew on their financing and resources to stop the West's assassins. There was none more dangerous than Cold Harvest.

Now he was close, so close. They had brought the war to his home, and he would bring it to theirs. He had everything he needed.

CHAPTER 37

Hayes leaned over the tailgate of his truck with a prepaid mobile phone in his hand. He'd taken it from the last man he'd shot outside the West Virginia trailer. Some dried blood flaked off the handset. All the other shooters he'd run across had wiped theirs, but this one was still working. Maybe the young gunman had hoped to get out a last message to whoever was handling him.

He'd traced the forest roads with his truck, but none went to the west. He'd need a dirt bike to chase Claire, and she was an expert rider, could race through tight-packed second-growth trees.

The search area was growing every minute. He'd called it in to Morgan to get a helicopter out here but needed to move on before any local law enforcement showed up and started asking questions about why he'd just dropped three people in the woods. He drove until he picked up a strong signal on the far side of the ridge, then called the NSA tech.

"Jonathan."

Hayes didn't bother introducing himself. The NSA always knew who was calling. "I have a bad guy's phone," he said. "Can you give me anything on it if I get it up on the system?"

"Plug it in and log in."

Hayes connected it to his laptop and then used his mobile data card to access a virtual private network.

"I can see it. I'm cloning it now," Jonathan said.

"Anything on it?"

"I can get the last number, but it looks like a relay."

"Can you trace it?"

"Not if it's done right, and this looks like a quality setup."

"And if I call it?"

"Hang on a minute."

Hayes waited, listening to the quiet tapping of keys.

"Okay," Jonathan said. "I've pulled everything off there. Go ahead with the call. It can't hurt. I'll try the trace."

"Ready?"

"Shoot."

Hayes put his phone down, then lifted the

dead man's and hit redial. It rang once, and the line opened, but then there was more ringing, a connection, another ring, as the call bounced from relay to relay. They might have been able to trace the killer's field teams, but whoever was on the other end of this, in command, was well insulated.

Finally, there was the slight static of an open line, and Hayes heard a distorted voice say, "Verify yourself." The person on the other end wanted an authentication code.

"Who are you?" Hayes asked.

There was no reply. He only hoped that by holding the line a little longer he might help trace the call.

"All of the men you sent to ambush me are dead," Hayes said. "What do you want?"

There was a rustle on the other end of the line, and then a new voice. Despite the distortion, Hayes could tell it was deeper, a man's.

"What do you want?" Hayes asked again.

"The same as you. To end the terror. To keep our families safe. You people are so blinded by your own myths. You never seem to understand. You're the violence."

The line went dead.

Three hundred miles away, Hynd stripped the back off the phone, pulled the SIM card

243

and battery, and handed them off. Three more of his contractors were dead, but there was some grace in it. Claire had met with this man from Cold Harvest, and they had both survived. Each might assume that the other had drawn him or her into an ambush. If Hynd played this right, he might be able to turn them against each other. Claire could not only lead him to his targets, but even act as his weapon.

CHAPTER 38

Claire felt the blood soak through her sock. It reminded her of the blisters she used to get during the endless marches that were used to weed out candidates for Cold Harvest.

The only roads out of those woods were to the east, so she had gone west. She had left the dirt bike near a river. She couldn't get it across.

She'd been walking for so long. What started as friction and heat in her heel had become a stabbing pain, and now it was only a wet nothing. The hiking had felt like a slog at first, and then a numbing rhythm as she cruised through the dark.

The bruise under her jaw grew, balled up like a swollen gland. Hayes, the only one she trusted, had drawn her into a trap and tried to kill her.

The people behind this were inside the program. And she had no idea who was innocent and who had been turned. *Everything is a cover. Everyone is suspect.*

How could she warn her teammates? How could she protect them when any of them was liable to put a knife in her back?

Run, she thought. *Forget about protecting the others. Just grab what you need and run.*

She'd tried to run before. She'd learned her lesson, a lesson Hayes would learn too. You can't quit. Because the violence becomes a part of you. You can't escape who you are.

It was after the Paris killings, the gut shot. Paul took care of her, but the doubts broke through. He was a war photographer. He'd seen enough gunshot wounds to know.

He started sleeping in the guest room, and Claire knew that if she fed him one more lie, he would leave. It was over if she didn't quit. She had to choose.

She went to Gray and said she was done.

"Take as much time as you need."

"I'm not coming back."

"You're going to live the cover?"

"Yes."

"You need this, Claire," he said, and he took a deep breath. "That life doesn't exist without this one. It's not who you are. You need both. You need the outlet."

The marriage license. The birth certificate.

They all bore a false name, but it was more real than anyone she'd ever been.

"I tell you this because I don't want you to get hurt. It's not going to work. You can't change who you are."

She walked out.

He was right, but she wouldn't learn it for some time. She lived the lie. And she was happy.

A month later she and Paul were on vacation in Chania, an ancient port town on the island of Crete. They had met while she was working in Turkey and gone to Crete for what was essentially their first date, a week-long trip together. During that visit, all the joy of falling in love had been cut through with the knowledge that it was all a lie, that it could never work.

This time it was pure, unsullied. They went in early September and stayed at the same *pension*. They would lie out on the small terrace, drive over the mountains to empty beaches of the southern shore, to a spot where the myths say the Cyclops lived, looking across the sea to Libya. She made plans. She wanted a garden like her mother had, instead of the cut flowers she had been buying for years, with no roots, ready to be discarded.

The old instincts never left her, sure, and

the old paranoia worked at the margins of every moment. She would see the same man twice and mark him as a foot surveillant, start searching every vehicle for a potential snatch team. But over time they ebbed.

One night, they went to a restaurant housed in a building that long ago had been a Turkish bath. Half the tables were down on the marble of the old pools. It was nearly closing time, and Paul had just convinced her to take a second shot of raki.

She raised her glass and paused, holding the clear liquor in the air. The windows were at street level, and she saw a pair of shoes out front move across, then back, and then stop. Good trackers follow the shoes. Jackets and hats are easy to switch. But shoes are too bulky to carry and slow to change.

She'd seen them before and cycled through the faces from their afternoon and evening, stored like Polaroids in her mind, matching them up to threats from her past: Mogadishu, Ukraine, Aceh.

You're paranoid.

Yes, she was.

"Excuse me for a second," she said.

"You okay?"

"I think so," she said, and she placed her hand on her stomach. She went toward the bathrooms, then passed the kitchen to a rear exit. She wanted to see the pursuer's face, the reaction. As she came out in the small alley between the stone buildings, she could see the watcher waiting outside the restaurant. He turned and walked away.

She looked through the window and saw her husband. That's why she didn't want to go, and why she had no choice. That was why the anger was a gift: it was the instinct to protect because she had failed to protect her mother.

Claire started after him, and the pace quickened. She worked the angles of the old city to block him. He must have not known the terrain, because he was moving into an area of fewer, not more, choices and, finally, a dead end, a long lane that was cut off not far from the water by the ancient warehouses along the port.

Her hand closed on her knife as she approached. It was her only weapon, a sturdy folder with a frame lock that she kept sharp enough to shave with. He was cornered. She marveled at how easy it had been to get the better of him, even after all her time away from the nonstop drilling, exercises, and training.

The man's route was amateurish almost. But what she had seen of him so far wasn't the work of an amateur. *A dead end.* She had cornered him. Or he had lured her into a trap. She flattened against the wall, looked back, and saw movement behind her.

She sprinted at it, watched the hands rise toward her and cut right down a side street just as a silenced shot lit the narrow lane red.

Run, run! her instincts screamed, but she stopped as soon as her shadow couldn't be seen from around the corner, then pressed against the wall and moved nearer to the gunman. She slipped back into a doorway and drew her knife. The target always runs. No one goes closer to the threat. Which was why she had.

As he came running around the corner she gripped the knife in her fist and drove it sideways into his neck, just below the ear. The gun clattered to the ground, and she lunged toward it.

But she was too late; the other man was a blur of black rounding the corner and coming at her in a sprawl. She pivoted out of his line, dropped down, then shot her palm into his upper lip and nose.

The shock of pain and then the quick jerk of his head stunned him. She kept pushing, shoving his face back, then down to the ground.

She could hear police sirens in the distance, echoing through the maze of streets, concealing their location. He fired an errant shot as she climbed on top of him, chest to his, arm around his neck. She had to keep him so close he couldn't get the gun between them to fire. Her cheek was against his. She raised his head with hers and slammed it back down against the cold stone.

She did it a second time, and the blow shook through the bones of her own face. A third, and the gun dropped. She had her arms around his head like a running back cradling a football to his chest, and she drove it against the cobbles.

There was no time to find out who he was or who had sent him. The sirens moved closer.

"Please," he whispered as she slammed his head once more and heard the nauseating crack as his skull caved in.

He started to plead again, but she brought him up, chest to chest, and thought only of her husband and the animal need to protect what she loved as she finished him against the roadway with one double-handed blow. She dragged her palms along the curb, smearing the blood against the worn stone, then picked up the pistol.

It was a long way back to the restaurant

with her following the gun around every corner. Paul was gone.

She called the Cold Harvest night-action line from a pay phone. No answer. The number had changed. She knew none of the codes to authenticate herself anymore anyway. She was boxed out. She'd gotten her wish, to go clear, and now she was on her own.

She washed her face and hands in the brass lion-head fountain in the central square, then walked back to the *pension,* shoved the double front door hard enough to overcome the cheap dead bolt, and went upstairs.

The room was empty.

She felt the anger return. There was no one on the terrace, and she swept back into the room with the pistol raised.

"Do you speak English?" Paul's voice. She hid the pistol in her waistband and covered it with a light coat, then came down the rear stairs. He was in the back hall with the phone to his ear, probably calling the police.

She pressed down the button on the receiver.

"Hello? Hello?" He turned. "Carol! Jesus. Where have you been?"

He wrapped his arm around her, and she angled away so he wouldn't feel the gun.

"We need to go," she said.

"What? What happened? Jesus. Were you mugged?"

"We *need* to *go.*"

He was putting them both in danger.

"Carol, if —"

"Now!" And she showed him, for an instant, the strength of her true self. He froze. This man who had stood in front of advancing tanks with his Canon 5D and taken shot after steady shot.

"Okay. Okay."

Some part of her thrilled to that feeling, of showing him the killer and seeing his fear. And that scared her as much as the men on her trail.

CHAPTER 39

She walked through the woods alongside the highway for four miles before she came to the truck stop. The yellow lamps in the parking lot seemed to burn like the sun after so much time in the dark.

She entered the convenience store from a side entrance and walked straight past the CB antennas and 12-volt accessories. She smelled bad. Her shoe was full of blood. The girl behind the checkout stared at her, not because she hadn't seen worse — there were plenty of tweakers who ran through here — but because Claire had no shame as she bought a change of clothes and strode calmly toward the bathroom.

She went to the showers, fed in ten dollars, and stood under the steam for all six minutes. Then she sat on the little bench out front and put antiseptic deep into the cut before heading back to the parking lot.

She looked over the cars, checking for

signs of long-term parking, good candidates for theft. Headlights came toward her. She kept walking. A Jeep Rubicon pulled up alongside her.

"You look like you could use a friend," the man said.

The car looked brand-new, no signs of hard use, but it was about the most capable off-road made.

His hand had a wedding ring on it, and a knife clip stuck out from the pocket of his jeans. She watched his eyes as he measured her body with his. He should have noticed the desperation on her, the convenience-store clothes. He probably did, but it only encouraged him. She seemed to be helpless. He looked like a soccer coach, but he was a predator.

Claire considered the Jeep. It would open up a lot of terrain where the police never go.

"I could," she said.

"You need a ride?"

"I do."

He gestured with his head to the passenger door.

She circled around the car and climbed in as he rolled up the window.

"You didn't ask me where I was going," he said, and he laid his hand on her thigh.

"Just a ride," she said, and she put her hand on his, stopping it. He smiled and reached between her legs. She gripped his forearm and drew him toward her. His instinct led him to pull back, and as he did she released his arm, and slammed her palm into the side of his neck. She caught the jaw from under and added her strength to his own momentum to drive his head into the window with a heavy *chunk,* like a bat connecting with a baseball.

He wailed as she pulled the knife from his pocket, flicked it open, and put it into the hollow of his throat.

"Get out of the car."

He cursed and called her every vulgar thing you can call a woman. "Put that down before you kill somebody."

It was a nice knife, a Spyderco with a grippy handle. She pressed it forward, just barely breaking the skin. A drop of blood ran down his neck.

"Get out of the car."

His hand found the door latch, and he stepped out. She opened the glove box and pulled the registration and a Ruger pistol. "I have your address here," she said. "You report this to the police in less than twenty-four hours and I come to your house and kill you."

He wiped the blood from his neck.

"Understood?"

He nodded.

"Say it."

"I understand."

"Good."

She climbed into the driver's seat, dropped the vehicle into gear, and made for the forest road.

CHAPTER 40

Kathryn Morgan could see only the top of Tucker's head on the monitor of the video teleconference. The candidate's face was down and his hands were wrapped around his skull like he was in an air-raid drill. Three deep breaths, and then he faced the camera.

"Do you know what my deputy told me today?"

Morgan didn't reply.

"A reporter, some nobody down in Virginia, was asking around to see if there were any terrorism connections to the lake-house shootings. Some neighbors heard explosions and were wondering why a bomb squad was there."

He straightened his shirt and swallowed a pair of pills dry.

"The press!" he went on. "Do you hear me? And now you're telling me that Hayes is on some kind of spree in the mountains?

You said you had him under wraps."

"I didn't know he was going there."

"Exactly. How many people did he kill?"

"Three."

"Jesus Christ. This is your one job. You had him, and he walked away. And now I have three corpses, and this psychopath Claire Rhodes is on the loose. Where is Hayes?"

Morgan cleared her throat.

"Where is Hayes?"

"He gave us what we need to know to help the Feds and local law enforcement with the search and then headed out."

"Where?"

"I don't know."

Tucker ran his hand through his hair and grabbed a fistful near the back of his head.

"He's out of pocket? He met with Rhodes right under your goddamn nose!"

"He *is* killing the people behind this."

"Have you lost your mind? I can't have an open war inside the United States. Whatever. I'm done. Option S the whole goddamn thing."

It was an emergency plan to wrap the program.

"You're sure?"

"Yes. Cold Harvest. All of it. Shut it down."

"You know that's probably what the people behind these killings want. And some of these operators are working covers that have taken years to set up. They're close to stopping —"

"I don't care. I can't have them in the field. I can't have more firefights in the middle of the U.S. I can't have them running around like Hayes. We can use the diplomatic security teams to go after them and bring them in."

"To Washington?"

"No. That'll attract too much attention. Where else?"

Morgan thought through the options. "New York. The flights will work, and we can start putting them at the Upper East Side annex. I think that's available."

It was a CIA safe house in Carnegie Hill, more of an apartment building, really, used to debrief foreign diplomats and officials that the CIA had turned when they came through New York.

"But what are you going to tell them?" Morgan asked.

"Me? Nothing. I'm going to be giving a campaign speech at Rockefeller Plaza, and I should be in Ohio by the time they're all here and *you* tell them. *You* are going to be point on this. How long will it take to bring them in?"

"A lot are in the U.S. and Europe. If we crash it and use the jets, we can have half of them here by tomorrow and almost all by Tuesday."

"Good. I'll be long gone then. Bring them in. Tell them it's about the death of Gray and the others. It's an emergency meeting about the future of Cold Harvest, something about their own safety and the safety of the other operators. That's the only thing they'll go for. And then once we get them here, we're going to shut them down and keep a lid on them until after the election. We need eyes on them."

"They won't go for it."

"Then they'll go to prison. They've been operating illegally for years."

"And the press?"

"If it gets out, and if the Congress and the media need a sacrifice for the killings, we'll feed them Hayes. He's perfect for it. Hide the rest in classifications. Claim national security is at stake. You know how this goes."

Morgan looked down at her desk. The cheap lunch she'd swallowed down from the buffet on the corner churned in her stomach. This was capitulation, giving the enemy exactly what they wanted. It was surrender.

"What is it?" Tucker asked, seemingly concerned. It was a tactic to elicit honesty. Any protest Morgan made would be fatal. Her fingerprints were all over Cold Harvest. Hayes was her fall guy, but if she didn't pull this off, she would be Tucker's.

In any scandal, there comes a moment where you decide how high up to make the cut, who gets thrown away and who survives. She had damn sure better survive.

The pilot in her balked, but that pilot had died in a field hospital in Kuwait after the crash.

"Nothing. I'm on it," Morgan said.

"Bring in Hayes. I don't care what it takes."

CHAPTER 41

The air-conditioning turned on, and a cool draft billowed into the hospital room. They had medevaced Drew Ochoa to this facility after the attack at the lake house. A woman sat in the chair beside Drew's hospital bed under a window looking over the building's atrium. Her eyes were red, as if she had finally exhausted herself crying.

Hayes stepped into the room and nodded to her respectfully.

Drew opened one eye.

"Hey," he croaked. "Hayes. Are you okay?"

"I'm fine."

"Good." The shot had missed Drew's heart by a few inches. He looked ghostly and had an oxygen cannula beneath his nose.

"Sharon," Drew said, looking to his wife. "This is my friend who helped us out at the house. We used to work together."

She smiled at him weakly. "Thank you."

It entered Hayes like a knife. He'd been too late. One boy's father had died, this woman's husband was in the ICU, and her son had seen things no boy should ever see.

"I'm sorry I didn't get there sooner," Hayes said and lowered his head.

"Hon, could you see if you can get me another one of these fruit cups?" Drew asked. There were two full ones on the side of his tray.

"Sure," she said; she squeezed his hand and walked out.

Downstairs, two FBI agents strode through the sliding glass doors. They were rushing, still panicked from Morgan's tone when she'd given the order. They'd missed Hayes last time. They would take him now.

Drew picked up the plastic tumbler of water, took a sip from the straw, and winced.

"So what are you doing here?" he asked Hayes.

"Seeing how you're holding up. I'm glad you made it."

"This is a social call, with everything you have going on?"

"Can you talk? Are you up for it?"

"If that's going to help you destroy the people who did this, I can talk all day."

Hayes could hear the strain in his voice.

"Did you get a read on the shooters?"

They had gotten nothing off the bodies at the munitions factory. The trace on the call was a dead end. But Hayes couldn't stop thinking about those distorted words over the phone. *Keep our families safe.* There was an answer in there if he could just see it.

Drew was the only one who had been eye to eye with the killers, and Hayes thought he must have seen something that could help him find out who they were.

"They were very well trained, and you can't pick up that gear at Home Depot. English was excellent. Slight accents. I figure them for El Salvador or Honduras."

"That's good," Hayes said.

"Yeah. Leaves about ten thousand candidates. What happened to you?" He looked at the fresh scratches on Hayes's cheek. "I see you're taking a much-deserved break."

"I went to see Claire up at the Dolly Sods camp. It was an ambush. When the shooters came, she was convinced they had followed me, that *I* had come to kill *her.* The look she had. She really believed it. Is there a chance she's a pawn in this?"

"It doesn't sound like it. There were a lot of questions about that car fire, the one that killed her husband. Half the guys thought she did it."

"Have you ever looked at the file?" Hayes glanced down at his laptop bag.

"I was gone. Is there any explosive stuff? Gas chromatograph?"

"I'm not going to put you on this now."

"I'm not going to sit on my ass while the people who killed my friend and terrorized my family run free." With his good arm he cleared a spot on the rolling table that extended over his bed, then shut his eyes against the pain. "Give."

Hayes pulled out the computer and slid it in front of him. "This is the arson investigation. Local law didn't find anything. Here it is, the chemical screen."

Drew ran his finger over the display. It took him about ten minutes to go through it.

"Oh yeah. Accelerants. This is awesome stuff."

"What is it?"

Drew pointed to two graphs.

"These are chromatograms, like fingerprints for any chemicals they could pick up at the scene. This" — he tapped the one on the left — "is decabutane. The Russians started fielding it recently. Used it to kill that journalist in Dagestan. We didn't figure out how to detect it until the last year or so because it blends in with burned plastics."

"After Claire's husband was killed."

"Yeah. Headquarters is always behind on this stuff. They use the FBI labs, and the field guys are closer to the action, ahead of them on new accelerants. A professional killed him. But everyone sort of knew that it wasn't an accident. The burn site evidence doesn't tell you much more."

Hayes looked at the screen and the evidence code under the graph. "That's not from where the car burned; that's from a test of her house."

Drew studied it for a moment, then looked through the window in the door toward his wife. She was standing over their son, his head slumped down on his chest, not talking.

"She killed him, man." Drew shook his head slightly. "Unbelievable."

"You really think we're the first ones to put this together?"

"Could be," Drew said. "Or maybe the bosses figured it out and kept it to themselves for whatever reason. Political fallout? But either way, Claire is dangerous. That always was her strength: believing the lies she told. That's why she seems so innocent. I know you were close. I know you were falsely accused, but she's part of this, Hayes.

I love that girl, but you have to take her out."

Hayes remembered raising his gun outside the trailer in West Virginia and aiming at a figure he thought was Claire. He heard that body hit the ground again.

"I tried today."

Killing his own. A commandment he would never break. Maybe whoever was doing this knew that weakness. The evil bastards. They weren't just using bullets. They were killing Hayes's people, using his own decency against him.

"You better get going, Hayes. I'm seeing some unfamiliar faces around here. Morgan's security. Are you on your own on this?"

"Partly. I'm not going back to her until I know who's behind all this."

"They have guards here, and I think it's more to keep me under wraps than to keep the bad dudes out. A couple of teammates called to check on me. They're bringing them all in, Hayes, shutting it down."

"Bringing them in where?"

"New York. They're getting everyone together. They said it's about Gray's death and the future of Cold Harvest. They won't say exactly where everyone's going, for obvious reasons."

Using our decency against us.

268

"How did you get to Burke's funeral? Where I saw you?"

"I drove. Why?"

Hayes shook his head. "I'm not sure, but—" He broke off as he noticed something through the window. Two men in suits were fast-walking across the atrium toward the elevators. They looked like Feds. Hayes's mind ran through the deaths, the dossiers, the map. The pattern finally made sense.

"Do not go to New York," Hayes said. He had to warn the others, warn as many as he could. "I'll call you later."

"Go."

He crossed the room, checked the window in the door, and started down the hallway. There was no time to explain, but now Hayes understood: the threat was coming for his own home, his family.

The elevator dinged. The two men stepped out. Hayes ducked behind one of the curtained dividers in an open bay near the nurses' station. He stopped and listened to their oxfords squeak by. He watched them from the back as they went toward Drew's room. Then he stepped out, moving toward the elevators.

He was halfway there when he saw Michael, Drew's son. He recognized him from the vacation house. The boy's mouth dropped open. He was about to say something. Hayes put his finger to his lips.

The kid swallowed, then nodded and glanced around as Hayes pressed the button to the elevator.

He went to the garage and rounded the corner to his truck. He was halfway there when a man in a suit appeared between two files of cars and stood between him and his truck. Another agent.

He held his hand out. "Stop there."

Hayes kept walking toward him.

"Don't," the man said.

There was no time to explain, and the man wouldn't listen anyway. Hayes didn't want to hurt him, but if he came between him and his family, he would do what he must. "I need to go."

"Hold on. It's not safe." He moved closer.

"Don't," Hayes said and shook his head.

The man's palm touched his chest. Maybe he thought this was going to be the normal blustering between soldiers.

It wasn't.

Hayes seized his wrist and turned it hard outward so the man arched back and opened his chest. Hayes struck him with an open palm to the solar plexus.

His mouth gaped open, as if he were yelling, but no noise came. His diaphragm was in spasm, the wind knocked out of him.

He stumbled and fell to the ground, and Hayes threw open the door of his truck and took off.

Hayes was already past the gatehouse before anyone had a chance to alert the guards. He raised his phone to call his wife.

CHAPTER 42

Lauren Hayes was standing in the open back door of the kitchen, two trash bags in her left hand, as she answered her cell.

It was John. "What's up, hon?" she asked.

"Do you remember what I told you? What we practiced? About getting someplace safe?"

"Yes."

"It's time. It may be nothing, but I'm not taking any chances. I'll call the people I have watching the house. They'll go with you, and I'll be there in three hours."

"All right," Lauren said, and she put the bags down.

"You okay?" he asked.

"Yeah. I've got this. Love you."

"You too."

She was ready. He wouldn't have made that call if it wasn't serious. There would be time for questions later, but right now she needed to move. She grabbed a few essentials out of her bathroom, then went to the hall closet, opened the gun safe, and took out a Mossberg shotgun. She put a Smith and Wesson pistol in a hip holster and placed the Mossberg in a duffel bag that she kept packed for moments like this.

"Maggie, let's go!" she shouted as she zipped it shut.

Her daughter walked down the hallway with a Matchbox car in her hand.

"Where are we going?"

"On a little trip," she said. She lifted up her daughter and threw the bag over her shoulder. She was halfway out the front door when she stopped, went back to the family room, and picked up Maggie's stuffed monkey.

She left the house, scanned the tree line along the side yard, and got in her car.

Hayes kept the truck pegged at eighty-five, going wide into each corner to keep his speed. In his mind was the map in his office, marked out with the site of each victim's funeral. He hadn't seen the pattern until he remembered the funerals. Each death was within driving distance of the previous burial. The killers moved across the country because Burke was killed in California but buried at Arlington.

They were staking out the funerals, looking for more Cold Harvest members. Driving distance. That was the key. You can track someone driving. Flights are too hard and require massive teams and advance notice. Every death was two to six weeks after the previous funeral. Enough time to scout and plan each. Then go to the next funeral. Rinse and repeat.

Human emotion. Understanding it was the most lethal weapon. A student had taught him that. He'd never seen anyone wield it so efficiently. Claire.

Hayes remembered Burke's funeral. The killers had been there. That's how they found Drew. Hayes had been there too, with his family. They had tracked Drew to his home, and now they might come to his.

Hayes always took precautions. He never drove straight home, never stopped looking for tails.

But that didn't mean they weren't watching.

He remembered Claire's warning. *You can't have two lives, Hayes. Eventually they touch, and then it all burns. The people closest to you get hurt.*

Or was it a threat?

CHAPTER 43

El Harrach, Algeria

The orders had come straight from the national security adviser. Two diplomatic security agents approached the steel-barred door of the workshop. It was in a suburb of Algiers, far from the main square with its old French city hall, palms, and sea breezes. This street was a tangle of alleys and one-story shops with crumbling stucco. Two scooters shot past.

The smell of solvents crept out the windows. Inside, Joshua Drake slipped a razor behind the cover of a passport and cleanly separated the backing from the photo pasted inside.

He was Cold Harvest, undercover for two years infiltrating a human-trafficking ring that, on top of all of the miseries it dealt out to migrants, stranding them and drowning them in the cold Mediterranean, had a sideline in smuggling weapons and militants into Europe.

He saw the two agents on the CCTV and pulled his pistol, a Russian-made Strizh 9-millimeter with no serial number. They pounded on the door, and as Drake gave a closer look to his security monitor, the killing instincts relaxed, replaced with disappointment and anger. He put down the gun.

"We're with the embassy," one said into the camera. "We need to talk."

He'd been here for two years with no contact and no support from the CIA station in Algiers. Those were the cocktail-party folks, using official covers as embassy staff, safe behind blast barriers on a hill by the presidential palace.

He looked at them in the camera. Boxy black suits. Tight-tapered haircuts. Military bearing. They were so obviously American they might as well have been wearing Iowa State sweatshirts and drinking Slurpees.

He thought of bringing them in and killing them. It would make him feel better, but the damage was already done.

This was El Harrach, a militant stronghold. Everyone was family. Everyone talked. Two American agents had walked up to his business, and in that instant the cover he had built for two years was blown, the target painted on his back.

Two years of missed birthdays, two years of sordid small crimes to stop the big ones, and now he had just lost his chance to decapitate the most dangerous trafficking outfit on the Mediterranean.

Somewhere, a ship carrying a group of twelve radicals sailed. He would never know where it landed.

Windows rose three stories over this narrow street. And there were eyes behind every one of them. The news would pass quickly from the watchers in the buildings to the powers in the back offices. He was done.

He buzzed them in.

"Drake?"

His name sounded so strange out loud after all this time. "We need to bring you back home."

He looked at them, then at the gun, but he picked up a bottle of acetone instead and splashed it over his desk, his files, the trash. Any sensitive information was kept in his head, not on paper, but he wasn't taking any chances, leaving any trace.

"You idiots. AQIM will be here in twenty minutes." Al-Qaeda in the Islamic Maghreb, the reigning militants here in the north of Africa, rich with ransoms they had wrung

out from aid groups and Western governments.

He took a book of paper matches from
the windowsill, lit one, then tucked it in
under the cover so the flame would burn
toward the other matchheads. He placed it
on the desk, above the expanding puddle of
acetone, then started fast toward the door.

"Let's go."

On it went, in Caracas, Bamako, Molen-
beek, Frankfurt, Beirut, and all the other
cities where Cold Harvest members were
deployed. Their bank accounts were frozen.
They were left without access to arms or
papers. One operative at a time, Morgan
and Tucker dismantled the program, the
most potent weapon the U.S. had against
threats that drones and the military couldn't
reach, and began gathering them all in one
place.

CHAPTER 44

Hayes crossed the gravel toward the barracks. The door opened, and his wife stepped out. Hayes wrapped his arms around her as his daughter walked onto the stoop.

In the distance, a helicopter flared for a landing and disappeared behind a stand of white pines.

"How are you doing?" he asked Lauren.

"I'm fine. Maggie's a little overwhelmed, but she's being good."

"The routine?"

"Every step."

Lauren Hayes and the security team at the house had driven a surveillance-detection routine, a planned set of evasions and reversals designed to draw out any tails. They made their way to a small base set in the most remote forests of Camp Peary, the CIA's classified training facility along the York River near Williamsburg, Virginia.

This part of the facility was used by the Special Activities Division, and most of the CIA clandestine-service trainees who came through Peary could only guess at what went on behind its high fences.

"They said they didn't pick up anyone behind us."

"Good," Hayes said.

A detonation shook the earth, and Maggie flinched back. The clouds to the south flashed red.

"What is this place?"

"A training base. We would practice here to get ready for operations."

He could hear, in the distance, the rush of helicopter blades and the soft pops of gunshots in controlled bursts.

A few soldiers, standing respectfully in the distance, kept watch.

Down the hill behind her, there was a Pashtun village with mud walls and a two-story minaret. Beyond that was a bunker complex modeled on North Korean facilities, and then ten acres of sandy, leech-infested marsh that could stand in for Indonesian jungles.

Drew used to call it Shithole Disney World, all the worst places on earth in one spot.

They would build a perfect model of the

target for a given operation and raid it, time after time, until they knew those walls as well as they knew their own homes, until they could perform the mission without thinking, could succeed with half the team killed or injured. It was known as a rock drill.

It was strange to see Lauren and Maggie here, in this mock-up war zone, with the blasts shaking his wife's words and the smoke rising behind them.

They had the two of them staying in the dormitory-style housing behind the obstacle courses and parade grounds.

"I'm sorry about this, Lauren. It won't be for long," Hayes said. He was going straight at the men behind this to force it to a conclusion.

"You work with these people?"

"I used to."

"Friends?"

"Closer than that."

They were special operations and CIA paramilitary officers, a small fraternity who knew Hayes's true role. Hayes had helped them refine their methods for classified direct-action missions. After his years in exile among the enemy, he had brought back lessons learned. He changed everything about how they infiltrated and took down threats.

"You're safe here," he said.

"What's happening?"

"I thought that the people I'm after might come for me, for the house. It was a precaution."

"The people who are killing your teammates? They know where we live?"

"I didn't want to take that chance."

"You're going after them?"

"Yes."

He knew their pattern now. Morgan was giving them what they most wanted, which was to gather everyone in one spot, where they could be killed in one blow.

That was good. Hayes could exploit that. He was finally a step ahead. He could use their plans against them.

A blast shook the trees in the distance. Maggie hugged her mother's leg. Her eyes narrowed, almost closed, and she began to cry.

Hayes kissed her on her forehead and she stopped crying and sniffled, though her mouth remained in a grimace.

"You're leaving again," Lauren said.

He had to. He was going to New York. The killers were raising the stakes, moving into open violence. They had taken innocents before. How many would they take to get all of Cold Harvest?

"Yes. But I always come back."

Hayes looked in his wife's eyes. Claire had been right. Hayes had to choose between his home and the fight. He couldn't have both.

He was comfortable around death, had lived beside it and tasted it. He respected it but didn't fear it. It was just another factor. The worst thing for him would be to stay here safe knowing he'd let others fall. It would be worse than dying, a kind of damnation.

Maggie started to whimper again. He'd thought he would come home, and all would be fine. He could go fight his wars and then lie down in his bed and rest easy. He was wrong. He had spent too long out there among the threats. They had come for him, come back with him. He remembered the distorted voice of the enemy on the phone. Part of what he'd said was true: he was the violence.

Lauren lifted Maggie up and soothed her, rubbing her hand over her back. A man in canvas work pants and a flannel shirt walked toward them and then stopped. He was clearly waiting for Hayes.

"You better get going," Lauren said. She'd sent him off on missions dozens of times, but something about this was different. It felt final, like a valediction. They both seemed to understand without a word.

He put his arms around her, then kissed her. A last squeeze of the hand, and then she stepped away toward the bunkhouse, leaving him there alone.

He walked to the gate, then turned and saw his wife at the edge of the gravel, their child on her hip, soldiers on both sides with M4 carbines on slings. This was no place for a family. It was too much to ask of anyone. He was losing her.

As soon as he was in the parking lot, he started calling the men he trusted, the men who still trusted him. He was going to New York. There was one way to stop this. He had to put himself between the killers and their target.

CHAPTER 45

Hynd ran his hand over the grimy steel of the tractor-trailer's underbody and felt the new welds. The shocks had also been reinforced to hide the bulk of the load. The bed was lined with marble slab to direct the blast up and out, more kills and less crater. Over that lay two dozen barrels of ammonium nitrate and nitromethane slurry, an explosive equivalent in power to TNT but far easier to procure. They were using Tovex as the primer.

The explosives alone would take out dozens of buildings, but they had followed the design of the bomb that had destroyed the Marine barracks in Beirut in 1983, the single deadliest day for the U.S. military since World War II.

Above those drums were thirty tanks of butane. To make something burn, you need fuel and air. Most explosives contain both, a fuel and an oxidizer. But the most powerful ones, known as thermobaric or fuel-air explosives, carry their entire load as fuel and mix it with the surrounding air to explode. That was how a single thermobaric hand grenade could topple a house.

This truck would turn the streets around it, the atmosphere, the bodies and breath of the bystanders themselves into a bomb.

The truck that killed the Marines in Beirut had driven through concertina wire to get close to the target. It had lifted the barracks fifteen feet in the air, shearing fifteen-foot foundations reinforced with steel rebar. The whole thing collapsed as it fell.

Americans had started putting up barriers around all their sites, but it was a classic bureaucratic response, the operating principle of all that had been done in the name of homeland security: react and overreact to the last attack. It's most important to be seen doing *something;* it doesn't matter if it's effective. The barracks would have fallen even if the truck had been stopped at the outer perimeter.

So the U.S. and its allies had built their Potemkin defenses and continued to die at the hands of this simple inevitable weapon, the truck bomb. Khobar Towers; the assassination of Rafik Hariri, the prime minister

286

of Lebanon; the first World Trade Center attack; Oklahoma City.

Thirty thousand pounds of TNT: that was the explosive power of this vehicle. Six times the size of the Oklahoma City bomb. It would destroy an area of five city blocks.

He moved across the concrete floor and picked up a switch from the workbench. It was made from two pieces of milled aluminum, hinged at one end like a bike brake and designed to fit in the hand. Its technical name was a pressure-release detonator, more commonly known as a dead man switch.

Near the hinge it had a safety — a pin with a ring hanging from it, similar to those on hand grenades.

Hynd weighed it in his hand; barely fourteen ounces. Such devices were normally used as backups for suicide terrorists. In case they were killed before they had a chance to trigger their charges, that switch guaranteed a detonation.

But this was a special use. Hynd had studied the American fighters carefully. Even if the truck wasn't able to reach its target, the plan would work. Timur just had to get within blast distance of bystanders and force a standoff. He knew the American soldiers' psychology. If they were in the vicinity, they would run to the threat, even if it meant dying, and all Timur would have to do was let go or let them take him out with a final shot. They couldn't help but play hero. They would kill themselves.

Vera approached him, carrying one of the encrypted phones. One of Hynd's intelligence contacts in Algeria had called in the tail number of a private jet that was owned by a CIA front company. It had just taken off, and the source suspected it had a Cold Harvest operative on board. There were similar reports from agents in other countries.

Cold Harvest had spent years practicing nearly perfect security, but now they were crashing the exfiltrations of their agents, bringing them home, blowing their covers. Its leaders were panicking, tipping their hands.

Based on the flights and sightings, he believed they were gathering somewhere near New York. They were being herded together, as he'd predicted. But where exactly? He had lost too many of his men to nail it down. Once the Cold Harvest members landed in the United States, he wouldn't have the resources to track them.

But he didn't need to. He had Claire.

"It's time to talk to Claire Rhodes," he said.

"Don't do it," Vera replied. She was afraid, and rightly so. Rhodes was a killer on fire with anger and revenge.

But that was all to the good. Hynd knew her better than she knew herself. He could control her. He had so far.

"Is this about killing them? Or controlling her?" Vera asked.

"It's the same thing," Hynd said.

"How do you know she'll lead you to them? She might just run, disappear."

"No," he said. She had tried to quit before and had failed. Even after her teammates rejected her, she wanted to protect them. That desire was strong, at the core of her broken nature. But in trying to shield them, she was leading him to them and helping him kill them one by one. "I can send her straight at them. She'll show us where they are."

"You're going to end up dead."

"I might," he said. He ordered Timur to ready the truck. They would station it within striking distance of New York City, and when Hynd found out the location of the gathering, they would take them all out.

Bombs and guns and hired hitmen. There had been so much killing at a distance. But this would be his hardest task: empty-handed and face to face with that lethal woman. It was what he lived for. He would make her his weapon.

"Let's go."

CHAPTER 46

The thorns tore at the canvas of Claire's work pants and carved welts across her arm. She paid no mind, counting steps as she moved among the trees. She fixed her position in the woods based on landmarks — the red light of the water tower and the church steeple in town. Memories can be deceptive. She knew that as well as anyone.

She needed the exact location to find the cache she had left up here, among the trees above her house. She needed money and a better weapon. She had left this cache when she fled. There were too many people watching her home after she'd killed the man who was posing as a U.S. Marshal.

She didn't keep the tools of her trade at home. She stored some and buried others as backup, hidden away nearby. Never let your two lives touch. It was the first thing you learned.

She ignored the gravestones, a churchyard

of a church long since gone. The weeds swallowed them up, and the acid rain left only the faintest impressions of the inscriptions. This one had died in the Civil War. The Battle of Port Republic.

Old cemeteries were the perfect spot for these hides. Out of the way, avoided by most, never redeveloped.

She had the jack handle from the second car she had stolen, a Dodge pickup. It was the only thing handy to dig with. She stooped among the fallen stones and drove the metal into the ground.

Claire felt the doubts inch in as she dug. She'd thought it was here, but she felt nothing. Things shift under your feet. Roots grow, water runs, the earth wears down. These Appalachian peaks were once as high as the Sierras.

She lifted the tool and drove it back in. The jack handle scraped against metal, a hollow thunk below the dirt.

Twenty minutes later, she pried out the metal box, a watertight medical chest, and opened it up. Among the gear inside, there was a Glock pistol and a broken-down sniper rifle in a nylon roll. She'd spent countless hours training on precision rifles, and while she was with Cold Harvest she had done extensive preparations, going over the details of taking out targets with long-range shots in American and European cities. The box smelled like a grave, but the gunmetal gleamed with oil. They should be fine.

A smaller case beside the guns held a flip phone with half a dozen prepaid SIM cards, a GPS unit, a high-powered flashlight, and nine thousand dollars in used twenties.

Would she run? It was the only move that made sense. But she had run before. She hadn't gotten away last time, because she was the problem. How could she protect the men and women she had worked with in Cold Harvest? It was strange. Normally Cold Harvest information never showed up on the intranets she could still access, but she had picked up some travel notices that used the old coded names for the program. They were getting careless. The flights and logistics suggested they were gathering somewhere near New York, although she couldn't be sure exactly where. But how could she warn them? She'd tried to warn Hayes, and he'd played sympathetic, drew her into a trap, and attempted to kill her.

Hayes, that asshole. He couldn't be the prime mover behind this, though. He was a soldier. Morgan and Tucker were the chiefs. Claire could try to cut it off at the top, to go after them. But there were too many questions. Why did they call off the investigation? Did they kill her husband? Kill the other members of the program? Was Hayes working for them? Why?

No. She couldn't put more bodies down until she was sure. She couldn't let the anger drive her, couldn't let the killing seduce her.

Her head ached. The broken blisters on her foot sent out a stabbing pain with every step. She needed sleep. She looked down the ridge at her home in the hollow. She had left it in switched-on, full-assault mode, indifferent to herself or the past. Never mix lives. Always be willing to let the cover die, to let your old self die. Never get attached.

She didn't know what came next, but it meant prison, exile, or death. Her old clothesline wavered in the breeze. Paul was such a cheapskate, hanging his laundry out on principle, like a pioneer's wife.

His face — sometimes she had trouble remembering it. The chin wouldn't be right. She'd forgotten her mother's a long time ago. She had a photographic memory for license plates and train schedules. The faces of her targets never left her, their bugged eyes and lolling tongues as they died. But she couldn't remember the only good people in her life. She wanted a scrap of them, some light to take with her into the dark that was coming.

This was going to end badly. That she knew. Everything changes. Everything disappears. The earth moves under your feet. She wanted to see them again.

They wouldn't be watching the house anymore.

No. It was a bad idea. She had a gun, money, her target. *Never cross lives. Leave the dead behind and go. Remember what happened, Claire.*

But the end was coming soon, and this wasn't about success on an op, then a homecoming. This was her last chance, her last self. And she didn't know who she was, but she knew that if she cut out the part of herself that wanted those memories, the good in her was already dead. And that would mean they had won, the men who had taught her how to kill and the men trying to kill her now.

She started down the hill toward her old home.

CHAPTER 47

Claire stood inside the open screen door, looked down, and saw the torn corner of a maple leaf on the ground. She'd wedged it between the door and frame before she left so she'd know if someone had entered.

Whoever it was could have come yesterday or five minutes ago. She listened, heard only the cicadas, and opened the back door. She moved fast in the dark, going from memory. Lights would bring attention. She stopped at the door to Paul's office and ran her fingers over the fake wood grain.

She had shoved all the photos in there, most of them in boxes. Her mother, her husband. She hadn't been able to look at them. Every time she did, she would hear their voices, hard and accusing, calling her out on her guilt.

Her pulse throbbed in her fingertips, and for a moment it was all she could think about, her heart and lungs slamming in her chest like a train's engine.

A low pop from the attic. The house settling with the evening cold.

She put her hand on the knob. It felt almost warm, like someone was inside, but that was nerves, just the flush of blood in her skin.

Love cut with dread; she knew this feeling from her last week with Paul. She'd told him who she was after they returned from Chania. There was no other way. She'd told him her real name for the first time.

He stormed out, mute with anger. He was gone for two hours in a cold drizzle. She was in bed, awake, when the front door opened. He came home, sat with his back to her, and asked if she was okay. Then he lay beside her. Accepted it. He was worried about her, even after all those lies. That night, she slept better than she could ever remember.

She had let the truth in, and they were still there, and alive, and safe. She was just Claire, a woman with a husband and a house and a garage full of crap and no more lies. They would be okay.

The next morning arrived like a hangover.

She woke before him, and the realizations came in as clear as the sunlight.

What if he talked? He was a journalist, for Christ's sake. Getting the truth out was in his blood as surely as hiding it was in hers. What would she do to protect her secret?

She followed him for four days, went operational against her own goddamn husband, lying through her teeth to him every morning and every night, feeling more insane every day, until the fifth, when she trailed him all the way to Washington, and he parked in front of an eight-story building on F Street a few blocks from the Treasury. It housed the DC bureau of the *LA Times.* He had friends at the *Times,* had shot photos for them in Iraq.

He was going to talk. People in Cold Harvest were already dying. If he talked, he might get her or her teammates or himself killed. What would she do to protect them? Who would she choose, her brothers or her husband?

The reaction came automatically. Her mind went to the suppressed .22 under her seat, the stick of M112 plastic explosive in her assault kit, and the impossible choice.

He died that evening.

She didn't do it, but she might as well have. She'd killed him when she brought him into her world, because she was weak

and selfish and thought she could have both
lives.

CHAPTER 48

She opened the door. Her legs threatened to fall under her, collapse like stacked cards, but she took a long breath in through her nose, exhaled through her mouth, four counts, four times, then she straightened herself up and stepped in.

The faces looked at her from a dozen different angles, a dozen photos, on the walls and piled in boxes.

And in an instant she was back in the nightmare, in that fire with Paul. The close air of the room was the burning fuel oil dripping over her body, flames twining red and yellow, and the hitch in her chest was a joist, forcing the air out of her lungs. She closed her eyes.

And then she was in her childhood home in Singapore, paralyzed with fear, as she heard her mother cry out and the crack of the belt.

Open your fucking eyes, Claire. The only

monster is you. The only one hurting anyone is you. They're dead and no one is here.

The carpet felt like sponge under her first unsteady step. She opened her eyes and took four more deep breaths.

She picked up a photo from their wedding day, a candid of her fixing Paul's collar. Then she lifted a faded shot of her mother, pregnant with her, twisting the spiral cord of a telephone around her finger. Claire ran her thumb over the cool gloss finish of the print and studied her mother's face.

No one reached for her. No one cried out, *Why did you let me die?*

She was just alone, in a home that she felt nothing for, with salt tears running down her face.

Eeee.

Hallway floorboard. A long nail. She knew that noise. The house wasn't settling. She wasn't alone. The training saved her. She shot across the room.

The photo fell to the ground as she drew her pistol to her chest and hauled open the door. She moved as if on invisible rails through the dark.

Whoever was in here was moving just as fast, must have had night-vision on, the way he was navigating through the house.

She closed on the thudding footfalls,

heard the sound of the bedroom door ahead of her creak open, then shut. As the lock rattled, she threw her shoulder into it and blew the frame out in splinters.

A black figure turned, silhouetted by the window, almost beside her, in too close for shots.

"Claire, no." But the gun was already driving toward his temple. She pistol-whipped him and landed with her full weight on his chest as he slumped to the ground.

She gathered a fistful of the man's shirt and pulled the body toward the light. She kept the pistol trained on his eye, an easy kill. Blood dripped from his temple across his face, onto the carpet. She smeared it away.

Her hand tightened, on the grip of her pistol as her teeth buried in her lower lip and her eyes grew wide with shock. No. That body was burned and buried.

Her whole arm trembled. She let him fall back and brought her left hand to the pistol to steady it.

"Claire," the man said.

She moved closer to him. The blood smelled like cast iron. There was no mistaking that face.

"Paul?"

CHAPTER 49

It was her husband. Joy edged in, and she stopped it. No. Too many questions. She had been taught that any doubt meant a trap, meant death. If there was any question, she should simply execute the target and go.

Her mouth drew tight, her eyes barely open. "No." She said it over and over and the gun shook in her hand.

Kill him, she thought. And that cycled instantly into guilt that made her feel more insane, like her skin was too tight and hot, like she was drying out in a kiln.

PTSD? No. She'd had visuals before, waking dreams. This was different. This was real.

"Oh God," he said. "I was wrong to come here. It *was* you."

"Paul. What's happening?"

He looked straight at her over the gun, didn't flinch, didn't plead.

"You started that fire. You tried to fucking

kill me then. I shouldn't have come back. Go ahead. Shoot. At least now I know it was you. No more secrets."

"I didn't, Paul. What is going on?"

He didn't say anything for a long moment, calculating, looking from her face to the barrel. She took her finger off the trigger, then stood over him and ran her left hand over her mouth. Her palm felt cold, clammy; shock coming on. But she kept breathing deeply, fell back on the training. One mistake could cost her life, cost her everything she had thought she had lost.

Careful, Claire, your emotions.

"Paul. You need to explain what's happening because I don't want to harm you but I need to understand what's going on or we could both get hurt."

He nodded.

"You understand?" she asked.

"I think so. Is that one reason you might let someone live? For answers?"

"Yes, it is. But that doesn't matter now. You survived the fire?"

Interrogation. This was her domain. She'd spent weeks patiently running through questions, teasing out answers, outplaying the world's great liars. The thought of it as work felt comfortable, brought her down.

He looked around the room, seemed to

be having trouble focusing. She reached down to the laundry basket to her left with her free hand and tossed him a clean T-shirt. He pressed it to the cut at his temple.

"We can take time and talk through all this later," she said. "But right now I just need the straight story of what happened. Okay? It's important."

He started to object, then caught himself. "Fine."

"Were you in that fire?"

He touched the fingers of his left hand to a patch of scar on his neck. "Yes. But would you put down the gun?"

"No. Soon. But I have to be sure. What happened? Just answer the questions."

He looked at the gun, then relented.

"I ran once the car started burning. I got away. Some debris —" He pointed to his neck. "Then I saw two men coming. I'd seen them following me before. I thought they had something to do with your job, that they'd set that fire, that they'd try to kill me. I thought they were with you, Claire."

"Why?"

"I saw you watching me that week. I know how to keep an eye out. You wanted to see where I would go, who I would tell. I thought you were all working together."

"I was following you to protect you. If you told anyone, it could have gotten us both hurt."

He laughed deep in his throat.

"Sure. And what if I were going to break your cover? What would you have done to stop me?"

"I don't know."

"Was it an accident, Claire? A warning?"

"I didn't set it off."

"You had me in the crosshairs, Claire. You were stalking me, like . . . like one of the people you kill. So I ran."

"Then why are you here? Why did you come back?"

"I heard about the shooting, the man you killed off the forest road. How you disappeared. I thought they were coming for you. I realized that you were a victim too. I thought you could help me, that we could help each other."

"Where have you been?"

"Outside Bozeman."

"What did you do for money?"

"Swung a hammer. Landscaping. It's cheap out there."

He'd been a rafting guide, a river bum until he was twenty-eight. It was possible.

"Who knows you're alive?"

"You. I didn't trust anyone."

"How did you find me?"

"You found me. I came here after the police left."

"Looking for me?"

"I thought you'd come back, for guns or money or something."

He wanted her caches, her help. "You needed money?"

He dabbed at his temple and looked at the blood. "Yes."

"There's nothing in the house."

She ran her thumb over the pistol's grip. "Whose ashes did I scatter?"

"I don't know."

A faint glow passed left to right across them. A car engine echoed up the hollow.

"We need to go. Someone may have seen you, or me. We can't be found."

"Where are you taking me?" Paul asked.

"I'm not forcing you."

He glanced at the gun, then shook his head, looked to the ground. "Not even a word."

"What?"

" 'Glad you're not dead. Good to see you. Sorry for ruining your fucking life.' "

"I am glad, Paul. I am. But I've been taught to assume every word is a lie, every identity a cover until proven otherwise, and this is all too much. So we need to go, and you need to tell me the story from beginning to end. I just have to be sure, Paul. God, I hope it's true."

Or else . . .

She brought the gun down to her side.

"An interrogation?" Paul asked.

"I just need to know."

"And how can I trust you?"

"Because you're still alive," she said.

"Is that what passes for trust in your world?"

"Yes. It's the only thing you can believe. And you can't always believe it. I told you, I'm done lying to you."

A ringing bell filled the house: the landline in the kitchen. Claire spun, the gun braced in both hands. Then she held her left arm out to him and helped him to his feet.

"Now," she said, and she gestured forward with the pistol. She covered him as he left the bedroom.

CHAPTER 50

Vera stood with her back to a tree on the ridge above Claire's home. She set her cheek against the cool polymer stock of her rifle and watched Hynd and Claire climb through the woods behind the house. The red dot in her optic danced on Claire's back, circling her heart and lungs as she tracked her through the pines. Claire stopped near her truck and turned to the side, and Vera centered the aim just behind Claire's jaw, on the brain stem.

Six pounds of pressure on the trigger, and the woman would be a carcass on the hillside, a bad memory.

Her finger reached inside the trigger guard, felt the curved steel, as she watched. She couldn't pull, not without Hynd's orders, and he was still standing beside Claire, still playing this insane game.

It was reckless for him to resume his old cover as Claire's husband this far along in the operation. Vera had tried to talk him out of it.

But they needed to know where the members of Cold Harvest were gathering. And so far, Claire had been an unerring, if unwitting, guide. She had given them both Gray's and Hayes's locations. But they had no time left. The rest were meeting soon. They needed to provoke her, send her straight after her teammates.

It made sense that Hynd would want to go back. He thrived on risk. He had started this operation years before as an ambitious outsider bent on revenge against the West's elite killers, simply hoping to gain access to a member of the program. He'd used Claire's neediness, her psych profile, her thirst for decency to get close to her. He'd succeeded far better than he could possibly have imagined. Another man would have panicked when things moved so quickly, when he got in so deep, but he rode it out and lived the lie with her in the heart of the enemy nation.

He went inside Cold Harvest, and that was what raised his profile to where it was today. The man who knew the names, faces, and addresses of those in a program so secret that most other countries' intelligence services were unaware of its existence. The man you would seek out if you wanted to eliminate that program.

That penetration was his greatest success, so of course he would want to return to it, like an actor reprising his signature role.

She kept the gun pegged on Claire as the woman put down the truck's tailgate. She could hear every word. Paul's phone was modified to have an open microphone, constantly broadcasting audio as well as a GPS beacon. She could hear and follow him and know if he was in trouble.

The bitch was going to kill him. She was sure. Every fiber urged her to take Claire down. But that wasn't how this worked.

Hynd gave the orders. There was a simple code to tell Vera to take the kill shot. All he had to say was "Fair enough." And as soon as he learned the location where the members of Cold Harvest were gathering, he would say, "I see. I see," and she would call in Timur and the truck. The bomb was done, waiting in an abandoned salvage yard in northern New Jersey, ready to move on New York as soon as they had the site.

Claire had been an excellent guide so far. While posing as her husband, Hynd had been able to follow her and find her caches, and he had fitted every device he could with GPS trackers. She had led them to Gray and to Hayes and to her old home tonight.

Even with backup and all the tech in the world, he was putting himself in the hands of a killer. Vera thought it was reckless, but he had proved her wrong before. Vera had warned him against coming to the United States under cover as Claire's husband, against staying in the role even after the first killings of Cold Harvest members seemed to point to Claire or him.

But he had a way out. He always had an exit before he committed to an operation. She remembered the prisoner whose remains they'd used to stand in for Paul's body in the car fire.

He was a clueless Englishman from Whitechapel, born to Bangladeshi parents. He'd traveled to Turkey, trying to join up with the struggle, play action hero, wave black flags, and shoot guns in the desert. If he wanted to die for the cause, so be it. He was the right size and build. They brought him to a gravel factory in Qatar and locked him in a belowground hold. Hynd ordered his vocal cords slit so he couldn't talk, because it would be a long captivity and guards and prisoners can build rapport.

They needed his body to match up to Paul's medical records. After they stitched up his neck, four men held him down in an old cream-colored recliner and drilled into his teeth, taking great care. They put in fillings, using the American composition. Three on the top and four on the bottom.

Then they braced his thigh against the brackets of a machine table, put the scissor jack from a car under it, and pressed, turn by turn, until the femur cracked.

They set the bone and put a cast on it. The doctor would check on him every day while he was healing, shoving himself around mute in that cave.

The prisoner stayed down there, hidden from the sun for four months, until the bone had healed. But his spirit was broken, and he didn't have enough fight left to struggle as they hauled him to his feet. Death was a deliverance.

Hynd stood eye to eye with this man, the same height, the same build. His double. Then he cut his throat, slowly, precisely, two small slices to the carotid on either side, to avoid any telltale cutting of the spine. The captive whimpered but barely tried to resist.

They burned the prisoner's body. A fuel-oil fire grows hot enough, like cremation, to leave behind only gleanings — melted metal, like fillings or surgical screws — and charred chunks of the long bones, the femurs and sometimes the humeri, from which no traceable DNA can be extracted.

When Paul needed to stage his death in the United States, they used the fuel-oil tank in the garage attached to his office. The structure crumbled, crushed the car, burned everything in it like an incinerator. He had already planted the double's remains in the vehicle.

When the authorities went through Paul's medical documents, they would find the records of the broken bone and the X-rays showing seven fillings. The remains offered enough forensic evidence — the gleanings and bone break — for a positive ID. They would match Paul's records, which had been counterfeited like the rest of his persona before he approached Claire, and were backstopped by the foreign intelligence services that had hired him to eliminate Cold Harvest.

All that work, and the coroner ended up making the ID from the ashes alone and Paul's missing-person report. No one even noticed the break repair on the femur.

Vera's grip on the gun relaxed as she listened to Hynd's and Claire's voices. Hynd told the story of his year on the run for a second time, and she knew Claire was starting to believe it.

Vera had never understood how he could stand it, living with her, being so close to the enemy. In Paris, Vera had been in the next room when Claire had killed Hynd's closest friend, then nearly shot Vera, and still Hynd had taken that woman back to his bed.

But now, as she listened, she could see it, how he could live both lives, how he could make her believe. It was amazing to see him work. How he could play up fear and make it a weapon.

Vera took her hand off the rifle and listened to Claire's voice softening in the earpiece. She could hear her turning, bit by bit.

Hynd was right. She put on that strong persona, but she was weak, so driven by the past, so easy to control. He had her.

They had started killing her teammates in Cold Harvest while Hynd was still undercover. And since he had found the victims through her, all the suspicion pointed to her after he was gone.

Hynd was glad enough to get out, but he had always wondered how much he could exploit the rift between Claire and her former bosses. Each suspected the other. If he kept the killing up, raised the pressure, perhaps he could even make them turn on each other.

Vera listened as he approached the most dangerous moment. They needed to give Claire a reason to go straight to New York, to wherever her teammates were gathering. She was driven by a need to protect, and if they were able to show her a clear threat to the others, she would have no choice but to lead them to the rest of Cold Harvest. But she was also ruled by anger, and if they played her exactly right, they might be able to use that, even provoke her into killing the leaders of Cold Harvest herself.

Hynd's next step was critical. Vera fixed the red dot in her sight on Claire's temple and put her finger on the trigger.

CHAPTER 51

Claire pulled the cache box from the bed of the truck onto the tailgate and ran her hand over the top, brushing dirt onto the ground. Paul stood beside her.

He had run through it twice, every detail. Money. Itinerary. Landmarks. Zip codes. Addresses. She ran it out of order, trying to find inconsistencies, pauses. She was trained to spot lies.

She found none. It all worked. There were good answers and, more important, holes, things he didn't know. It wasn't too perfect.

"Here," she said, and she patted his hand on the tailgate. "I'll clean that up." The cut at his temple was still welling with blood. She pulled a butterfly bandage from her first-aid kit and pinched the skin closed, ignoring his wince of pain.

"Thanks," he said, and he stepped down.

She felt the hope coming back to her, clouding her mind, and she laid one hand on the latch of the metal chest.

He smiled at her, then seemed to think twice about it and cast his eyes to the ground. It was like he had forgotten who he was dealing with for a moment.

"What is it?"

"Is it easy for you now? Killing?"

"I don't want to talk about this, Paul."

"You do it up close? Face to face?" She knew where he was going with this. *As close as we are?*

"They were terrorists. It's not easy, but it has to be done. I told you. I kill bad men."

"Yeah." He shook his head. "The assassin with a conscience. What a cliché. And I believed it."

"It's true."

"Reza Dinari."

"What?"

"Reza Dinari. He was a lawyer, an Iranian exile in London. He died at home in late April three years ago. You were traveling at the time. You told me you were in Scotland."

Her face went hard. "Paul, what are you doing?"

"Sara Khouri. Died in Corsica. Did you go there right before we went to Crete?"

They were all people she had killed. "What is this supposed to be?" Claire asked.

"I had a lot of time on my hands in that

trailer in Montana. I knew your old travel schedule. I looked for the victims. They were innocent, Claire. A human rights activist. A political dissident. She was killed before she could expose corruption in the house of Saud. Did you know?"

She picked up the gun, looked for reassurance in its weight in her hand.

"No. I can't talk about this, but we were surgical, better than the drones. We couldn't afford mistakes."

But the intelligence. It came from Cold Harvest. She'd checked every target a dozen times, but they could have fed her false intel. There was no way to verify the lethal findings. They came from special access programs.

"No," she said. She clamped her jaw like a vise.

She had wondered why the bosses of Cold Harvest would be killing their own soldiers. It started to make sense. If Cold Harvest had been taking down innocent people, if the program had been corrupt, then they would need to get rid of them to keep the truth from coming out.

What if all the victims were innocent? Jesus, it made sense. The world seemed to tint; the blacks and whites of the night forest took on colors, reds and blues. She put

319

her free hand against the cap of the truck.

The day they buried her mother, her father ran his hand through her hair and said, *You're a good girl, Claire.*

People misunderstood her. What fueled her wasn't revenge — it was the need for atonement. She killed to take the evil out of the world, to protect. It drove her so strongly because she had failed to protect her mother. She had done nothing that morning even as she heard her cry out. She had let an innocent die.

"Claire, the gun." Paul stood and stepped back.

She had it ready in front of her, looked at it strangely.

It was her worst fear come true. Her whole life, she'd run from the injustice of her father's getting away with his crime, trying to use that anger to do something decent, but it had taken her in the end. She was just like him. She had become the corruption. And the killings of her teammates finally made sense.

They had always wondered how Morgan commanded such sway in foreign capitals, how Tucker, a stuffed suit, managed so many foreign policy breakthroughs. Did he use Cold Harvest to trade favors, to kill for the oil dictatorships and repressive regimes?

It explained why they would be wiping the program now: to cover their tracks. Her mind was moving too fast, the adrenaline pushing her to act.

She felt her breath coming in and out too quickly, tried to focus to slow it down, but the faces of the dead crowded in. The pistol went back into her holster.

She turned and opened the box, and Paul looked over the contents: a case for electronics, four hand grenades, six flash-bangs, and a Remington concealable sniper rifle. There were four hundred rounds of ammo, one hundred for the rifle and three hundred for the pistol.

She didn't know what to believe. Part of her wanted to put a hole in Paul's eye and roll him into the river and forget everything he had said.

That would be her life, wouldn't it, to kill the one decent thing in her world because she couldn't accept decency as anything but betrayal in disguise?

God, they'd fucked her up.

The wilderness of mirrors. What if Paul was telling the truth? Maybe they had tried to kill him because he knew about the program, or maybe they'd been trying to kill her. He had been driving Claire's car that day.

She knew her former teammates were gathering in New York. If what Paul was saying was true, she needed to get to New York and stop Morgan and Tucker before they killed them all.

And if Paul was lying? That meant he'd been lying the whole time. If he was some kind of mole, if this was all a trap, if he had the resources to pull off a con like that, his story would seem every bit as true. It would be backstopped and rehearsed until there were no holes. Only the Russians went this far with their long-term undercover spies — known as illegals — but it was conceivable.

If he was lying, she needed him alive. If he was lying, he wasn't working alone, and they would kill her as soon as she tried something against him. She needed to move fast, to get him out of his comfort zone. She needed to stay with him to find out what he was doing, who he was working for, and what sort of threat they posed. If she lost him, she would never be able to clear her name. If he was lying, she needed to play along.

She had to keep him close no matter what. She brushed a speck of dirt from one of the grenades, then shut the case and shoved it back.

Lies or the truth. Both roads led to the

same place. She needed time to read him, to draw him out. She had her husband back, and she had six hours to decide what she believed and whom she was going to kill.

"Get in the truck," she said; she slammed the tailgate closed and circled to the driver's seat.

"Where are we going?"

"New York."

CHAPTER 52

Hayes took a circuitous route through the underground garage at Rockefeller Center to remain in the security cameras' blind spots. Their lines of sight were as clear to him as picket fences.

Morgan had sent him the message: Meet her people in Manhattan by eight p.m. "Let's make this easy on everyone."

Hayes knew what that meant. Knew what the hard way was — the FBI would keep coming after him. His name was still sketchy as hell. They could just lock him up. Everything he'd done was illegal. There was no formal presidential finding for his actions, no permission slip from the top. He was a criminal.

He didn't like anything about the spot where she had told him to go for the meeting, far uptown, near the northeast corner of Central Park in East Harlem. It was a good place to take someone down.

He wasn't going to walk into an ambush or let her set the terms. He didn't think that she was behind the killings, not directly, but he still wasn't taking chances. Hayes had chosen instead to surprise her here because she wouldn't try anything this close to a political rally.

Hayes slipped past the NYPD officer watching the northeast stair. Hayes had served on presidential security details dozens of times. He knew their routes, their radio calls and routines. And they didn't have a full Secret Service team up for a candidate like Tucker, though Hayes was surprised to see how large a detail he did have. He was protecting himself because of the attacks.

He waited for a moment until his target appeared, then crossed quickly into the long service corridor and staging area for the ballrooms. He'd followed Morgan for the last hour. They were in the third basement of Rockefeller Center. She paused when his shadow passed her — good instincts.

She turned and made a strangled noise.

"Hayes. What? The meeting is at — you can't be here!"

"I was in the neighborhood. I thought I would push it up." He was putting himself in a dangerous spot, but he had to at least try to get her to see the truth, talk to her face to face. She'd been an army officer and had sworn the oath. He knew her. She wouldn't let her own people get killed. And if she did try to haul him in, he would improvise.

"You're making a mistake, Kathryn," he said. "Don't gather Cold Harvest together. You're playing into the killers' hands."

"Don't you —" she said, then stopped as the door ahead opened. Tucker stepped out, a Starbucks cup and a sheaf of papers in his hand. He saw Morgan first.

"What are you doing out here?" Tucker asked. "We have —"

Then he caught sight of Hayes.

"What is this?"

"Good," Hayes said. "We can all talk."

Tucker craned his neck around, looking for Secret Service and finding none. Hayes stepped closer. Tucker was terrified but trying not to show it.

"You killing us all, Tucker? Everyone in Cold Harvest?"

"How dare you? You and this program are shut down. There has been enough bloodshed. You have failed in the mission."

Hayes ignored him. A grand conspiracy, organized by ruthless and far-seeing masters? Hayes didn't think so. It would be almost reassuring to think people that competent were in charge, but no. The real enemy wasn't usually one twisted kingpin. The enemy was everywhere, in everyone. It was everyday weakness — cowardice and ass-covering. The political players he met in DC were afraid to openly disagree with their bosses, let alone order up a few homicides of American personnel that they'd taken twenty years and as many millions of dollars to train.

Their presence here was what finally convinced him. Tucker and his deputy wouldn't be anywhere near such a gathering of Cold Harvest if they were really going to kill, or let someone else kill, the rest of the team.

"No. I didn't think it was you," Hayes said, ignoring Tucker's last remark. "It seemed too bold. You're more the type for sins of omission."

They had simply turned a blind eye to the killings, hoping it would all blow over. And, God, they were so wrong-footed by trying to put a lid on the program. They were gathering everyone, offering a perfect target. Maybe the killers were counting on this sort of weakness.

"You're done," Tucker said. "And Cold Harvest is done. This violence all came because of this program, and we end it by ending the program."

"Do you really believe that? That surrendering and giving the enemy exactly what they want will end this?"

"You're cut off. We're bringing you and everyone else in the program in and parking you until this blows over. It's finished. Morgan's making the announcement tomorrow."

"You want to tell them yourself?"

Tucker's head moved back a few inches. Morgan scanned the staging area.

"Jesus," she said.

A tall man with black hair stepped out from behind a pillar. It was Josh Drake. Two more came out at the end of the corridor, and others emerged from a side hallway. There were six of them in total, Cold Harvest operators. Hayes and Drew Ochoa had called them. They found out Drake was already in New York after Morgan pulled him out of his undercover role in Algeria.

Hayes had liked Drake from the day he'd met him eight years ago, fighting in Somalia. He was a West Coast SEAL and Team Six operator. The guys constantly gave him shit about his looks — he could have been a movie star — and called him Hollywood or sometimes just Wood. It fit the stereotype that SEALs, especially the West Coast teams, were a bunch of vain beach bums. During force-on-force simulations, other guys would sneak hair gel into the California guys' magazine pouches as a prank.

Drake had helped reach out to the others who were already in New York. Hayes had wanted to come alone, but they weren't going to let him walk into a potential trap without backup, and they wanted to see this go down.

"You brought them *here?*" Tucker seethed. "What is this, a coup?"

"*You* brought them here. And you did a bad job. Blowing covers in daylight, using known CIA assets."

"How did you get away from the security team?" Morgan asked.

Drake gave her a *Come on* look.

"You're all going to prison," she said.

Hayes shook his head. "You don't see it, Morgan. They found us by following the funerals. They've been able to kill us because we gathered together. Now you're offering them a perfect target."

"Even if they did attack, how would they be able to overcome a few dozen of our most experienced operators in the best-policed city in the United States?"

"They've been successful so far. You put a target on all of our backs by rushing this and breaking people's covers. It would have been easy to trace. When will the rest of Cold Harvest be here?"

"You're not asking questions," Tucker said.

"Tuesday," Morgan said.

He watched Morgan's eyes as she glanced from his team members to her boss, thinking it through. A bloodbath on her watch, on American soil. It wasn't a moral turn; it was a cold look at the optics. She'd misstepped.

"You want us to call it off?" she asked.

"No," Hayes said. "It's too late. We can use it to our advantage, set up a decoy to bring whoever's behind this into the open. We'll change the location to someplace far from population centers. Do a bad job concealing where it's happening. There's a safe house in the mountains near Ramapo."

It was an old business travelers' hotel that the Agency had bought and fitted out with bulletproof glass and standoff barriers disguised as planters.

"That will draw them out," Hayes said, "and we can lure them into a trap and take them down."

"Who?"

"Us. Cold Harvest. We'll take that fight. We'll win."

They were all solo operators, but they would meet this threat together, die together if need be. Let them come with everything they had. Hayes was ready.

"You're out of your mind, Hayes. You're going to go to war on American soil?"

"The war's already started."

Two Secret Service agents stepped out from the double doors behind Tucker. They saw the men ringing Morgan and Tucker and drew their sidearms.

"Vince," Hayes said and gave one of the men a nod. He knew him well. They'd spent six weeks together working a detail through Southeast Asia.

"What's going on? Tucker, are you okay?"

"No. These men need to be placed under arrest —"

"Hold on, Tucker," Morgan said.

"You want to go to prison too?"

"Fuck off," Morgan replied, and Tucker stammered in indignation. "You don't see it?" she asked her boss. "Whoever's behind this could be on the way here now. I'm fine with politics, but I'm not getting any more of our people killed."

"Sir?" the Secret Service agent said to Tucker. The candidate's face screwed up for a moment as he tried to process what he'd just heard.

"What are you saying, Kathryn?"

"The security on pulling everyone from the field was rushed. And there might be leaks in the office."

"The attackers could be coming to New York now?" Tucker asked.

"Yes," Hayes said.

"Sir?" Vince asked again.

"One second," Tucker barked. He checked his phone. "I'm going onstage right now."

"Cancel it," Morgan said. Tucker didn't move.

"She's right," Hayes said.

The only thing that surpassed Tucker's cowardice was his ambition. He was behind in the polls and running on his national security record. This was his big moment on foreign policy, the day before the Fourth of July. He couldn't afford to look weak.

"No," Tucker said to Hayes. "Don't move. I want you on security upstairs."

Tucker had been planning to lock up Hayes and the others, but now, suddenly, they were the best chance he had. He needed to put them between him and the violence.

"We're cut off, remember?" Hayes said. "We don't work for you."

"Give him what he wants," Morgan told Tucker. "This has to end."

"You're on in two minutes," the agent said to Tucker.

"I need you watching out," Tucker said to Hayes.

Jesus, Hayes thought; he had him now. Tucker would go on, knowing that other men would catch his bullets for him. No matter. If the enemies of Cold Harvest were out there, Hayes would find them. He could keep watch while staying out of sight.

"I will if you let Cold Harvest fight this," Hayes said.

Tucker rocked back and forth for a moment.

"Fine. Come on."

Tucker turned, and Morgan, Hayes, and the other operators flanked him and headed toward the stairs and Rockefeller Plaza.

CHAPTER 53

Timur sat in the driver's seat of the truck. They were staging for the attack from inside a prefabricated industrial building in Woodbridge, New Jersey. It was set on the back lot of a salvage yard beside the Arthur Kill, the snaking body of water that separates New Jersey from Staten Island.

He ran his finger around the split ring on the dead man switch and let it dangle against the pin. Satisfied with his last inspection of the trigger, he handed it off to the man in the passenger seat, a younger fighter named Alex who had helped him with the preparations. He was nervous, Timur could tell. Timur would drive, and Alex would hold the switch.

Everything was ready, though he was planning to go over the radio protocols one more time with Alex. Timur rested his head against the seat. He had worked through the night and was tired, so tired, but the end was coming soon.

He stepped out of the truck and walked to the window, which had been covered with a tarp. He eased it to the side and looked out.

Over the rusting fences of the yard, the sky glowed yellow in the distance: the lights of New York City.

Soon. All he needed was the call.

CHAPTER 54

Two blocks north of Rockefeller Plaza, in an underground garage, Claire sat in the back of the truck under the cap, cross-legged, sorting gear from the cache box into a backpack and a duffel. She stripped down to a tank top and pulled on a black form-fitting vest that held an extra magazine of .308-caliber rifle rounds. She clipped two mini-frags to the left side above her first-aid kit. They were Dutch hand grenades the size of golf balls. They'd been discontinued in the regular army because of their short fuse, but Claire always carried a couple on shoots like this in case everything went sideways.

She slid the Remington concealable sniper rifle into the backpack. Broken down, it could easily fit into the schoolbag. Tucker would go onstage soon. She pulled on a light synthetic running jacket.

She felt the pulse racing in her neck. She knew that her people were gathering in New

York. She wanted to protect them, but there was no one she could trust. She had reached out to Hayes and been ambushed. They thought she was the killer. If she tried to get close, they would likely take her on sight before she had a chance to explain anything.

She had to protect them from afar. If Tucker and Morgan were behind this, there really was only one choice: to take them down. Unsanctioned operations like the one Tucker and Morgan were running were easily stopped with one attack. Take the head, the body dies. The killers lose their patron.

Assassination. American soil. It felt surreal to be making the call on her own, but the rest was just part of her job. She had killed politicians before, even a prime minister in West Africa. It could be done. As part of Cold Harvest, she had sniper scouting information on most of the major venues in Manhattan.

Police response time was eight minutes. She would be gone in six at the most. The holiday crowds would help.

It was doable. She slipped the thin dagger into her vest. The knife's contour was slightly curved from resharpening over the years, the handle worn, the razor's edge glinting in the light. It looked like an antique, but it was only six years old. It had seen a lot of use.

She zipped the jacket up over her gear. Paul stood watch outside. She picked up a small pouch, then stepped out of the car and handed it to him.

"Paul, I want you to take this. There's money inside. I can get you out of the country. There are people I know. You shouldn't have come back for me."

"I'm not leaving you alone surrounded by these people."

"I don't want you to see me work."

"I can handle it."

She had continued to sound him out on the ride up. Not a word out of place. If he *was* playing her, manipulating her, provoking her into attacking her own people, her plan was to go along so easily that he would drop his guard. If she teased him with what he wanted most, she could find the cracks in his cover.

She was beginning to trust him. The habits seemed stronger than her doubts. She even caught herself turning her back to him once. As her suspicions diminished, her anger grew about what her bosses might have done, tensing her muscles and driving her forward like amphetamines.

He looked at the bag, the bulk of the broken-down sniper rifle. "Are you sure about this?" he asked.

"Yes."

She wasn't. But her choices had been reduced to one option. If he was telling the truth, Tucker and Morgan and Hayes deserved to die.

"You should go, Paul."

He picked up the backpack. "I'm staying with you. You ready?"

She looked to a mid-rise on Forty-Sixth Street, the best vantage spot on Rockefeller Plaza. All roads led to that tower.

She shook out her hands but couldn't burn off that feeling, the unceasing push to move, to run, to break things. Was she lost in the lie again? Was she drawing him out? Was she really going to kill them?

She didn't know.

Movement is life.

She would decide in the moment, and trust her instincts.

CHAPTER 55

Hynd shouldered the backpack that Claire had given him and scanned the crowd as they walked down Fifth Avenue in the dusk. Vera was nearby, unseen but watching, with a field team of five other shooters. As soon as they had the location where the Cold Harvest members were gathering, Hynd and Vera would take Claire out and then give the order to Timur to hit the site with the truck.

He had exploited Claire's trust in him perfectly and used her anger to master her. Everything he had told her — about his time in exile, and about Cold Harvest killing innocents — was a lie, but she believed him.

For all the posturing and cynicism, she wanted to believe in something, like the rest of them. That's what made them weak. She was his weapon now.

"Hang here," Claire said. Police vans were

parked on the corners. Generators with tower lights stood halfway down the block.

"What are you doing?" he asked, but she was already gone, holding a plastic water bottle in her hand, knifing through the crowd toward an idling delivery truck. She crouched slightly as she moved past it, then circled back to him, blending in with the tourists streaming by.

"What was that?" he asked.

"Go."

She moved with the crowd, ignoring him as he walked with her, his head craned back. "Lower your profile, Paul. Relax. It's fine. No one's going to get hurt. Not yet."

Claire slowed just past Fiftieth Street, then turned and walked down the plaza toward the main stage. It was barricaded off at the end.

A low pop, like a small-caliber pistol, came from the far corner of the plaza. Murmurs of surprise came from the crowd as people flinched back, but Claire kept her eyes fixed on the stage. She watched the men in suits rush toward the noise, and among the people in the crowd, she caught the well-practiced reactions of the undercover Secret Service.

"Good," she said. She'd placed a sealed

water bottle behind the truck's tire. It popped when the vehicle backed up.

"What was that?" Paul asked.

"I have their security." She scanned the rooftops and then started walking south again. It felt good to be operational, to let the thousand details of threat and defense fill her mind and block out the rage and the endless nagging doubts.

They passed the Diamond District and cut around a few barkers offering deals on stones, then Claire turned right down a side street of discount clothes stores, Turkish and Brazilian restaurants, and ninety-nine-cent-pizza-slice shops. There were a variety of architectural styles, mostly buildings from the late nineteenth century. This was a part of Manhattan that the glass towers hadn't touched.

She stopped outside an electronics store.

"Here?" he asked.

"Yes. Mixed-use commercial. Non-jewelry. No central security. Best position on Rock Center."

She walked up to the metal door beside a loading dock and from her entry kit pulled a thin wire hook with a precise bend at the end. She could open most older commercial door locks with it by reaching all the way through the locking mechanism to pull the latch back directly. She popped the lock open and led him through the loading area.

The freight elevator had no cameras, and its shaft offered access to her sniper hide: the elevator machine room on the top of the building. The roof itself was too exposed, too easy for countersnipers to see, but the small boxy room on top of it was perfect for a shot at the plaza.

The elevator arrived on their floor. She stepped in, and when Paul tried to follow, she put her hand on his chest. "No." She tapped a button on the panel inside, then slid out as the doors nearly closed on her arm.

As the elevator descended to the floor below them, Claire pulled out a small metal cylinder with a hinged tab on the end, known as a drop key. There was a hole in the left panel of the closed elevator doors, and she slid the drop key into it and twisted it, releasing the lock. She stuck her fingertips into the crack between the doors and pulled them apart with little effort, giving them access to the open shaft and the roof of the elevator cab.

Claire stepped on top. "Come on," she said. "When this starts, it will cut you in half. Move."

He stepped in beside her. "Couldn't we

have gone from the inside?"

"No. That's a movie thing. The ceiling access is always bolted shut from the outside."

There were service controls on the top of the elevator, a standard feature. One of the basic approaches to embassy break-ins was to enter on business during the day, get on top of the elevator, and ride the damn thing until the guards had gone home. She'd used the tactic on the Tempest job in Paris.

She pressed a button, and the elevator started to rise; the floors shot past them. Forty feet up, he started to ask a question but she seized his arm and pulled him toward her as a counterweight — two thousand pounds of stacked steel plates — came flying past them like a guillotine blade. People working in these shafts called those weights the silent killers.

"Keep your eyes up," she said. The concrete ceiling of the shaft seemed like a giant granite stone plummeting toward their heads.

"Is there room?"

"Yes."

It came closer and closer. Paul crouched down, eyes shut tight, as the car closed on two girders that ran across the top of the shaft.

"Step back," Claire said, and she moved

344

toward the edge as the steel bars passed between them.

She climbed onto the beam. A chime sounded next to Paul's leg. The elevator was about to descend. "Here," she said. She put her hand under his arm and pulled him onto the girder just as the elevator began dropping. They had to leave the elevator in operation or else it might alert the security staff.

The girder was about four inches wide. Looking down at the elevator cab dropping away gave her the vertiginous feeling of flying into the air, and suddenly they were at the top of a hundred-and-fifty-foot drop. Paul was staring down. "Look at the wall," she said. She didn't need him puking or passing out.

A small square access above them led to the machine room. She grabbed the ledge on one side, jumped, took it at the waist, and hauled herself up.

"The bags," she said, and he handed them up. She reached back down for Paul, clasped his wrists, and helped him up as he dragged his toes down the wall, trying for traction.

She grabbed him under the armpits, and he managed to pull himself up on the ledge.

The machine room was a concrete-block box on the top of the building with frosted-glass windows on four sides and a locked steel door that exited onto the flat roof.

Claire slipped off her jacket. She pulled a small glass cutter from her bag, walked to the corner, and scored a rectangle in the pane. Using the metal ball on the other end of the tool, she tapped the rectangle twice, and the glass cracked. She worked the shard back and forth till it came out, giving her an eight-by-eight-inch hole.

This was known as a loophole. If the shooter kept back from it far enough for the muzzle flash to remain entirely inside the room, he or she could kill without ever being seen.

"You can't see anything."

"Not from there."

She unfolded the stock of the rifle and locked in the barrel. To her left, a four-foot wheel ringed with elevator cables spun vertically as the motors hummed beside it. In the center of the room there was an electrical box, a four-by-four-foot square platform about knee-high off the ground. When she climbed on top, the small sight picture through the opening showed only the sides of skyscrapers, but once she put herself all the way forward, she could see it, between two buildings and just over another beaux arts structure to the north — Rockefeller Plaza.

CHAPTER 56

It was known as a keyhole shot, a small column of empty space reaching from her to her target. It was hard to make, and harder to spot. Through her scope, she could see the Secret Service ringing the stage. A woman sang beside the podium, readying the crowd.

Paul stood to the side while Claire placed a sock filled with beans on the edge of the electrical box, placed the rifle barrel on it, and then started raising the stock inch by inch to line up her target.

She popped a piece of gum in her mouth and snugged the rifle against her cheek as she lay prone. Different snipers used different things — gum, tobacco, seeds — to occupy them and keep the concentration up. Her instructors' superstitions — and long-range shooters were a superstitious bunch — had rubbed off on her. Never change it up. She chewed Big Red.

"That scope's for you," she said. "Up here."

Paul lifted the spotting scope. "Where?"

"Lie beside me. I'm on target." That was how it was done. She'd seen 240-pound Marines spoon for eight hours at a stretch. If the enemy was watching and one of them had to piss, he would just roll to one side.

Paul stretched out next to her.

"That button on the side is the range finder. It's just like shooting photos. I need you to spot the targets. Aim at the middle of their faces."

They waited in silence for fifteen minutes. An opening speaker took the stage.

After a moment, behind a partition, hidden from the crowd's view, she saw Hayes appear and, on the other side, Josh Drake.

"Who is that?" Paul asked.

"You recognize him?"

"On the right behind the barricade. He was following me the week before the fire."

He was talking about John Hayes. Good tactics, keeping his face out of sight. Only this God's-eye view would reveal it.

Her even breath hitched. She counted three more Cold Harvest operators that she could see, all out of sight of the audience and the press. Tucker and Morgan stood offstage with Hayes, behind the partitions.

What the hell was going on? Hayes and Drake were protecting those two traitors like a Praetorian guard.

She didn't want to believe what Paul had told her. Didn't want to believe that Hayes had drawn her into that ambush. But why else would he be there with Morgan? She knew he had met with her. Was he working for her? Doing her bidding in order to clear his name once and for all? Was he Morgan's assassin? The insider killing his own brothers? How many others had he co-opted?

Claire's finger rested on the trigger, and she moved the scope from one face to the other. The first kill would be easy. The supersonic bullet would hit a moment before the suppressed crack of her rifle could even be heard down there. Give them half a second of reaction time, generously, to grasp that they were being taken out. She ran the numbers in her head, and, given the spread and the recoil, she figured she could take those three — Tucker, Morgan, and Hayes — before they could reach cover.

Morgan and Tucker moved to the side behind the partition. She wanted to wait for them all to get closer together so that she could definitely take them in one go. The calculations, automatic and long-practiced, soothed her. It was so much easier than the doubts.

Hynd couldn't believe it as he lay next to Claire and studied the faces in the spotting scope. He had thought that the assembly of Cold Harvest members would take days, but they seemed to be gathering here, now. He could take them. He needed to signal the others to call the truck bomb into the city. He had the open mic. Vera would understand.

"Those are your team members," he said. "They're here now with Tucker. What's going on?"

Claire didn't respond.

"I see. I see. Fair enough," he said.

The open mic picked up every word, and on the corner of Fifth Avenue at Forty-Fifth Street, Vera listened, stunned. *Fair enough;* that was the code to kill Claire. And he had given the location of the targets as well and said *I see* twice, which meant he was calling in the truck bomb now. But this was too soon. It didn't matter. She lifted her microphone to relay the order to Timur.

"Roll."

"What?"

"They're here. In Manhattan. Near

Rockefeller Plaza. Are you ready?"

"Now?" he asked. She heard him moving, heard voices echoing in the garage. "Is it all of them?"

"I'm not sure, but Hynd gave the order and the location. They must be close. Get that truck into midtown and we'll give you further instructions. We can hit them where they are hiding or draw them out. They'll run toward a threat. It's how they are trained."

"I'm on my way," Timur said. "I can take the Lincoln Tunnel. The middle tube is open to trucks."

"Get moving."

The engines started. She killed the radio and pictured the truck picking up speed, moving toward the heart of the city.

CHAPTER 57

Enough of this madness with Claire, Vera thought as she walked quickly up Fifth Avenue. The woman had given them what they needed, the Cold Harvest location. Now they could get rid of her.

Vera had left the rest of her team closer to Rockefeller Plaza. They were dressed to blend in with the crowd and could keep an eye on the rally and track the Cold Harvest members there. She would see to Claire personally. She checked the GPS she had on Hynd and turned toward the building where he and Claire were set up on the roof.

Vera buzzed the door. As she waited outside the loading dock, she loosened a button on her blouse. Her face seemed to melt from a hard old-world glare into something soft, inviting.

And just as she buzzed again, the heavy steel door opened.

"Yes?" answered the guard, a South Asian

man with a mustache.

"Oh, thank God, someone's here," she said as she stepped inside and glanced at the building directory behind him. "These goddamned servers picked the absolute worst time to go down."

It was a perfect Midwestern American accent, with a slight gravelly inflection at the end of each sentence, as she had heard the younger women use in this country. She barely paid attention to him as she rummaged through her purse.

"My client called me in. Their website is down. He's on five. Of course he can't make it out here himself on a weekend, so he said the building manager could let me in. I can get you his number. It's GTR Engineering."

She cursed and lifted a pack of tissues out of her purse, searching for her phone. A set of keys fell to the floor and skittered farther in.

The man, of course, reached down for them, and as he did she slammed the door shut behind him, timing it to cover the suppressed report of her 9-millimeter Glock.

He dropped to the ground, clutching his genitals. It wasn't a fatal shot, but the pain and shock had caused him to fall, cracking his head. He dragged himself along the floor with his free hand and the only leg that seemed to be moving.

"What are you doing? Oh God!"

He crawled toward the desk with the office phone, but he couldn't reach it.

"Keys. I need the keys." The suppressor hovered a few feet from his face, aimed straight at his eye.

His lower lip shook as he tried to speak. He pointed to a box on the wall. "Th- there."

She reached for them with her left hand, barely looking away, keeping the gun level.

"The roof?"

"The key hanging at the top left. The Medeco. The access is at the top of the west stairs."

She lifted it up. "This?"

He nodded his head. She fired twice and turned away as he fell and his skull cracked against the linoleum floor.

She locked his body in the office, took the elevator to the twelfth floor, then went to the stairs and climbed up to the roof access. The key worked. As she crossed the flat roof, she could hear the low buzz of electric motors inside the elevator room. It matched the background noises in her earpiece. They were inside.

Hynd had said that he let Claire live to use her, but Vera had always wondered if maybe he didn't have the strength to kill her himself. She needed to be up there to make sure he put her down.

She raised her pistol and moved toward them.

Fifty feet away, inside the machine room, Hynd adjusted the focus on his scope.

"They're getting ready," he said, and he watched a pair of tall Secret Service agents step toward Tucker, one on either side. Claire rested her cheekbone on the stock. Hynd knew that her attention was absorbed entirely by the shot; she would be an easy kill.

"I have them," she said.

Hynd thought of letting her pull the trigger. The chaos afterward would bring all those heroes into the open where Vera's ground team could engage them and hold them down long enough for the truck to arrive and take them all.

More than that. He wanted to watch her kill, to see his years of work realized, his mastery confirmed. He felt their bodies rise and fall together. Some part of him even thought that the anger, the killer in Claire, was stronger than any allegiance. Her country had burned her. He thought he could turn her, bring her over to his side openly. They were so much alike.

No. Prudence. Better to take her now. It would take only a quarter of a second to get control, to put his arm across her throat while she stared through the optic and clamp it from the rear, a naked choke that would crush the arteries on both side of her neck and cut off all blood to her brain.

It was a shame. She'd been one of his favorite girls.

Claire slowed her breathing. It all looked so simple through that sniper scope. Her anger was a strength, not a flaw. The trigger made problems go away. All she ever wanted, she could have with a single pull: the old life, with her husband back beside her.

The rifle felt so right in her hand. The actions came without thinking. The endless hours of drills took over.

Her life with him was a lie, but she'd never been so happy as she'd been in that lie. Afterward, when he was gone and she was alone with nothing to hide behind, she'd had to look at herself as she was.

She didn't like the woman she'd met. She'd choose the lie. One more act of killing. A last sacrifice. And then she was done.

"I know, Paul."

"What?"

"I know you're not what you say you are."

She turned her head, and their eyes were a few inches apart.

"I don't care," she said.

He started to say something, then stopped. Claire put her finger on the trigger and let the act speak for itself, an offering to him, a proof of her faith.

Three targets. Three shots. Two seconds.

She could take them all. She scanned with the rifle, fixing their position in her muscle memory, timing the countdown with her breaths.

Three, two, one, fire.

She eased the trigger straight back.

CHAPTER 58

Tucker scanned the crowd, picking out faces at random, looking deep into each one's eyes as he spoke. He pointed to the art deco facade of Rockefeller Center rising high behind him.

"In this building, seven decades ago, a small group of Americans started working in secret. It was the beginning of the Office of Strategic Services, the forefather of the CIA. They operated in the shadows, sent men and women behind enemy lines, and rolled back the Nazis and the Soviets.

"We may never know the full extent of their sacrifice, but they kept us safe."

Hayes walked behind the partition and scanned the crowd through a narrow gap. He could pick out the undercover Secret Service officers. Their eyes never stopped moving, and they held their gun arms slightly out to the side to keep anyone from bumping into their concealed weapons.

Tucker had ordered them to loop Hayes in on their communications, and he carried a radio with an earpiece.

The enemy could have two shooters in the front row right now. The people behind the attacks had been able to operate untroubled in the United States for so long. They knew their baselines, how to camouflage.

Tucker's voice rose and he moved his hand like a blade, cutting through the air.

"I know what it takes to keep us —"

The air cracked, a sound like dry wood splitting.

Without even thinking, Hayes started counting as he moved to cover.

A low boom echoed off the buildings.

Crack-bang, countersnipers called it. The first sign of a bullet was the supersonic crack as it passed by. An instant later, the bang from the gun barrel caught up, because the sound moved more slowly than the bullet. With a fast count, each second meant a hundred yards. Hayes reached four. Expert distance. Or maybe an amateur at expert range. Why the miss?

The agents swarmed the stage, pulled Tucker down, and rushed him off.

Crack-bang.

Another shot, another miss, but Hayes had already slipped to the side of stage. He wasn't running away. He was trained to always move toward fire. He dropped under the stage. The panicked footsteps beat the boards over his head like a bass drum.

Light streamed through a hole overhead where the bullet had punched through the flooring. Rock Plaza was relatively well protected — it was set back from the long avenues and surrounded by tall buildings with few decent sniper positions, all of them requiring difficult high-angle shots.

He saw the shattered concrete to his right and lined up the hole through the stage. It pointed to a roof with a low parapet and a boxy machine room on top: his shooter's location.

The high-angle shot, the narrow band between surrounding buildings, the perfectly disguised hide; it could easily have been Claire's work. She'd done one just like it in the Republic of Georgia.

Hayes came out on the far side of the stage and sprinted across the long exposed distance between him and the southern end of the plaza, heading toward the sniper.

Chapter 59

In that moment before the shot, Claire counted down: *Three, two, one, fire.*

She pulled the trigger.

Her words to Paul had made him hesitate as he thought through just what he was hearing. He started to say yes. He had gone along with the whole plan too easily, without the nervousness she would expect from a man unaccustomed to violent work. Then she caught the tension in his body as he prepared to move on her, and through the frosted window, she saw a shadow moving outside. It was all she needed to understand what the truth was.

The stock of her rifle was raised slightly, and she dropped her shoulder before she fired.

Every action has an equal and opposite reaction. It's a shooting lesson that becomes paramount as you move into the heavy calibers: the more lead you throw downrange, the harder the stock of the gun comes back at you.

The blast was deafening in the small space, and the muzzle flare was a tongue of fire reaching for the hole in the glass.

She missed. She'd wanted to miss. The stock flew into Paul's jaw and the side of his neck as he was moving in to choke her.

Her words before the shot had been the last lie. She'd had to believe it herself to sell it to him. Paul had thought she would play along. He thought he could control her. Thought the anger would control her. He was wrong on all counts. And in his arrogance, he'd tipped his hand, and now he was going to die.

In the half second of chaos after the shot, as the gun drove into the side of his neck, she threw her right elbow into Paul's windpipe, and he started back in a long choking inhalation.

He grabbed for the rifle, and it kicked back, sending a bullet flying. She went for his hand to lock up his arm, but as she rose up, he drove his thumb into her eye. The dusty nail dug into her tear duct. As she flinched, Paul shoved her back and drew her pistol.

She ignored the pain and clamped her hand down on his on the gun. The barrel was aimed at her face.

She twisted her hand around the meat of his thumb and the grip of the pistol and shoved it away as he pulled the trigger, deafening her with a hot breath of flame.

The bullet went wide, but she couldn't hear anything except a high whine at the center of her skull.

He stood and brought his left hand onto the grip of the gun. She was kneeling on top of the box, and he easily forced her wrist back.

If she were standing, she could have tried blows with her knee, but she was stuck on top of this goddamn box and watching as the bore of the pistol came toward her. There was nothing she could do. He had thirty pounds on her. Slowly, slowly, he wrested control away from her.

"Claire!" he croaked. "What the hell are you doing?" A long shallow gasp. "Let go of the gun." He brought it around, put both hands on the grip. She looked down the black eye of the barrel.

Then she dropped to one side, toward the edge of the box. With all his effort pushing the gun toward her, when she changed direction suddenly and added her strength to his, it was enough. She drew the gun toward her head and over and threw him to the side. He landed on his ribs, and the gun fell from his hands.

He leaped to his feet, and Claire was already off the box, closing in on him. She pulled a slender metal blade from her vest, and as he stood she lowered it slightly, then drove the knife into his belly.

It tore through his diaphragm and entered his heart as she raised her arm like someone hoisting a glass for a toast. He came off his feet, then slumped over her shoulder as she pinned him against the wall.

He'd believed what he wanted to believe: that she was weak, that he understood her, that she needed him. Even to the end, he'd needed to know that he could control her. Maybe he even wanted to be with her somehow, to have the old life back. He never committed, never chose a side. He wanted it all, believed in nothing but himself. He thought it made him stronger than the men below, men whose convictions were so strong they would sacrifice themselves and run toward gunfire without a second thought. But he was wrong.

"You have no idea who I am," she said as she dropped him to the ground and moved toward the pistol.

A gunshot popped outside, and the window

blew in. Stinging pain tore across her face, her eyes. She fell back, reached up, and felt the edges of skin, flaps along her eyebrows.

Blind. I'm fucking blind, she thought before she even hit the concrete. The glass had cut her. The blood pooled in her eyes. The shot had come from her left. She scrambled across the broken glass until she hit an electrical box.

She crouched behind it, the last cover she could remember. But she had no idea if the gunman had already come around to the other window and was now staring down at her helpless form.

Her fingers found the pouch of her first-aid kit, always within reach, even with one hand. She moved past the tourniquet and felt the gauze impregnated with QuikClot.

As she blinked, she could make out shapes, a dark swirl, like the room reflected in night water. She pressed the cloth to her forehead. The clotting agent burned, smelled like rusting steel. She ran her hand gently across her eyelids, fearful of making any cuts to her eyes worse, but now she could see. She blinked away the blood.

Her fingers touched the bandage, and the pain made the whole world waver; she was on the edge of blackout. It was a deep laceration around the orbital bone, but at least one of her eyes was okay.

She looked for the rifle, for her pistol, for anything. But there was only broken glass. The guns must have fallen on the far side of the box and were lying under the shattered window where the shot had come from. If she went over there, she would be in the open, an easy kill. All she had were the two mini-frags.

She could hear the gunman moving outside. The north and south windows were blown out. Another shot, and the window to her side shattered in. It sounded like a silenced pistol. Bullet by bullet, he was eliminating any cover, readying for the final kill. She had to get out. She had seconds. She pulled the ring and dropped the grenade through the window above her head, just outside the machine room.

She threw herself through the low broken window on the other side of the room and landed hard on her shoulder on the building's roof. She rolled over, feeling the sharp edges of glass bury in the meat of her back as the frag shook the air and chunks of metal rained down.

She saw the shooter coming. It was a woman. Claire pulled the pin on her second and last frag and rolled it toward her, then stumbled around the corner of the machine room, so the wall was between herself and the bang.

She looked around for better cover as the sulfur smoke of the explosion drifted toward her. Fifty feet away, there was another concrete-block box sticking out from the roof, the stair access, and beyond that just a parapet and the hundred-and-fifty-foot drop to the street. She started to run toward the stairs, long unsteady strides, trying not to puke from pain.

The grenade blew behind the machine room. She listened for cries but heard only silence. After a moment, there were footsteps, the crunch of glass. The other woman was still alive, and armed. And Claire had only her knife and nowhere to go but down.

CHAPTER 60

Hayes moved against the crowds of tourists heading toward the river as he approached Forty-Sixth Street on Fifth Avenue. The sound of small explosions echoed off the building facades rising above him. It made it hard to fix a location, but he was sure from his initial sight of the sniper: they were coming from that tower.

The Secret Service counterassault team had swarmed Rockefeller Plaza. This was the part of the Secret Service you didn't see until something went very wrong. They waited in the SUVs with the heavy guns and full assault gear and covered the protection detail as it hurried the principal out of the way.

Hayes was up on the communications network shared by the Secret Service and NYPD. He keyed his radio. "We have a shooter on top of the art deco midblock with the shields in the parapet. Between

Forty-Seventh and Forty-Sixth Streets."

"Two emergency service unit squads rolling in now," the commander responded. Those were the NYPD's tactical teams.

"I'm heading in on the north side," he said, and described his clothes. "Don't kill me, all right?"

"Rog."

As he neared the building, he watched the crowds hunkering down in front of the storefronts, some people crying. He crouched in front of a woman and helped her to her feet, then directed the others to keep moving.

A man passed him, head down, and Hayes went twenty feet before a detail called back to him: the lean jaw and bulk around his waist — it didn't match. Hayes turned, but the man was already drawing his weapon, and Hayes dropped him with two shots.

"They have shooters on the streets too. They're blending in with the civilians," he radioed.

Hayes knew the textbook response to a scenario like this. His former unit used to work closely with the Secret Service — whenever the president deployed overseas, a Delta team was there. The police would block off the surrounding streets and search the people within the area one at a time while the SWAT teams closed on the building the shots had come from and cleared it room by room.

But the enemy was using their tactics against them. Hayes put himself in that tower, watched the crowds fleeing like ants.

What would you do? How would you kill yourself?

If he were the sniper, he would already be running from that building. That was the standard guerrilla tactic: shoot and scoot. And then what? A mass attack, the bigger the better — suitcase, backpack, car. A cordon would lock in only innocents, agents patting each one down, searching every bag. It would corral Hayes, his team, and a lot of civilians close enough together for them to be taken down in one blast.

"I think our sniper is probably already on the move. We need more people. Keep the perimeter a quarter mile out, no choke points. Cue on vehicles, maybe large backpacks. Get every explosives dog and detector you can in here."

He told them to keep the searches fast. Pros would ditch anything incriminating anyway. The idea was to get bystanders away from the target and inspect every vehicle and trash can for a bomb.

He neared the front entrance of the building the shot had come from and scanned the doors and the street ahead. Had she already run?

Where are you, Claire?

A woman stumbled as she ran, and he helped her up, rushed her along. Then a man across the street craned his head to the sky, and his mouth fell open. Hayes looked up but saw only a blur: a person plummeting from the tower that the sniper had been using. Then the ground shook with the impact, and blood splashed along the concrete and onto the hem of his pants.

Hayes ran toward the body, and he could tell it was a woman. He knelt down beside her — dead in an instant — and reached down to check if the face was recognizable. His fingers touched the blood-matted hair, and then the shadow crossed him, and he looked up to see a pistol aimed at his head.

CHAPTER 61

Moments before that body hit, Vera, up on the roof, ducked behind the corner of the machine room as the second grenade blew. The shock wave punched her in the lungs. She heard what she thought was another one landing, and she ducked down. She counted to ten, but there was no blast.

She lifted her phone and used the reflection on the blank screen to look around the wall. Where she thought the grenade had landed, there was only a chunk of concrete.

Smart. Claire was out of bangs, so she'd thrown that rock to trick her and buy extra time. It had worked. Claire might be defenseless now, but Vera wasn't taking any chances. She raised her gun and stepped out.

There was only one place for Claire to hide, the stair access near the edge of the roof. Vera followed the trail of blood toward it and then came around the corner. Claire wasn't there. Vera's radio earpiece crackled.

"What's happening? The truck's forty minutes out, coming up on Newark."

She ignored the voice and crept to the far side of the stair access, the last place Claire could have taken cover.

On top of the stair-access structure, Claire wrapped her fingers around the handle of the knife, and moved her weight onto the balls of her feet. Just as the woman rounded the last corner and saw the ladder leading to her perch, Claire threw herself forward, at the shooter's shoulder. She brought the blade down, aiming for the soft triangle between the clavicle and jugular. The woman turned at the last instant. The knife-point dug into her clavicle and was deflected away. Claire hit the ground hard, slamming her knees and cracking her teeth.

The knife slipped to the end of her fingers as the woman took a long sidestep and turned to aim the pistol at Claire, but Claire was already rising, moving toward her, settling the knife into an ice-pick grip. She came at the woman's side, knocked the gun away with her left hand, and drove the blade up to its hilt into her back with her right.

The woman, stunned by pain, dropped the pistol, and it came down hard on its rear sight. Vera jumped away from the blade by reflex with a long stumbling step. The shock was too much. She lost her footing and hit the low wall at the top of the cornice, then went over.

Claire picked up the gun, scanned behind her, and came to the edge. The woman's body was hung up in the cast-iron ornaments: Greek shields sticking up from the lower part of the cornice like twists of wire at the top of a chain-link fence. Her torso draped over them, and her legs hung in empty space.

"What are you planning?" Claire shouted. She reached out with her left hand. Her blood was up, and all she wanted was to kill, but answers mattered more than revenge.

The woman tried to raise her arm. Claire closed her fingers around the blood-slicked palm. For a second the woman managed to grip it, and Claire dug her feet in and began to pull her from the narrow ledge.

Then the woman's hand went limp and slipped from Claire's. Her eyes were open but showing only the whites. Dead.

Claire leaned out and took her radio, a push-to-talk handset with an earpiece dangling from it, then saw the emergency service unit truck nosing through the panicked crowds. She put in the earpiece to pick up on whatever they were planning and walked to the stair access on the other side of the roof. It was open.

She returned to the machine room for her backpack. The rifle lay on the ground near Paul's body but she didn't see her own pistol. She didn't have time to look for it, so she would have to use the woman's silenced handgun. She went back to the stairs and took the steps down in a sprint, then stopped, grabbed the rail, and retched on the landing.

She counted backward until it passed and then kept on, slower now, until she reached the ground floor. She washed off the blood with water from a plastic bottle she had in her bag, then pulled on a Yankees cap and a jacket to cover her crimson-stained shirt. She pushed open the emergency exit bar and hit Forty-Sixth Street. The tactical teams' vehicles blocked both ends.

She tried to think. When she was being chased in a city, she liked to run fast in one direction and then slow and circle back. Pursuers would just keep going on their initial course, and she would either pick them off on her back trail or disappear in the opposite direction. The grind of a police helicopter echoed between the buildings.

Claire felt warm blood soaking her shirt near her lower back. The cuts from the glass must have opened up.

She watched Hayes help a woman along near the front of the building.

"Stay down," he said. "Go! Go! Go!" Claire ducked into a doorway. He was coming her way. In the glass vestibule, she could catch his reflection.

She felt the ground shake with a thump behind her. She turned and saw the body, destroyed on the sidewalk. It was the woman from the roof. Her body had finally slipped loose.

Then she saw Hayes reach down to check it. Behind him, a woman moved closer, another scared tourist. But then her manner changed, and she reached into a tote and came up with a pistol, aimed it squarely at Hayes's head. She was part of Paul's backup.

Claire strode toward her and took aim. She pulled the trigger smoothly twice as Hayes turned and trained his weapon on the attacker. Claire's shots hit the woman in the chest and head, and she fell. Hayes pointed the gun at Claire, looking back and forth between her and the woman on the ground, clearly trying to make sense of what had just happened. He decided in an instant and took his aim off her.

"Claire, your eight o'clock. Twenty-five meters." She turned and saw the gunman coming at her, but Hayes already had him — three shots to the chest.

Hayes moved toward her with the controlled quickness of a well-trained shooter. Without talking, Hayes and Claire went back to back, scanning sectors, searching for other threats to materialize from the crowd.

"Mag," Claire said. Hayes pulled one from his waist holster with his nondominant hand and reached it back without looking. She dropped hers to the street — one round left — then drove the fresh magazine in and racked the slide.

"I'll cover the corner on the right," Hayes said. "What the hell is happening?"

She felt cold all of a sudden, and the street seemed to tilt and move far away. The adrenaline had been the only thing keeping her going.

She had heard Paul's team talking on the radio. There was an attack on the way. She needed to tell Hayes, to warn him. "There's a truck coming. I'm sorry, Hayes, I'm sorry."

She had pushed too far, lost too much blood, and her hand went limp on the gun. She watched it as the world shrank to a pinpoint. She tried to stand, but her legs seemed like they were far away, unattached to her body.

She tried to hold on but couldn't. At least she had warned them.

Her skin felt cold, and as she fell back, Hayes caught her with his left arm, keeping his gun out with his right.

"Medical! Medic up!"

CHAPTER 62

Hayes knelt beside Claire while Drake covered the street to the east. Blood pooled beneath her on the sidewalk. She was cut on the back somewhere.

He rolled her over as her clothes stuck to the concrete and put pressure on the wound. "What truck, Claire? What did you do?"

"I heard them. It's coming from the south. The turnpike. Trace it."

Her fingers reached for her pocket, but her arm began to shake as two medics arrived, and one took a knee beside Hayes.

"Where is the truck?"

"A half hour away," she managed to say. "They said it was on a dead man." Hayes saw the push-to-talk radio sticking out of her pocket, under her fingers, and put one hand on hers. He took the radio with the other. She tried to talk, but the words were slurred. She licked her lips.

The EMTs put her on the stretcher.

"I'm sorry. I didn't know who to trust." She grabbed his hand. "Do you . . ." She trailed off.

Hayes thought of the woman Claire had shot. Claire had saved him. He'd been doubted before. And he was alive only because one man had trusted him.

"I believe you," he said. But she couldn't respond. Her eyes closed, and her head slumped to one side. "BP's tanking!" the medic shouted. "We've gotta move!"

Hayes stood and searched the street, saw the police and emergency responders filling in. It was just what the killers wanted, to pin them down and take them in one go. He lifted the handset, walked back to the communications truck, and approached the Secret Service agent who had stayed behind to coordinate with the NYPD.

"I need a trace on this handset. There's a truck bomb coming in from the south."

"Where?"

"The turnpike. We might have time to cut it off before it hits the city."

Hayes needed to run straight at that truck. He was facing a mass attack in the middle of the most densely populated stretch of the United States, a truck bomb on a dead man switch that was almost impossible to disarm.

The agent lifted his radio and called to the operation center. It was a bunker in midtown, with eight-foot-thick concrete walls, positive-pressure ventilation, and radiation shielding, where commanders from different agencies could oversee the incident response. Morgan and Tucker had been taken there. He could hear Morgan's voice in the background.

The agent turned to Hayes. "What do you need?"

Hayes looked at an NYPD helicopter circling overhead. There might be a way.

"A ride."

CHAPTER 63

Timur kept the truck going steady at fifty-five miles an hour and handled the push-to-talk.

Alex sat beside him in the passenger seat, a hinged piece of aluminum in his hand: the dead man. Wires from it ran underneath the seat.

The refineries near Linden rose to his left, a thousand yellow lights spread across the pipes, and red burn-off flames flared into the night.

Alex looked in the side-view. The slanting headlights to the right looked like they belonged to a late-model American sedan, maybe unmarked police. He saw another farther back.

"They're coming for us," he said.

Timur checked his mirrors. "Arm it."

Alex took a deep breath in and exhaled. He dried his left hand on the cheap upholstery of the passenger seat, lifted the switch with his right hand, and held it tight. Then he put his left index finger inside the split ring and pulled.

He laughed nervously. "It's hard."

"Go again," Timur said.

Alex pulled again, and the metal squealed as it came out. The pin hung from Alex's finger. Timur looked over Newark Bay toward the Manhattan skyline. He could pick out the Freedom Tower and the Empire State Building.

Hynd had told him, and he wasn't sure whether to believe it, that the Americans would come to him. That they would sprint toward their own deaths. They would know somehow that it was suicide, but they wouldn't be able to help themselves. Honor, sacrifice: they called futility by other names.

CHAPTER 64

The East River heliport didn't look much bigger than a tennis court. It was a stretch of asphalt right on the river, tucked in beside FDR Drive. As the NYPD helicopter touched down, its rotors came within feet of a billionaire's Sikorsky on the next pad over. The pilot didn't even throttle down as Hayes and Drake ran in a crouch, holding their rifles on slings across their bodies, and climbed into the cabin.

Hayes pulled a headset on and sat on the deck with his legs hanging out the open door.

"Ready?" the pilot asked.

"Ready," Hayes said.

The turbines pitched to a high whine. The pilot pulled back on the collective, and they lifted off.

"You guys were briefed?" Drake said. "We're running straight into the fire."

The copilot looked at him, unimpressed,

and tapped the NYPD emblem on his shoulder. "That's what we do."

Hayes's belly went heavy as they climbed and spun. The skyscrapers whipped to the left, and they banked hard over the water and rose above the Manhattan Bridge.

Hayes had never had good luck with helicopters. He tied a piece of webbing across the handles of his open door as the wind buffeted him. It would form a rest for the sniper rifle he carried, an SR-25 semi-automatic. It was an update on a classic rifle, and he'd used the military version extensively in the Marines and Delta.

As the towers of Lower Manhattan snapped by in front of him, Hayes spoke into his radio headset to the operations center.

"Do we have a fix on the truck yet?"

"Northbound turnpike. Coming through Newark. We can shut the road down."

"How big is it?"

"Tractor-trailer."

Hayes cursed under his breath. That meant almost a one-mile blast radius. He surveyed the New Jersey Turnpike, the chemical plants and petroleum tanks clustered on both sides of the road. Hayes could see the cities running south along the pulsing red and white veins of the turnpike:

Newark and Elizabeth, dense with people. If they stopped the truck and it blew, thousands would die.

He traced the turnpike north, to where it ran on a long bridge over the twists of the Hackensack River and the surrounding grasslands and landfills. That was where he needed the truck. It was the only chance. If he wasn't able to stop that bomb, he could at least isolate it, and the bridge was the one place where that could work.

"Tell the state troopers not to approach it," Hayes said. "We need them to cut off the southbound traffic at the north end of the bridge, and then be ready to cut off the northbound traffic behind the truck. Is that doable?"

Hayes heard cross talk in the ops center, then Morgan came back. "It's doable. But how are you going to stop it from blowing?"

He wasn't. "Just wait for my word."

They crossed over Jersey City, and the low-rise urban grit gave way to warehouses and heavy industry and, beyond them, the Meadowlands.

"Cut off the southbound lanes," Hayes said. "Don't let the civilians anywhere near that bridge. Go."

He watched the turnpike north of the bridge. A minute later, police flashers lit up and Hayes watched the lights cut across the lanes. The police cars slowed, one in each lane, as the traffic stacked up behind them and the cars ahead cruised over the bridge, leaving those lanes empty. Just past the northern terminus of the bridge, there was a chlorine plant. He couldn't let the truck get that far. That span of elevated roadway was his one shot.

"Where's the truck?" Hayes asked.

"Half mile from the bridge."

"Cut off the traffic behind him."

Hayes saw more flashers move out in a chevron along the northbound lanes, light up, and block the road behind the truck.

CHAPTER 65

The last northbound cars that the police had let through sped past in a column over the bridge. And at the tail, Hayes saw the truck, heavy and slow on the uphill grade at the southern end of the bridge. It fell behind the others. It was isolated.

They raced toward it in the helicopter. "Do you want me to circle around to pace the truck?" the pilot asked. The easiest shot would be to reach it, turn, and take it out while running at the same speed alongside.

Hayes eyed the distance. They didn't have time. It would take a while for that truck to stop, and he couldn't let it get to the other end of the bridge, where the southbound traffic was stalled.

"No time. We need to cut him off. Can you put us in a hover over the roadway ahead of him?"

"Yes." They came in fast over the turnpike. The pilot rotated the helicopter ninety degrees, flying sideways, so Hayes's open door faced the semi.

"Closer," Hayes said as the last north-bound car shot underneath them. The bridge was now empty except for the truck.

"There," he said, and they stopped, hovering a quarter of the way across the span. He rested the rifle's hand guard on the webbing, looked through the optic, and watched the truck speed at him, growing in the lens. He was too far for headshots. The 7.62-millimeter round might be able to kill the engine, but it wasn't a sure stop by any means.

He eased the trigger back, and the gun kicked into his shoulder. The noise was deafening inside the cabin, and his hot brass bounced off the ceiling.

He steadied the gun and saw the blown truck grille, steam billowing out. He fired again, and saw a flash of red from inside the engine. The truck was still moving fast, coming at them.

"You're too close" came a voice over the radio from the op center. "Pull out. I say again, pull out."

"Don't," Hayes said to the pilot. Behind them, stacked up in those cars, there were families like his. He and this helicopter were the end of the line; he didn't care what it cost.

But the pilot hadn't moved anyway. He kept them locked twenty feet above the road. The cabin stank of the heavy cartridges' fumes, and Hayes raised the rifle slightly and centered it on the driver's-side windshield. The glass flashed like a signal mirror as it came under each streetlight, but he could see the driver's shape now, bouncing in his sight as the wind buffeted the helicopter.

Time seemed to slow even as the truck careered toward them. Hayes fired again and then saw the hole in the shattered truck windshield. He could make out the head now, a glimpse of the driver gritting his teeth in determination or pain. He centered the reticle on his face. The crosshairs moved in a figure-eight pattern while he kept the gun as steady as he could and eased back the trigger.

The gun shoved him again but he held it close and looked through the scope. The driver, his head mostly gone, slumped to the side, and the truck moved left as a cloud of black smoke belched out from under the hood. It slowed, but it was still coming way too fast. The second man reached for the wheel and Hayes put the crosshairs on his ear and fired once, then again as the man ducked down, and then a third time. Before he could check for a hit, the cab was twisting sideways in his scope.

Hayes lifted his head and saw the cab strike the guardrail, sending off a torrent of sparks. The heavy trailer shoved it from behind, and the truck jackknifed, the cab grinding against the rail as the trailer swept sideways across the roadway and began to tilt.

"It's down," Hayes said.

The pilot was already pulling back, and as Hayes looked at him he saw that his face was white as porcelain. He felt suddenly heavy on the deck as the helicopter turned and rocketed north as if it had been jerked on a fishing line.

The voice came in his ear. It was Morgan from the op center. "Was that it? Is it over?"

Not yet, Hayes thought. *Not yet.* He could see a last glimpse of the truck through the window as the helicopter turned to the north. In an instant, the semi was gone, like someone had changed a slide, and all he could see was a black cloud with red at its heart, growing silently for an instant. The air wavered around it in an expanding sphere, and Hayes went to brace himself, but the shock wave took him, blasted in his ears and tore at his lungs. For a moment he floated weightless inside the cabin, then he smashed into the deck as fire filled the aircraft and the explosion swallowed the bridge.

CHAPTER 66

It was Independence Day, twenty-six hours after the truck had blown, and the Macy's fireworks had just finished. In a hospital room in NYU Medical Center, Claire Rhodes stood at a window with a view of the East River.

The bandages pulled tight across her brow. All that was left of the pyrotechnics were barges and starburst trails of smoke. The crowds filing away from the water looked like moving shadows from this height. The NYPD had found the last of the attackers and in the end the city decided not to cancel the display. She had watched it in silence, and now wiped the tears from her cheeks.

Behind her, Hayes lay on a hospital bed, his eyes closed.

A man in a rumpled suit stepped into the room and instinctively Claire put herself between him and Hayes. She moved awkwardly, though, babying the stitches in her back as the pain from her cut arced through her torso.

The new arrival had bright blue eyes and there was something precise about his movements. "It's Cox, right?" she asked.

"Yes. Long time. How are you holding up?"

Claire didn't answer for a moment. She waved her hand toward the bandage. "Fine. This is the least painful part of it. I let him inside. Those deaths are on me. You want to lock me up, go ahead."

Police guarded every entrance to this floor.

"Your husband?" Cox asked.

The words still stung her.

"Your story checks out, Claire. We have the body. We're going through his old records. We think he was an illegal. His cover was almost perfect."

"Did you find out who he was working for?"

"Not yet."

"His name?"

"No."

She looked down.

"I should have known."

Cox put his hand on her shoulder.

"You weren't the only one who missed it. How's Hayes doing?"

"Partially collapsed lung. They may have given him something for the pain." She looked at Hayes, laid out behind her, bandages over the burns on his neck and shoulder from where the blast had entered the NYPD helicopter.

"Why don't you let him go?" she asked Cox.

"Go?"

"Clear his name. After everything he's done. Isn't that the deal? You can't afford to lose him. If he works for you, you'll finally fully exonerate him. What does the poor bastard have to do? Just let him walk."

Cox nodded along until she was done. "It was his idea, Claire."

"What?"

"After he stopped the Washington attack. He offered himself up. He told us to pin the whole thing on him. To confirm the worst rumors about him."

"Bullshit. Why?"

"You think he cares what anyone at the Pentagon thinks? The people who know him know him. The last thing he wanted was attention. He'd built up the perfect cover, because it was true, because we screwed up and hunted him for two years, believing the accusations against him.

"If he kept that cover, he could go out

among the enemy. They murdered the closest thing to a father Hayes ever had. They nearly got his wife and daughter killed. He was a man on fire, Claire, and he'd do anything to hunt down the people who came for him. It was his call."

"Jesus."

"I shouldn't have let him. I told him . . ."

"What?"

"He's on the kill list now. They'll never stop hunting him. I warned him, but —"

He broke off. Claire had heard it too, a change in Hayes's breathing. He was awake.

Hayes kept his eyes closed and spread his hands on the sheets. They felt cool and clean. His body was still on fire, pain tearing at the skin of his neck and shoulder, but he could breathe now. He took a long breath in, and something cut at him inside his chest.

"Hayes?"

He opened his eyes, and a man stood over him. It was Cox.

"You missed the fireworks, John," Cox said.

Hayes waved his hand, dismissed it. "I'm good on fireworks for a while, thanks."

He pushed himself up in the bed and looked to Claire.

"You make it out all right, Rhodes?" he asked in a hoarse whisper.

"I'm okay, but you shouldn't be talking."

"I've had pneumos before. It's not too bad. You did a good job getting us up on that truck. How are Drake and the pilots?"

"They survived. Those NYPD boys saved you. Most would have panicked and pulled up, but they kept the helicopter ten feet off the road and put you at the edge of the lethal range."

"Helicopters," Hayes said, and he shook his head. "Always a helicopter."

"You can add the Bell 429 to your list of confirmed kills, and the Hackensack River Bridge."

"Oh shit."

"I wouldn't go back to New Jersey anytime soon."

"Not a problem. You see Drake?"

"Broke his left leg, but he looked okay overall. He had some nurse in there chatting him up."

"That's my boy," Hayes said. He examined Cox's face for a bit. The older man's lips were cracked and chapped and he had dark rings under his eyes, like he'd been out on a two-week patrol. "Where the hell have you been?"

"South China Sea. Off the grid. Don't

even ask. They'll declassify in fifty years and that'll be too soon. I'm sorry I couldn't be here for you."

"We sorted it out."

"You need another handler."

"Like Morgan? No, thanks."

Cox put his hand on Hayes's good shoulder. There was a lot to work out, but that could wait.

Hayes looked back and forth between Claire and Cox, then raised his eyebrows.

"So what were you saying about me?" Hayes asked.

Cox's and Claire's eyes met.

"For God's sake. You both look guilty as Judas. I thought you knew how to lie."

"Is it true?" Claire asked.

"What?"

"You kept your name dirty."

Hayes laid his head back.

"It was the best way to get at the people who did this. It's how I found out they were hunting down Cold Harvest in the U.S."

A phone buzzed in the pocket of Cox's suit. He reached for it. "I have to answer this, get you taken care of," he said. "You all need anything?"

Hayes and Claire shook their heads, and he stepped into the hallway.

Hayes looked at her, the skin beside the bandages still stained with Betadine.

"You'll be all right, Claire. You've been through worse. They'll clear you."

"You think so?"

"A hundred percent. They'll probably offer you a job."

She crossed her arms over her chest and looked out the window. "And you?"

All he could think of was his wife and daughter, of how close the killers might have come and what that meant for his home. Would Lauren and Maggie have to move again? To run with him?

"I'll be all right."

"I should have known about Paul."

"You can help me go after the people he was working for. There's someone above him."

She turned back to him. "I'm done, Hayes. I've been done for years. I thought I could use the anger, make some good of it, but you were right. It ended up controlling me. I tried to quit before, but it was disappearing into a lie, you know?"

He nodded.

"You can stop," she said. "You've given

them more than anyone could ask."

But he knew the truth. He'd made his choice. And even if he'd wanted to walk away, he couldn't. This had gone too far.

CHAPTER 67

It was August, six weeks after the chaos at Rockefeller Plaza. Tucker looked out the window at the parking spot on the corner of Q Street that the Secret Service had occupied for the past six months. They were gone, but the media had arrived, dozens of reporters. They weren't asking about his campaign anymore, angling for access to the future president. Now they were working the scandal: How had the national security adviser fallen so far? When did he suspect that Americans were being killed and what had he done about it? Who was culpable for that blast in the Meadowlands?

The normally tidy condo was a mess of takeout containers, and Tucker's skin felt like it was covered in a thin layer of oil.

He couldn't leave the house. He had a target on his back because of Cold Harvest, and now there was no one left to protect him.

The lawyers cost thirty thousand dollars a month, and the real investigations into what he had done hadn't even begun. There was no money left to pay for private security. After all those years writing out the kill list, Tucker now felt what it was like to be hunted.

"Tucker," Morgan said. She was standing behind him as he gazed out the window. She tried to draw his attention, get him to focus. He turned, and she pressed the papers to his chest.

It was a statement of reason revoking Tucker's security clearance. "Sign this," Morgan said, and she gave him the pen.

He scrawled a line along the bottom without looking.

"What are you doing?" he asked Morgan.

"About what?"

"Security. How do you sleep at night knowing they're out there?"

"I don't, really. I have the dog. But if they want me, they'll get me." She shrugged. "It's okay. They're pros. We won't even see it coming."

"But who is going to look out for us?"

"That's the promise, you know — you look out for the guy next to you and he looks out for you. That's why everyone wants to be in the elite units. It's not just

403

pride. It's basic common sense. You want the best men and women watching your back."

"Good," Tucker said, nodding, then he stared out the window again, feeling for the first time like he could take a full breath. "So what do we do?"

"Nothing. We broke that trust. We're on our own."

"When do we get to stop looking over our shoulders?"

"Never," she said. "I have to go." She picked up the form he had signed and turned.

"Morgan," Tucker said as she walked down the hall. But the only reply was the front door closing.

He stood for a moment, looking through the window at a clear Georgetown morning, then he pulled the shades and sat alone in the dark.

CHAPTER 68

Hynd's eyes stared blindly at the ceiling. Claire looked into them and tried to recognize the man she knew as Paul.

The corpse lay in a cardboard cremation box on top of a metal gurney. All the evidence had been taken, and his index fingers had been neatly clipped off to be held for future reference and DNA testing.

This was no funeral-home wake, no churchyard burial. This was the body of a ghost with no family and no nation — the less said about it, the better.

"Hynd," she said out loud. "Niko Hynd." It had taken him so long to learn her real name, and now it chilled her to call him by his.

They'd waited a decent interval to ask her for a final identification of the cadaver, after weeks of subjecting her to endless hours of debriefings and polygraphs.

She'd seen plenty of bodies in her day,

but this one was different. Standing here, she was ready to be overwhelmed, prepared for anything to come at her. But she was surprised to feel little more than the lingering anger, sadness, and guilt over those who had died. She felt that every day. She suspected it might never go away.

She asked Cox what would happen next, after the final identification of Hynd's body. When he told her, she had insisted that she be here for this. She wanted to watch him burn, not to appease that anger, but to know that he and the evil he carried were gone.

She nodded to the technician — a man in a black suit and a white shirt with no tie — and stepped back.

He moved toward the body and she put her hand on his. "Hold on," she said.

The ring. She'd never taken it off. She never noticed it anymore. It was just a part of her. She slipped it over the knuckle and looked at the skin beneath it — paler and smooth, like scar tissue. The skin felt strangely cold. She put the ring on his chest, just beside the stitches of the Y incision, and stepped back.

A moment later, the conveyor carried the body away. Through a plate-glass window she watched the flames rise, bright blue. She let all the rage — from Paul, from the past — burn away with it. She'd given a power of attorney to sell her house to a local real-estate agent she knew from the bakery. She picked up a few photos of her mother and left the rest of her belongings to be auctioned or given away.

She was done. She would leave it all behind and begin again, like she had a dozen times before, but this time it wouldn't be as a new cover.

The hot August air wrapped around her as she stepped outside. She had a backpack with two changes of clothes and a few necessities.

Cox had sent a car for her, and she climbed into the back of the Suburban. An older black man looked at her in the rearview. "Where are we going today, ma'am?"

He had a Creole accent — Belize, she guessed.

"Dulles," she said. The international airport.

Someplace warm. She had a ticket to St. Lucia. She had found a cheap spot away from the crowds and was going to take a break, to heal. And then — she didn't know. She wanted a place she could plant a garden, a place she could keep horses. Maybe she'd try some executive recruiting.

"All right, then," the man said. "My name is Gerald. Pleased to meet you."

She looked at him, and it took all of her will to push back against the lessons they had forced on her: *Erase yourself; never give them your name.* She smiled.

"You too. I'm Claire."

CHAPTER 69

Hayes waited until he was sure Lauren was asleep. He stared into the darkness for another twenty minutes as she flinched slightly, then settled in to rest. Her breath slowed, became deep and even.

He couldn't sleep. He'd met with Cox in Washington the week before. There was good news: They had been able to trace back the patterns of Hynd's communications and movements, and he had never come within fifty miles of this house, never laid eyes on it.

His family was safe, for now. His feet touched the cold hardwood floor and he moved silently through the doorway, then downstairs. If he stayed beside Lauren when he couldn't sleep, she would always wake, always feel the restlessness in him.

Hayes stopped at the window, and his reflection seemed to float out ahead of him in the inky contours of the maple trees.

There were four men he trusted like brothers hiding in the woods with SIG rifles, ready to kill anyone who came for his family. He'd run a two-hour countersurveillance routine to get here from the meet with Cox.

Cox had offered to bring them all onto a base, but that was a prison with no end in sight, and Hayes had already asked too much of his family. It was his war, not theirs.

He ran his hand over the window trim. It was laid in straight, and in the corner he saw the coping fit perfectly, without room for a hair. Lauren had finished it while he was out there, hunting the men behind these attacks.

Cox had shown him a list. It was true. There was a bounty for Hayes's life. He was the number-one target of the network that had paid Hynd to kill Cold Harvest. Hayes would never be safe, and anyone near him was in danger.

It was hubris that led him to think that he could build this place, could sit at home at peace and take the war pick-and-choose like most of his countrymen. No. He hadn't even finished painting before the violence came for them. He'd tried to protect them, and twice he had brought the threat to their door.

"You want what we all want, to be with

your family and to keep them safe," Cox had said.

And Hayes knew without being told that he had to choose one or the other: being with his family or keeping them safe. The enemy would never stop hunting him. Protecting them meant leaving.

The sound was barely audible — a soft footfall — but Hayes spun and his hands came forward.

His daughter came down the stairs, one careful step at a time. The black dog padded down beside her.

"Hey, sweetie. What's going on?"

"I couldn't sleep."

"Me neither. Something scare you?"

"No. Did it scare you?"

He laughed quietly and looked at her for a long moment. "No," he said, and he lifted her into his arms.

He checked the clock. Four thirty in the morning, and here she was, ready to roll and looking out for the other guy. "You'd be a good Marine," he said, and he kissed the top of her head.

"Don't even start on that," a voice said. Lauren was coming down the steps. "You all right?" she asked.

"Yes, but you all should go back to bed. It's late."

"Or early," she said as she came over and stood next to him. Maggie fidgeted and Hayes put her down. She went to the kitchen and climbed onto one of the stools at the island.

Hayes put his arm around his wife's waist and brought her to his side.

He'd spent his whole life living out of a backpack, with foster families and group homes, and he'd joined the Marines when he was seventeen. There was ugliness in his past, but it didn't poison him. It made him clear-eyed, unsentimental, and grateful, above all. A clean, safe place to live, a family, food, love; they seemed like mirages, and even now he never expected them to last. He didn't get to have this. And that was fine. He'd never thought he would.

It had been tough, coming home, but he and Lauren were finding their way. The time in exile had changed him, hardened him. They didn't have to talk about it all, because the choice had been made. He couldn't stay.

He would still see them, would always be a part of their lives, but it would be on bases, with protection running so that the people who were hunting him wouldn't ever come near his family. He couldn't live here. The job would be his home, as it had been for so long. Even before his exile, the deployments and training had kept him away three hundred days a year. Lauren had been the first to point it out — the new arrangement wouldn't be all that different.

He told her she didn't have to wait, that he understood if she needed a change, and she told him to be quiet. He knew she couldn't think about that now, couldn't stand to hurt him.

She was strong and could hold down this family and this house without him. Her father had been U.S. Army, Tenth Mountain Division. She knew about the work, and they'd always been straight with each other. She would be fine without him. He could see her strength in his daughter too. They would be okay.

The sun was rising, tinting the gray morning red. The shadows of the trees resolved out of the dark and began to stretch out toward him, his home, his family.

He leaned over and kissed her temple. One day he could come home and rest, when his body was too broken down to go on or after he killed the men behind this. But now the trail was going cold, and the fight was calling.

ACKNOWLEDGMENTS

Thanks go first to my toughest customers, my family — Heather Burke and Ellen, Greg, Peter, and Michael Quirk — and my agent, Shawn Coyne. Together they saved the day on this one.

And thanks to my editor, Emily Giglierano, for her spot-on revisions. To Pamela Brown, Zea Moscone, and Sabrina Callahan, for introducing John Hayes to the world. To Tracy Roe, a topflight copyeditor *and* a doctor, for her fantastic work on the manuscript, to Lauren Harms for a terrific cover, and to Mary Tondorf-Dick, Peggy Freudenthal, and Pamela Marshall for keeping everything running smoothly. And to Josh Kendall, Reagan Arthur, and everyone at Mulholland Books, Little, Brown, and Hachette. It's a hell of a team, with a phenomenal bench of authors, and I'm enormously grateful to be part of it.

Thanks to the bookstores and communities of readers who welcomed me on the road over the years at Mysterious Galaxy, One More Page, Book People, Murder by the Book, Book Court, Politics and Prose, Rainy Day Books, powerHouse Books, the Holmdel Barnes and Noble, Book Carnival, Vroman's, and Poisoned Pen.

Thanks to Joe Finder, Alex Berenson, Gregg Hurwitz, Jesse Kellerman, Marcia Clark, Michael Koryta, Ben Coes, Dorothy Fortenberry, Chris Holm, Kim Fay, David Swinson, Kristen Kittscher, Maggie Shipstead, Steph Cha, and Steven Pressfield, for great books and support.

Thanks to Dr. Drew Wilkis and Dr. Steven Davis, Niko Gubernator, Tony Matthews, Captain Cornell Riley, Lieutenant Colonel James Hannibal, Roger Pardo-Maurer, Abe Sutherland, and Sadiqullah Sadiq (whom I also have to thank for introducing me to *tapas,* the Afghan folk poems). And to Billy Miller, for taking me shooting and offering technical advice on the manuscript.

Thanks to Adam Kushner, Mike Melia, Dan Wagner, Mandy Simon, and Jennie Rothenberg; to Joe and Colleen Euteneuer, for a grand welcome to Kansas City; to John MacGaffin and Peter Higgins, of the FBI and CIA, for sharing their stories. I'm also particularly indebted to Sean Naylor's *Re-*

lentless Strike and Mark Mazzetti's *The Way of the Knife* for inspiration and background.

I took a few liberties in the text, and I'm sure I managed to sneak in a few mistakes despite all this help.

Finally, thank you to those who will go unnamed here and to everyone who does the selfless work, in its many forms, of looking out for the rest of us.

ABOUT THE AUTHOR

Matthew Quirk studied history and literature at Harvard College. After graduation, he joined the *Atlantic* and spent five years at the magazine reporting on a variety of subjects including crime, private military contractors, terrorism prosecutions, and international gangs. Quirk's bestselling first novel, *The 500,* has been translated into twenty languages. He lives in San Diego.

The employees of Thorndike Press hope you have enjoyed this Large Print book. All our Thorndike, Wheeler, and Kennebec Large Print titles are designed for easy reading, and all our books are made to last. Other Thorndike Press Large Print books are available at your library, through selected bookstores, or directly from us.

For information about titles, please call:
  (800) 223-1244

or visit our website at:
  gale.com/thorndike

To share your comments, please write:
  Publisher
  Thorndike Press
  10 Water St., Suite 310
  Waterville, ME 04901